Alice Cary, Phbe Cary

Early and Late Poems of Alice and Phbe Cary

Alice Cary, Phbe Cary

Early and Late Poems of Alice and Phbe Cary

ISBN/EAN: 9783337407421

Printed in Europe, USA, Canada, Australia, Japan

Cover: Foto ©Andreas Hilbeck / pixelio.de

More available books at **www.hansebooks.com**

EARLY AND LATE POEMS

OF

ALICE AND PHŒBE CARY

PUBLISHERS' ADVERTISEMENT.

BOTH Alice and Phœbe Cary were apparently indifferent to the fortune of their poetical writings. They wrote freely and published in a number of different periodicals. From time to time they collected some of their poems into volumes, but these volumes were not always kept in print. After their death, the late Mary Clemmer, in writing the memorial of their lives, preserved a few of the scattered poems, and a tolerably full collection of the poems written by the sisters after their reputation had been well established was published and continues to be published as "The Poems of Alice and Phœbe Cary." But this volume does not contain those poems which were brought together in the first considerable collection of Alice Cary's poems, published by Ticknor & Fields in 1859, now long out of print, but including verses, like "Pictures of Memory," which have become established favorites, and have been preserved in anthologies and in the memory of readers ; neither does it contain all of the poems which, in the later years of the sisters, were contributed to the leading periodicals.

There have been repeated calls for poems not accessible to readers, and it has seemed desirable, therefore, to take the body of poetry written by Alice and Phœbe Cary, and to select from these two sources, the early poems and the late, such as have acquired a special hold upon the public and such as represent the ripest powers of the poets, and to present them in a volume, companion to the one long accepted as the treasury of their poetical writings, but entirely independent of that volume, since no poem is common to both volumes. The topical division adopted in the standard volume has been followed also in this, as far as regards Alice Cary.

CONTENTS.

ALICE CARY.

RELIGIOUS POEMS AND HYMNS.

ALICE CARY.

BALLADS AND NARRATIVE POEMS.

A NORLAND BALLAD.

THE train of the Norse king
   Still winds the descents,
Leading down where the waste ridge
   Is white with his tents ;
The eve star is climbing
   Above where they lie,
Like hills at the harvest-time,
   White with the rye.

Who comes through the red light
   Of bivouac and torch,
With footsteps unslackened
   By fasting or march ? —
Majestic in sorrow,
   No white hand, I trow,
Can take from that forehead
   Its pale seal of woe :

Past grooms that are merrily
   Combing the steeds,

To the tent of the Norse king
He hurriedly speeds ;
A right noble chieftain, —
That gloved hand I know,
Has swooped the gerfalcon
And bended the bow.

Outspeaks he the counsel
He comes to afford :
" As loves this engloved hand
The hilt of my sword —
As loves the pale martyr
The sacrament seal —
My heart loves my liege lord
And prays for his weal.

" I once wooed a maiden,
As fair to my sight
As the bride of the Norse king
I plead for to-night ;
As thou dost, I tarried,
Her fond faith to prove,
And the wall of the convent
Grew up 'twixt our love.

" Hold we to our marching
Three leagues from this ridge,
And we compass our rear-guard
With moat and with bridge :
Give one heart such shriving
As priest can afford,
And a sweet loving lady
The arms of her lord !

" Oh felt you sweet pity
  For half I have borne,
The scourgings, the fastings,
  The lip never shorn ;
You fain would not linger
  For wassail's wild sway,
But leaping to saddle,
  Would hold on the way."

Outspoke then, the Norse king,
  Half pity, half scorn,
" Go back to thy fasting
  And keep thee unshorn ;
No tale of a woman
  Pause I to divine ; "
And from the full goblet
  He quaffed the red wine.

Then fell sire and liegeman
  To feasting and song ;
I ween to such masquers
  The night was not long :
And but one little trembler
  Stood pale in the arch,
When gave the king signal
  To take up the march.

If danger forewarn him,
  The omen he hides,
And mounting right gaily,
  He sings as he rides :
" Now, bird of the border,
  Look forth for thy chief ;

By the bones of St. Peter,
Thy watch shall be brief!

"Stand forth, wretchèd prophet,"
He cries in his wrath,
As his foam-covered charger
Has struck on the path
Leading down to his castle:
"Stand forth! here is moat,
Here is drawbridge — we charge
Back the lie in thy throat!"

"Pause, son of the mighty,
My bode is not lost
Till the step of the master
The lintel has crossed;
And then if my counsel
Prove ghostly or vain" —
The king smiled in triumph
And flung down the rein.

Lo! passed is the threshold,
None answer his call;
Why starts he and trembles?
There's blood in the hall!
His step through the corridor
Hurriedly dies,
'T is only an echo
That answers his cries.

One soft golden ringlet
That kissed the white cheek
Of the beautiful lady
They find as they seek:

There was mounting of heralds
In hot haste, I ween,
But the bride of the Norse king
Was never more seen.

LEGEND OF SEVILLE.

THREE men that three gray mules bestrode
Went riding through a lonesome road —
Dust from the largest to the least
Up to the fetlock of each beast.

The foremost was a stripling pale ;
" Comrades," he said, " within our hail
I see a hostel, white as snow —
'T is nightfall — shall we thither go ? "

" Nay," said the other two, " in sooth
'T is white enough, but of a truth,
Too lowly for our courtly need —
We 'll gain a fairer with good speed."

So, past the hostel white they rode,
These men that three gray mules bestrode,
Till led the pale young moon afar,
By her slim silver horn, one star.

Right wistfully then looking back,
Cried out the middle man, " Alack !
I spy a rude black inn — shalt see
If the host have good wine for three ? "

" Now," said the hindmost, " by my troth
Shamed is my knighthood for ye both." —
So, pricking sharply, on they rode,
These men who three gray mules bestrode.

Close where a whimpering river lay
Stood huts of fishers ; all that day
Drying their loose nets in the sun,
They told how murders might be done.

A moorish tower of yellow stone
Shadowed that river-bridge, o'ergrown
With lichen and the marish moss —
Forward the stripling rode to cross :

Close came the others man by man,
But farther than the shadow ran,
The legend says, they never rode,
These men who three gray mules bestrode.

JESSIE CARROL.

I.

At her window, Jessie Carrol,
    As the twilight dew distils,
Pushes back her heavy tresses,
    Listening toward the northern hills.
" I am happy, very happy,
    None so much as I am blest —
None of all the many maidens
    In the valley of the West,"

Softly to herself she whispered ;
Paused she then again to hear
If the step of Allan Archer,
That she waited for, were near.
" Ah, he knows I love him fondly ! —
I have never told him so ! —
Heart of mine, be not so heavy,
He will come to-night, I know."

Brightly is the full moon filling
All the withered woods with light,
" He has not forgotten surely —
It was later yesternight ! "
Shadows interlock with shadows —
Says the maiden, " Woe is me ! "
In the blue the eve-star trembles
Like a lily in the sea.
Yet a good hour later sounded, —
But the northern woodlands sway . —
Quick a white hand from her casement
Thrust the heavy vines away.
Like the wings of restless swallows
That a moment brush the dew,
And again are up and upward,
Till we lose them in the blue,
Were the thoughts of Jessie Carrol
For a moment dim with pain,
Then with pleasant waves of sunshine,
On the hills of hope again.

" Selfish am I, weak and selfish,"
Said she, " thus to sit and sigh ;
Other friends and other pleasures
Claim his leisure well as I.

Haply, care or bitter sorrow
    'T is that keeps him from my side,
Else he surely would have hasted
    Hither at the twilight tide.
Yet sometimes I can but marvel
    That his lips have never said,
When we talked about the future,
    Then, or then, we shall be wed ! —
Much I fear me that my nature
    Cannot measure half his pride,
And perchance he would not wed me
    Though I pined of love and died.
To the aims of his ambition
    I would bring nor wealth nor fame.
Well, there is a quiet valley
    Where we both shall sleep the same ! "
So, more eves than I can number,
    Now despairing, and now blest,
Watched the gentle Jessie Carrol,
    From the Valley of the West.

II.

Down along the dismal woodland
    Blew October's yellow leaves,
And the day had waned and faded,
    To the saddest of all eves.
Poison rods of scarlet berries
    Still were standing here and there,
But the clover blooms were faded,
    And the orchard boughs were bare.
From the stubblefields the cattle
    Winding homeward, playful, slow,

With their slender horns of silver
  Pushed each other to and fro.
Suddenly the hound up-springing
  From his sheltering kennel, whined,
As the voice of Jessie Carrol
  Backward drifted on the wind —
Backward drifted from a pathway
  Sloping down the upland wild,
Where she walked with Allan Archer,
  Light of spirit as a child !
All her young heart wild with rapture
  And the bliss that made it beat —
Not the golden wells of Hybla
  Held a treasure half so sweet !
But as oft the shifting rose-cloud,
  In the sunset light that lies,
Mournful makes us, feeling only
  How much farther are the skies, —
So the mantling of her blushes,
  And the trembling of her heart,
'Neath his steadfast eyes but made her
  Feel how far they were apart.

" Allan," said she, " I will tell you
  Of a vision that I had —
All the livelong night I dreamed it,
  And it made me very sad.
We were walking slowly seaward,
  In the twilight — you and I —
Through a break of clearest azure
  Shone the moon — as now — on high ;
Though I nothing said to vex you,
  O'er your forehead came a frown,

And I strove, but could not soothe you —
Something kept my full heart down ;
When, before us, stood a lady
In the moonlight's pearly beam,
Very tall and proud and stately —
(Allan, this was in my dream ! —)
Looking down, I thought, upon me,
Half in pity, half in scorn, ´
Till my soul grew sick with wishing
That I never had been born.
' Cover me from woe and madness ! '
Cried I to the ocean flood,
As she locked her milk-white fingers
In between us where we stood, —
All her flood of midnight tresses
Softly gathered from their flow,
By her crown of bridal beauty,
Paler than the winter snow.
Striking then my hands together,
O'er the tumult of my breast, —
All the beauty waned and faded
From the Valley of the West ! "

In the beard of Allan Archer
Twisted then his fingers white,
As he said, " My gentle Jessie,
You must not be sad to-night ;
You must not be sad, my Jessie,
You are over kind and good,
And I fain would make you happy,
Very happy — if I could ! "
Oft he kissed her cheek and forehead,
Called her darling oft, but said,

Never, that he loved her fondly,
  Or that ever they should wed;
But that he was grieved that shadows
  Should have chilled so dear a heart;
That the time, foretold so often,
  Then was come — and they must part!
Shook her bosom then with passion,
  Hot her forehead burned with pain,
But her lips said only, " Allan,
  Will you ever come again ? "
And he answered, lightly dallying
  With her tresses all the while,
Life had not a star to guide him
  Like the beauty of her smile ;
And that when the corn was ripened
  And the vintage harvest prest,
She would see him home returning
  To the Valley of the West.

When the moon had veiled her splendor,
  And went lessening down the blue,
And along the eastern hill-tops
  Burned the morning in the dew,
They had parted — each one feeling
  That their lives had separate ends ;
They had parted — neither happy —
  Less than lovers — more than friends.
For as Jessie mused in silence,
  She remembered that he said,
Never, that he loved her fondly,
  Or that ever they should wed.

'T was full many a nameless meaning
  My poor words can never say,

Felt without the need of utterance,
That had won her heart away.
Oh, the days were weary! weary!
And the eves were dull and long,
With the cricket's chirp of sorrow,
And the owlet's mournful song.
Out of slumber oft she started
In the still and lonesome nights,
Hearing but the traveller's footstep
Hurrying toward the village lights.

So, moaned by the dreary winter —
All her household tasks fulfilled —
Till beneath the last year's rafters
Came the swallows back to build.
Meadow-pinks, in flakes of crimson,
Through the pleasant valleys lay,
And again were oxen ploughing
Up and down the hills all day.
Thus the dim days dawned and faded
To the maid, forsaken, lorn,
Till the freshening breeze of summer
Shook the tassels of the corn.
Ever now within her chamber
All night long the lamp-light shines,
But no white hand from her casement
Pushes back the heavy vines.
On her cheek a fire was feeding,
And her hand transparent grew —
Ah, the faithless Allan Archer!
More than she had dreamed was true.

No complaint was ever uttered,
Only to herself she sighed, —

As she read of wretched poets
    Who had pined of love and died.
Once she crushed the sudden crying
    From her trembling lips away,
When they said the vintage harvest
    Had been gathered in that day.
Often, when they kissed her, smiled she,
    Saying that it soothed her pain,
And that they must not be saddened —
    She would soon be well again!
Thus nor hoping nor yet fearing,
    Meekly bore she all her pain,
Till the red leaves of the autumn
    Withered from the woods again;
Till the bird had hushed its singing
    In the silvery sycamore,
And the nest was left unsheltered
    In the lilac by the door ;
Saying, still, that she was happy —
    None so much as she was blest —
None of all the many maidens
    In the Valley of the West.

III.

Down the heath and o'er the moorland
    Blows the wild gust high and higher,
Suddenly the maiden pauses
    Spinning at the cabin fire,
And from out her taper fingers
    Falls away the flaxen thread,
As some neighbor entering, whispers,
    " Jessie Carrol lieth dead."

Then, as pressing close her forehead
　To the window-pane, she sees
Two stout men together digging
　Underneath the churchyard trees ;
And she asks in kindest accents,
　" Was she happy when she died ? "
Sobbing all the while to see them
　Void the heavy earth aside ;
Or, upon their mattocks leaning,
　Through their fingers numb to blow,
For the wintry air is chilly,
　And the grave-mounds white with snow.
And the neighbor answers softly,
　" Do not, dear one, do not cry ;
At the break of day she asked us
　If we thought that she must die ;
And when I had told her, sadly,
　That I feared it would be so,
Smiled she, saying, 'T will be weary
　Digging in the churchyard now ! '
' Earth,' I said, ' was very dreary —
　That its paths at best were rough ; '
And she whispered, she was ready,
　That her life was long enough.
So she lay serene and silent,
　Till the wind, that wildly drove,
Soothed her from her mortal sorrow,
　Like the lullaby of love."
Thus they talked, while one that loved her
　Smoothed her tresses dark and long,
Wrapped her white shroud down, and simply
　Wove her sorrow to this song:

IV.

Sweetly sleeps she : pain and passion
  Burn no longer on her brow —
Weary watchers, ye may leave her —
  She no more will need you now !
While the wild spring bloomed and faded,
  Till the autumn came and passed,
Calmly, patiently, she waited —
  Rest has come to her at last !
Never have the blessèd angels,
  As they walked with her apart,
Kept pale Sorrow's battling armies
  Half so softly from her heart.
Therefore, think not, ye that loved her,
  Of the pallor hushed and dread,
Where the winds, like heavy mourners,
  Cry about her lonesome bed,
But of white hands softly reaching
  As the shadow o'er her fell,
Downward from the golden bastion
  Of the eternal citadel.

ANNIE CLAYVILLE.

In the bright'ning wake of April
  Comes the lovely, lovely May,
But the step of Annie Clayville
  Falleth fainter day by day.
In despite of sunshine, shadows
  Lie upon her heart and brow :
Last year she was gay and happy —
  Life is nothing to her now !

When she hears the wild bird singing,
  Or the sweetly humming bee,
Only says she, faintly smiling,
  What have you to do with me?

Yet, sing out for pleasant weather,
  Wild birds in the woodland dells —
Fly out, little bees, and gather
  Honey for your waxen wells.
Softly, sunlit rain of April,
  Come down singing from the clouds,
Till the daffodils and daisies
  Shall be up in golden crowds ;
Till the wild pinks hedge the meadows,
  Blushing out of slender stems,
And the dandelions, starry,
  Cover all the hills with gems.
From your cool beds in the rivers,
  Blow, fresh winds, and gladness bring
To the locks that wait to hide you —
  What have I to do with spring?

May is past — along the hollows
  Chime the rills in sleepy tune,
While the harvest's yellow chaplet
  Swings against the face of June.

Very pale lies Annie Clayville —
  Still her forehead, shadow-crowned,
And the watchers hear her saying,
  As they softly tread around :
" Go out, reapers, for the hill-tops
  Twinkle with the summer's heat —

Lay from out your swinging cradles
  Golden furrows of ripe wheat !
While the little laughing children,
  Lightly mixing work with play,
From beneath the long green winrows
  Glean the sweetly-scented hay.
Let your sickles shine like sunbeams
  In the silver-flowing rye,
Ears grow heavy in the cornfields —
  That will claim you by and by.
Go out, reapers, with your sickles,
  Gather home the harvest store !
Little gleaners, laughing gleaners,
  I shall go with you no more.

Round the red moon of October,
  White and cold the eve-stars climb,
Birds are gone, and flowers are dying —
  'T is a lonesome, lonesome time.
Yellow leaves along the woodland
  Surge to drifts — the elm-bough sways,
Creaking at the homestead window
  All the weary nights and days.
Dismally the rain is falling —
  Very dismally and cold ;
Close, within the village graveyard
  By a heap of freshest mould,
With a simple, nameless headstone,
  Lies a low and narrow mound,
And the brow of Annie Clayville
  Is no longer shadow-crowned.
Rest thee, lost one, rest thee calmly,
  Glad to go where pain is o'er —

Where they say not, through the night-time,
"I am weary," any more.

IN THE SUGAR CAMP.

Upon the silver beeches moss
  Was drawing quaint designs,
And the first dim-eyed violets
  Were greeting the March winds.
'T was night — the fire of hickory wood
  Burned warm and bright and high —
And we were in the Sugar Camp,
  Sweet Nellie Grey and I.

'T was merry, though the willows yet
  Had not a tassel on;
The bluebirds sung that year, I know,
  Before the snow was gone.
Through bunches of stiff frosty grass
  The brooks went tinkling by;
We heard them in the Sugar Camp,
  Sweet Nellie Grey and I.

Broken and thin the shadows lay
  Along the moonlit hill,
For like the wings of chrysalids
  The leaves were folded still.
And so, betwixt the times we heaped
  The hickory wood so high,
When we were in the Sugar Camp,
  Sweet Nelly Grey and I.

I said I loved her — said I 'd make
A cabin by the stream,
And we would live among the birds —
It was a pretty dream !
I could not see the next year's snow
Upon her bosom lie —
When we were in the Sugar Camp,
Sweet Nelly Grey and I.

RHYME OF MY PLAYMATE.

ALAS ! his praise I cannot write,
Nor paint him true for other eyes ;
For only in love's blessèd light
Could you have known him good or wise.

Beside him from my birth I grew,
E'en to the middle time of youth,
And never was there heart so true,
Though shy of all the shows of truth.

Silent he often sat, and sad,
While on his lips there played a smile,
Which told you that his spirit had
Some lovely vision all the while.

Like flowers that drop in hidden streams,
Low under shelving weights of ground,
His thoughts went drooping into dreams
Though never trembling into sound.

The common fields, the darkening woods,
The silver runnels and blue skies,

He mused of in his solitudes
And gazed on with a lover's eyes.

The hollow where we used to stray,
  Gathering the rush with purple joints —
Till from the haycocks thick and gray
  The shadows stretched in dusky points;

And homeward with their glittering scythes
  The mowers came, and paused to say
Some playful reprimand (the tithes
  Of our thus idling all the day) —

Lay green beneath the crimson swaths
  Of sunset, when I thither came,
And the thick wings of twilight moths
  Flitted in circles all the same.

And the brown beetle hummed upon
  The furrow as the day grew dim,
As when in sunset lights long gone
  I trod the meadow-side with him.

The swallow round the gable led
  Her fledgling brood, but far and near,
O'er wood and wold there seemed to spread
  A dry and dreary atmosphere.

Unpraised but in my simple rhymes,
  With sullen brow and footsteps slow,
Along the wilds of burning climes
  Alone, unloved, I saw him go.

No heart but mine his memory keeps —
The world will never hear his name,
Dreamless he lingers by the steeps
Whereon he might have climbed to fame.

THE WOOD LILY.

BETWIXT the green rows of the corn
Ne'er grew a wild blossom so sweet —
Her mother's low cabin was gay
With the music that followed her feet :

Combing now the white lengths of the wool
With hands that were whiter than they ;
Spinning now in the mossy-roofed porch
Till the time when the birds go away.

Her hair was as black as the storm ;
No maiden in all the green glen
Was so pretty, so praised, or so loved :
We called her the Wood Lily, then.

The church wall, so gray and so cold,
Is streaked with the vines which she set,
And her roses beside the arched door,
In summer half smother it yet.

And often with pitiful looks
They pause, who put by the lithe shoots,
As if something said, " It were well,
If Lily lay down at the roots."

Dull spiders reel up their white skeins
On the wheel where she comes not to spin,
And her hands have pulled all the bright flowers
From the locks that are faded and thin.

And if you go near to the door,
You will choke with the coming of sighs,
For by the dark hearthstone she sits
All the day, singing low lullabies, —

So low, they may scarcely be heard,
While the smile of her lip and her brow,
Like sunbeams are gone under clouds —
And this is our Wood Lily, now.

THE DESERTED FYLGIA.[1]

LIKE a meteor, radiant, streaming,
    Seems her hair to me,
And thou bear'st her feet like lilies,
    Dark and chilly sea!

Wannish fires enclasp her bosom,
    Like the Northern Light,
And like icicles her fingers
    Glisten, locked and white.

[1] " A Scandinavian warrior, having embraced Christianity, and being attacked by disease which he thought mortal, was naturally anxious that a spirit who had accompanied him through his pagan career should not attend him into that other world, where her society might involve him in disagreeable consequences. The persevering Fylgia, however, in the shape of a fair maiden, walked on the waves of the sea, after her Viking's ship."

On the blue and icy ocean,
    As a stony floor,
Toward thy boat, O dying Viking,
    Walks she evermore !

Like a star on morning's forehead,
    When the intense air,
Sweeping o'er the face of heaven,
    Lays its far depths bare —

Is the beauty of her smiling,
    Pale and cold and clear —
What, O fearful, dying Viking,
    Doth the maiden here ?

Moaningly his white lips tremble,
    But no voice replies —
Starlight in the blue waves frozen
    Seem his closing eyes.

Woman's lot is thine, O Fylgia,
    Mourning broken faith,
And her mighty love outlasting
    Chance and change and death !

THE HAUNTED HOUSE.

THE winds of March are piping shrill,
    The half-moon, slanting low,
Is shining down the wild sea-hill
    Where, long and long ago,

Love ditties singing all for me,
Sat blue-eyed Coralin —
Her grave is now beneath the tree
Where then she used to spin.

Three walnut trees, so high and wild,
Before the homestead stand —
Their smooth boles often, when a child,
I 've taken in my hand ;
And that the nearest to the wall,
Though once alike they grew,
Is not so goodly, nor so tall,
As are the other two.

The spinning work was always there —
There all our childish glee ;
But when she grew a maiden fair,
The songs were not for me.
One night, twice seven years 't has been,
When shone the moon as now,
The slender form of Coralin
Hung swinging on the bough

That 's gnarled and knotty grown ; in spring,
When all the fields are gay
With madrigals, no bird will sing
Upon that bough, they say.
And through the chamber where the wheel
With cobwcbs is o'erspread,
Pale ghosts are sometimes seen to steal,
Since Coralin is dead.

The waters once so bright and cool
Within the mossy well,

Are shrunken to a sluggish pool ;
 And more than this, they tell,
That oft the one-eyed mastiff wakes,
 And howls as if in fear,
From midnight till the morning breaks —
 The dead is then too near.

THE MURDERESS.

ALONG the still cold plain o'erhead,
 In pale embattled crowds,
The stars their tents of darkness spread,
 And camped among the clouds ;
Cinctured with shadows, like a wraith,
 Night moaned along the lea ;
Like the blue hungry eye of Death
 Shone the perfidious sea ;
The moon was wearing to the wane,
 The winds were wild and high,
And a red meteor's flaming mane
 Streamed from the northern sky.

Across the black and barren moor,
 Her dainty bosom bare,
And white lips sobbing evermore,
 Rides Eleanor the fair.
So hath the pining sea-maid plained
 For love of mortal lips,
Riding the billows, silver-reined,
 Hard by disastrous ships.

Why covers she her mournful eyes ?
 Why do her pulses cease,

As if she saw before her rise
    The ghost of murdered Peace ?
From out her path the ground-bird drifts
    With wildly startled calls,
The moonlight snake its white fold lifts
    From where her shadow falls.

Ah me ! that delicate hand of hers,
    Now trembling like a reed,
Like to the ancient mariner's,
    Hath done a hellish deed ;
And full of mercy were the frown
    Which might the power impart
To press the eternal darkness down
    Against her bleeding heart.

GLENLY MOOR.

THE summer's golden glow was fled,
In eve's dim arms the day lay dead,
Over the dreary woodland wild
The first pale star looked out and smiled
    On Glenly Moor.

Nor lonely call of lingering bird,
Nor insect's cheerful hum was heard,
Nor traveller in the closing day
Humming along the grass-grown way
    Of Glenly Moor.

No voice was in the sleepy rills,
No light shone down the village hills,

And withered on their blackening stalks
Hung the last flowers along the walks
    Of Glenly Moor.

Within a thin, cold drift of light
The buds of the wild rose hung bright,
Where broken turf and new-set stone
Told of a pale one left alone
    In Glenly Moor.

All the clear splendor of the skies
Was gathered from her meek blue eyes,
And therefore shadows dark and cold
Hang over valley, hill, and wold
    In Glenly Moor.

And the winged morning from the blue
Winnowing the crimson on the dew
May ne'er unlock the hands so white
That lie beneath that drift of light
    In Glenly Moor.

ROSEMARY HILL.

'T was the night he had promised to meet me,
    To meet me on Rosemary Hill,
And I said, at the rise of the eve-star,
    The tryst he will haste to fulfil.

Then I looked to the elm-bordered valley,
    Where the undulous mist whitely lay,
But I saw not the steps of my lover
    Dividing its beauty away.

The eve-star rose red o'er the tree-tops,
   The night-dews fell heavy and chill,
And wings ceased to beat through the shadows —
   -   The shadows of Rosemary Hill.

I heard not, through hoping and fearing,
   The whippoorwill's musical cry,
Nor saw I the pale constellations
   That lit the blue reach of the sky.

But fronting despair like a martyr,
   I pled with my heart to be still,
As round me fell, deeper and darker,
   The shadows of Rosemary Hill.

On a bough that was withered and dying,
   I leaned as the midnight grew dumb,
And told my heart, over and over,
   How often he said he would come.

He is hunting, I said, in dim Arnau —
   He was there with his dogs all day long —
And is weary with winging the plover,
   Or stayed by the throstle's sweet song.

Then heard I the whining of Eldrich,
   Of Eldrich so blind and so old,
With sleek hide embrowned like the lion's,
   And brindled and freckled with gold.

How the pulse of despair in my bosom
   Leapt back to a joyous thrill,
As I went down to meet my dear lover,
   Down fleetly from Rosemary Hill.

More near seemed the whining of Eldrich,
  More loudly my glad bosom beat;
When lo! I beheld by the moonlight,
  A newly made grave at my feet.

And when with the passion-vine lovely,
  That grew by the stone at the head,
The length of the grave I had measured,
  I knew that my lover was dead.

NELLIE, WATCHING.

You might see the river shore
From the shady cottage-door
Where she sat, a maiden mild —
Not a woman, not a child ;
But the grace which heaven confers
On the two, I trow was hers :
Dimpled cheek, and laughing eyes,
Blue as bluest summer skies,
And the snowy fall and rise
Of a bosom, stirred, I weet,
By some thought as dewy sweet
As the red ripe strawberries
Which the morning mower sees ;
Locks so long and brown (half down
From the modest wild-flower crown
That she made an hour ago,
Saying, " I will wear it, though
None will praise it, that I know ! ")
Twined she round her fingers white —
Sitting careless in the light,

Sweetly mixed of day and night —
Twined she, peeping sly the while
Down the valley, like an aisle,
Sloping to the river-side.
Blue eyes! wherefore ope so wide?
They are fishers on the shore
That you look on — nothing more.

Pettishly she pouts — ah me!
Saucy Nellie, you will see
Ere an hour has fled away,
Little recks it what you say —
That those eyes with anger frowning
Darkly, will be near to drowning,
And the lips repeating so
Oft and proudly " Let him go ! "
Will be sighing.
                    Ah, I know!
I have watched as you have done
This fair twilight, pretty one,
Watched in trembling hope, and know,
Spite of all your frowning so,
That the wave of sorrow, flowing
In your heart, will soon be showing
In the cheek, now brightly blushing, —
Hark! 't is but the wild birds hushing
To their nests — and not a lover
Brushing through the valley clover !

Purple as the morning-glories
    Round her head the shadows fall ;
Is she thinking of sad stories,
    That, when wild winds shriek and call,

And the snow comes, good old folks,
  Sitting by the fire together,
Tell, until the midnight cocks
  Shrilly crow from hill to hill —
Stories, not befitting ill
Wintry nights and windy weather?

The small foot that late was tapping
On the floor, has ceased its rapping,
  And the blue eyes opened wide,
  Half in anger, half in pride,
  Now are closed as in despair,
And the flowers that she would wear
Whether they were praised or no,
On the ground are lying low.

Foolish Nellie, see the moon,
Round and red, and think that June
  Will be here another day,
  And the apple-boughs will grow
Brighter than a month ago:
  Beauty dies not with the May!
And beneath the hedgerow leaves,
All the softly-falling eves,
When the yellow bees are humming
And the blue and black birds coming
In at will, we two shall walk,
Making out of songs or talk
Quiet pastime.
                    Nellie said,
" Those fine eves I shall be dead,
  For I cannot live and see
  Him I love so, false to me,

And till now I never staid
Watching vainly in the shade."

"In good sooth, you are betrayed!
    For I heard you, careless, saying,
' 'T is not *I* for love that pine,'
    And I 've been a long hour staying
In the shadow of the vine!"

So a laughing voice, but tender,
Said to Nellie : quick the splendor
    Of the full moon seemed to fade,
For the smiling and the blushing
    Filling all the evening shade.
It was not the wild birds hushing
    To their nests an hour ago,
But in verity a lover
Brushing through the valley-clover.

Would all watches maidens keep,
When they sit alone and weep
For their heart-aches, ended so!

ROSALIE.

FROM the rough bark green buds were breaking;
The birds chirped gaily for the taking
    Of summer mates ; April was trilling,
Like a young psaltress, to the wind,
That stopt from dancing to unbind
The primrose ; for the thawing weather
The runnels brimmed.   We were together —

I singing out aloud, she stilling
Her hurried heart-beats. While, that day,
 Idly I hummed the poet's rhyming,
Her thoughts were all another way,
 Where the white flower of love was climbing
Through sunshine of sweet eyes — not mine !
 We were divided by that light :
The selfsame minute we might twine
 Our distaffs with new flax — at night
Put by our wheels at once ; the gloaming
Fall just the same upon the combing
 And braiding of our hair — in vain !
Our hearts were never one again.

Beneath the barn-roof, thick with moss,
 Rumbled the fanmill ; uncomplaining,
 The oxen from its golden raining
(One milky-white, the other dun)
 Went the long day to plough across
The stubble, slantwise from the sun.
 The yellow mist was on the thorns,
And here and there a fork of flowers
Shone whiter than, athwart the showers
 Of winnowed chaff, the heifer's horns.
And while the springtime came and went
 With showery clouds and sunny gleaming,
 We were together : she a-dreaming,
I scarcely happy, yet content.

Alone, beside the southern wall
 I digged the earth ; the summer flowers
 In pleasant times, betwixt the showers,
I sadly planted, one and all ;

And when they made a crimson blind
    Before the window, with their bloom,
    I spun alone within the room —
Right hardly did the wisps unbind,
    So wet they were with tears.   Ah, me!
Blithe songs they said the winds were blowing
From where the harvesters were mowing —
    I only cared for Rosalie.

'T was autumn ; gray with twilight's hue,
    The embers of the day were lying ;
    Athwart the dusk the bat was flying,
And insects made their faint ado.
So evening sloped into the night,
    And all the black tops of the furs
    Shone as with golden, prickly burrs,
So small the stars were, and so bright.
Close by the homestead, old and low,
    A gnarled and knotty oak was growing,
    And shadows of red leaves were blowing
Across the coverlid of snow.

Awake, sweet Rosalie, I said,
    The moon's pale fires run harmlessly
    Down the dry holts — awake and see !
She did not turn her in the bed.
My heart, I thought, must fall abreaking :
    All — all but one wild wish — was past :
    For that white sunken mouth, once speaking,
To say she loved me, at the last !
Two comforts yet were mine to keep :
    Betwixt her and her faithless lover
    Bright grass would spread a flowery cover ;
And Rosalie was well asleep.

RINALDO.

A FISHERMAN's children, we dwelt by the sea,
My good little brother Rinaldo and me,
Contented and happy as happy could be —
      Of blossoms no other
Was fair as the bright one that bloomed on his cheek,
And gentle — oh never a lamb was so meek —
I wish he were living and heard what I speak,
      My lost little brother!

One night when our father was out on the sea,
We went through the moonlight, my brother and me,
And watched for his coming beneath an old tree,
      The leaves of which hooded
A raven whose sorrowful croak in the shade
So dismally sounded, it made us afraid,
And kneeling together for shelter we prayed
      From the evil it boded.

At the school on the hill, not a week from that day,
The thick cloud of playing broke wildly away,
And the laughter that lately went ringing so gay
      Was changed to a crying,
And leaping the ditches and climbing the wall,
'Twixt home and the schoolhouse came one at our call,
And told us the youngest and best of them all,
      Rinaldo was dying.

There was watching and weeping, and when he was dead,
'Neath that tree by the seaside they made him a bed;
A stone that was nameless and rude at his head —
      His feet had another;

And the schoolmaster said, though we laid him so low.
And so humbly and nameless, we surely should know
For his beauty, where only the beautiful go —
   My good little brother.

CHANGED.

ALAS, the pleasant dew is dry,
 That made so sweet the morn;
And midway in the walk of life
 He sits as one forlorn.

I knew the time when this was not,
 When at the close of day
He brought his little boys the flowers
 Ploughed up along his way.

The ewes that browsed the daisy buds
 Erewhile (there were but twain),
Are now the grandams of a flock
 That whiten all the plain.

The twigs he set his marriage-day
 Against the cabin-door,
Make shadows in the summer now
 That reach across the floor.

The birds with red brown eyes, he sees
 Fly round him, hears the low
Of pasturing cattle, hears the streams
 That through his meadows flow.

He sees the pleasant lights of home,
  And yet as one whose ills
Seek comfort of the winds or stars,
  He stays about the hills.

The once dear wife his lingering step
  A joy no longer yields ;
No more he brings his boys the flowers
  Ploughed up along the fields.

WURTHA.

THROUGH the autumn's mists so red
  Shot the slim and golden stocks
Of the ripe corn ; Wurtha said,
  " Let us cut them for our flocks."

Answered I, " When morning leaves
  Her bright footprints on the sea,
As I cut and bind the sheaves,
  Wurtha, thou shalt glean for me."

" Nay, the full moon shines so bright
  All along the vale below,
I could count our flocks to-night ;
  Haco, let us rise and go.
For when bright the risen morn
  Leaves her footprints on the sea,
Thou may'st cut and bind the corn,
  But I cannot glean for thee."

And as I my reed so light
  Blowing, sat, her fears to calm,

Said she, " Haco, yesternight
  In my dream I missed a lamb,
And as down the misty vale
  Went I pining for the lost,
Something shadowy and pale,
  Phantom-like, my pathway crossed,
Saying, ' In a chilly bed,
  Low and dark, but full of peace,
For your coming, softly spread,
  Is the dead lamb's snowy fleece.' "

Passed the sweetest of all eves —
  Morn was breaking, for our flocks :
" Let us go and bind to sheaves
  All the slim and golden stocks ;
Wake, my Wurtha, wake " — but still
  Were her lips as still could be,
And her folded hands too chill
  Ever more to glean for me.

THE SHEPHERDESS.

Sat we on the mossy rocks
  In the twilight, long ago,
I and Ulna keeping flocks —
  Flocks with fleeces white as snow.
Beauty smiled along the sky ;
  Beauty shone along the sea ;
" Ulna, Ulna," whispered I,
  " This is all for you and me ! "

Brushing back my heavy locks,
  Said he, not, alas ! in glee,

" Art content in keeping flocks
    With a shepherd boy like me? " —
Shone the moon so softly white
    Down upon the mossy rocks,
Covering sweetly with her light
    Me and Ulna, and our flocks.

Running wild about our feet
    Were the blushing summer flowers —
" Ulna," said I, " what is sweet
    In this world that is not ours ? "
Thrice he kissed my cheek, and sighed,
    These are dreary rocks and cold —
Oh, the world is very wide,
    And I weary of my fold !

Now a thousand oxen stray
    That are Ulna's, down the moor,
And great ships their anchors weigh,
    Freighted with his priceless ore.
But my tears will sometimes flow,
    Thinking of the mossy rocks
Where we sat, so long ago,
    I and Ulna, keeping flocks.

WASHING THE SHEEP.

" OH, Jesse, go and wash the sheep —
    The hills are white with May,
The mossy brook is brimming full —
    'T is shearing-time to-day.

And I will bring my spinning-wheel,
  And tie the bands anew,
And when to-night the lilac buds
  Break open with the dew,
I 'll come and meet you, as I used,
  The summer eves ago,
When first you loved me, Jesse dear —
  Or when you told me so."

'T was Emily, the fair young wife
  Of Jesse thus who spake ;
And, kissing her, he straight became
  A shepherd for her sake.
She heard him singing to the sheep,
  Across the hills, all day,
As one by one he plunged them in
  The rainy brook of May.
But ere the eve, the shadows fell,
  The sun in clouds was gone,
And dreary through the western woods
  The windy night came on.

Her gold curls beaten straight beneath
  The rain that wildly drove,
Sad Emily along the hills
  Went calling to her love ;
And calling by the brooks of May,
  The grassy brooks o'erfull,
What sees she 'mid the new-washed lambs
  Gleam whiter than their wool ?
Oh never winter frost, nor ice,
  So filled her heart with dread ;
And never kissed she living love
  As then she kissed the dead !

GEORGE BURROUGHS.[1]

OH, dark as the creeping of shadows,
  At night, o'er the burial hill,
When the pulse in the stony artery
  Of the bosom of earth is still —
When the sky, through its frosty curtain,
  Shows the glitter of many a lamp,
Burning in brightness and stillness,
  Like the fire of a far-off camp —
Must have been the thoughts of the martyr,
  Of the jeers and the taunting scorn,
And the cunning trap of the gallows,
  That waited his feet at morn,
As, down in his lonesome dungeon
  The hours trooped silent and slow,
Like sentinels through the thick darkness,
  Hard by the tents of the foe.

Could he hear the voices of music
  Which thrilled that deep heart of gloom?
Or see the sorrowful beauty
  That meekly leaned by the tomb?

[1] No purer hearts or more heroic spirits ever perished at the
stake than some crushed and broken on the wheel of bigotry
during the Puritan Reign of Terror. Among them, I would in-
stance the Rev. George Burroughs, who prayed with and for his
repentant accuser the day previous to his execution, and whose
conviction demonstrated the righteousness of God to the Rev. Cotton
Mather. After his execution, to which he was conveyed in an open
cart, Mr. Burroughs was stripped of his clothing, dragged by the
hangman's rope to a rocky excavation, in which, being thrown
and trampled on by the mob, he was finally left partly uncovered.

Could he note in the cold and thin shadow
    That swept through his prison bars,
The white hand of the pure seraph
    That beckoned him to the stars,
As, roused to the stony rattle
    Of the hangman's open cart,
He smothered, till only God heard it,
    The piercing cry of his heart?
Can Christ's mercy wash back to whiteness
    The feet his raiment that trod,
Whose soul, from that dark persecution,
    Went up to the bosom of God?
Hath he forgiveness, who shouted,
    " Righteously do ye, and well,
To quench in blood, hot and smoking,
    This firebrand, which is of hell "?

Over fields moistened thus darkly
    Wave harvests of tolerance now —
But the tombstones of the old martyrs
    Sharpened the share of the plow!

LOCHMARLIE.

SHE stood, the hoping and fearing wrought
To one consummate and sovereign thought,
    A dear little dimpled maiden.
But she did not watch for the boat on the tide,
With the black nets dragging over the side,
    And the silver herrings laden.

The waves lay quiet about her feet,
And she made the weed-strewn beach so sweet,
  Both she and her song together;
The two little shoulders out of her gown
Peeping timid, and rosy-brown
  As her Glenfern hills of heather.

All out of the West the scarlet fell,
And the gold and the gray like a chasuble,
  On the moaning and dark Lochmarlie,
And over the red and the gold and gray
The song from the young mouth rippled away,
  And the glad refrain was Charley!

No sounds were heard but the fisher's oar,
As his boat came scudding in to the shore,
  Her nets like a black veil wearing,
And his shout, as he lightly leaped to the land;
But what to the maiden there on the sand
  Was the prize of silver herring!

She hid her shoulders deep in her gown,
And dropt her careless eyelids down
  To the water of dark Lochmarlie;
And over the fisher and nets and all
Her song went on like the beach-bird's call,
  And the wild refrain was Charley!

Slow the night came over the dew,
But never a sail the mist breaks through —
  " Sweetheart, can you thus dissemble?"
And fainter and fainter the love-song grows,
Till it breaks as the raindrops break in the rose
  To a soft and soundless tremble.

Now all is still as still can be,
And the bell strikes one, and two, and three,
    And the morning, whitening over,
Casts the moon in the sea like a ring,
Which a maid might out of her window fling
    To her mad and moaning lover.

The strong-armed fisher comes to the shore,
And heads his slighted boat once more
    Where the silver prize is lying;
But it seems to him that the wild green wave
Turns as the grass turns over a grave,
    And his wrecked heart fills with sighing.

'T is many a year since the maiden's lay,
With the gold and the scarlet, died away
    From the water of dark Lochmarlie;
But still with the night do the tides return
To the heathery hills of wild Glenfern
    With the wail of Charley! Charley!

THE BETROTHED.

I HAVE acted as they have bid me, he said that he was
    blest,
And the sweet seal of betrothal on my forehead has been
    prest;
But my heart gave back no echo to the rapture of his
    bliss,
And the hand he clasped so fondly was less tremulous
    than his.
They praise his lordly beauty, and I know that he is fair,

Oh, I always loved the color of his sunny eyes and hair !
And though my bosom may have held a happier heart
than now,
I have told him that I love him, and I must not break
the vow.
He called me the fair lady of a castle o'er the seas,
And I thought about a cottage nestled in among the
trees ;
And when my cheek beneath his lip burned not, nor
turned aside,
I thought how once a lighter kiss had left it crimson-
dyed.
What care I for the wind-harps breathing low among
the vines,
I better love the swinging of the sleety mountain pines ;
And to track the timid rabbit in the snow-shower, as I
list,
Than to ride his coal-black hunter with the hawk upon
my wrist.
And I fain would give the grandeur of the oaken-shad-
owed lawns,
And the dimly-stretching forest where the red roe leads
her fawns,
To gather the thistle and the fennel's yellow bloom,
Where frowning turrets cumber not the path with gor-
geous gloom.
Let them wreathe the bridal roses with my tresses as
they may ;
There are phantoms in my bosom that cannot keep
away ;
To my heart, as to a banquet, they are crowding, pale
and dread,
But I told him that I loved him, and it cannot be unsaid.

THE WIFE OF LUMLEY MOORE.

HAVE you not seen her many a day,
  Leaning out of her door,
List'ning and looking far away —
  The wife of Lumley Moore?

The leaves of the rooftree, thick and dim,
  Trembling through and through,
And little birds with necks stretched slim,
  As if they listened too?

Have you not seen the air a-hush
  And tender with her praise,
And the squirrel hide in his hazel-bush
  Ashamed of his clumsy ways?

Her timid glances all alert,
  As if her peace was gone,
And her step as light as she feared to hurt
  The grass she trod upon?

Have you not heard her piteous sighs
  That reached to other years,
And seen the light of her sweet, sweet eyes
  Going out in tears?

Poor lady! when at midnight dark
  The death-watch beats his drum,
She turns no more in her bed, to hark
  For feet that do not come.

The brier its thorny arms all wide
Has thrown across her door,
And the lizard slips where lived and died
The wife of Lumley Moore.

THE PEASANT PAVO.

A STORY FROM THE SWEDISH.

ON a sterile farm in the northland
The peasant Pavo lived,
And for seven sweet years together
His crops and his cattle thrived ;
For he wrought with a hand untiring,
And wrought with a heart at peace,
And the merciful Lord and Master
Gave back the good increase.

His boys were rathe and ruddy,
And his girls as fair as the morn,
With hair as bright as the yellow light
In the ears of harvest corn.
And Pavo's wife was comely,
And she never stayed to sigh,
But spun at the wheel, and ground the meal,
And baked the cakes of rye.

The high bleak moors were alway
With Pavo's furrows crossed,
And white as snow in the reeds below
The horns of his cattle tossed.
So seven sweet years together
The prosperous sheaves were bound,

And then the sliding snow-drifts
They froze the seed in the ground.

"Good man, good man!" cries Pavo's wife,
"Our work no more God speeds,
And the silver horns of our cattle
They are drooping under the reeds ;
And the heads of our darling children
They are drooping too," she said.
"Take staff and away, good man, I pray,
Or else we shall starve for bread ! "

"Nay, nay ! " said the peasant Pavo,
"Let us better courage take ;
God tryeth the trust of his servant,
But he will not all forsake !
So sing, good wife, at the cradle,
And sing at the distaff still,
And henceforth, mark, put half of bark
And half of rye, in the mill !

"For me, I will set my furrow
Down deeper by half, nor cease
To break in the morn my cake of corn
And bark, in the sweetest peace."
And the hand of the wife, like a lily,
It fluttered against the pane,
To beck him away from his plow that day,
But all and all in vain.

He digged between the snow-drifts,
And harrowed the sweet seed down,
Till all the high, bleak moorlands
Were green instead of brown.

But the sleet and the hail descended
  All bitter and sharp one day,
And cut from the fair young corn-stalks
  The tender ears away.

Then Pavo's wife fell fretting,
  And would not be at peace ;
" You have sowed," she said, " but where is the bread ?
  God giveth us no increase !
I tell you, man, there hath fallen
  A curse on the plow this day ;
So let it stand and rust in the land,
  And take your staff and away ! "

" Nay, nay ! " said the patient Pavo,
  " God doth but his servant try ; "
And his lambs he sold from out their fold,
  And bought him seeds of rye.
And set his plow yet deeper,
  And deeper harrowed the grain,
And the high, bleak moorlands blossomed
  With a living green again.

And the gracious Lord and Master
  He blessed the tireless hand,
And all like a yellow sunset
  The harvest shone in the land ;
And the wife of the peasant Pavo
  Her cheeks they burned like flame,
And she bound her sheaves with willow-leaves,
  In token of her shame.

MARY AND THE MILLER.

" WHAT are you thinking of, Mary?
Wilful and wise little Mary —
Tell me, my sly little fairy,
    What are you thinking of now? "
" Of my new Easter dress
    In the rose-scented press —
    Of that, and my little brown cow !"

" What are you looking at, Mary?
Glad little golden-haired Mary,
Tell me, my sunshiny fairy,
    What are you looking at now? "
" At a poor silly moth
    I took out o' the froth
    Of the milking-pail, mother, I vow ! "

" What are you harking to, Mary?
Dear little dewy-eyed Mary —
What do you hark to, my fairy,
    With such a wild, wondering look? "
" To the breeze on the hill, mother,
    Not to the mill, mother —
    Not to the mill by the brook ! "

" Why are you sighing so, Mary?
Poor little, pale little Mary —
And is it about the young fairy
    The miller has married but now? "
" It is not for her ring —
    That is no such great thing —
    There are six on the horn of my cow ! "

" Why are you weeping so, Mary ?
Sad little, sweet little Mary —
Sad little, sick little Mary,
 Why are you weeping so, dear ? "
" Oh, I think I shall die !
If I do, let me lie
Where the mill-stream will sing all the year."

PIERRE RAVENAL.

AMONG the rocks and glaciers,
 Where the summer never came,
There lived, one time, a hunter —
 Pierre Ravenal by name.
He had a hut in the mountain,
 And a little red-cheeked wife,
But to chase and kill the chamois
 Was the pleasure of his life.

And he did not love his fireside,
 Nor love the milk of his goats,
Nor love his cloak of camel-cloth,
 As he loved their silken coats.
His eye was all undazzled
 By the plume of the rarest bird,   ·
If he happed to cross in the snow-fields
 The trail of a chamois herd.

One day, when over the glacier
 The wind blew bitter and chill,
Pierre Ravenal shouldered his carbine,
 And tramped away with a will.

And the good little wife by the chimney
  She carded her flaxen wisp,
And left the quarter of rabbit
  To broil on the coals to a crisp.

Ah ! what was the blazing fagot,
  And what was the savory meat,
When Pierre, her hunter and husband,
  Was off in the freezing sleet !
But he loved to chase the chamois
  As well as he loved his life,
Nor ever dreamed of the trouble
  In the heart of the good little wife.

So, while she sat by the chimney,
  And carded a shirt for her Pierre,
He laughed to himself, and shouted,
  For the grandest luck of the year.
He had chased a herd of chamois
  Up, up through the jagged blocks,
To the ledge where they fell sheer downward,
  Four hundred feet of rocks !

When all at once, beside him,
  A dwarf, with a hand of ice,
Stood close, and clutched and held him,
  As if with an iron vice.
Oh, never was seen a monster
  So black, and of shape so ill ;
And the tones of his speech they grated
  Like stones that are crunched in a mill.

And his beard it shook and rattled
  Like withered reeds in a storm,

As he held poor Pierre, head foremost,
By all the length of his arm ;
And backward and forward swung him,
With his ugly face in a frown,
As if he were ready to dash him
Four hundred feet sheer down.

" I 've caught you killing my chamois ! "
He cried, " as I knew I should ;
And you, for the sake of justice,
Shall give back blood for blood ! " —
" Have mercy, oh, have mercy !
Good King of the Dwarfs," cried Pierre,
" For the sake of my starving children, —
For the sake of my wife, so dear !

" They are faint with cold and hunger,
In our poor hut under the snow, —
Good King of the Dwarfs, have mercy,
And for love's sake, let me go ! " —
And the heart of the monster softened
When he heard the piteous call,
And he dragged the hunter in across
The jagged top of the wall.

" Go back ! " he said, as he crushed him
All up in his arm, like a sheaf,
" Go back to your hut; but I tell you,
You are none the less a thief ! "
And then the dwarf, still growling,
Dropt down upon his knees,
And digged from under the snow-cakes
A golden-rinded cheese.

"Take this to your wife and children,
  And by my kingly grace,
Whenever they eat a mouthful,
  Another shall come in its place;
But only just so long," he said,
  " As you hold your honor good;
For if I catch you here again,
  I will have back blood for blood ! "

Then Pierre took up his carbine,
  Saying, " Stand our bargain so ! "
And buttoned the cheese beneath his coat,
  And tramped across the snow.
And seven long years together
  His good little wife and he
Lived in their hut by the mountain side,
  As happy as they could be.

And still, as they ate their supper
  Of cheese, and went to bed,
The golden rind grew whole again,
  The same as the dwarf had said.
And what with the cup of goat's milk,
  And the Alpine flower or two
Sold now and then to a traveller,
  They were well enough to do.

But the little wife had all the while
  A thorn in her bosom hid,
For Pierre would keep his carbine bright,
  Whatever else he did.
" To scour the lock so often,
  It is a foolish thing to do ! "

She would say, because in secret
  She feared the worst was true.

One day, as by the chimney
  She sat at her wheel and sung,
With her face away from the rafter
  Where the polished carbine hung,
Pierre Ravenal slipt it lightly
  From off the beam so low,
And with it slung on his shoulder
  Went tramping through the snow.

And when a herd of chamois
  Before him leaped and ran,
He straight forgot the bargain
  With the dwarfish little man,
And scurried over the snow-fields,
  And up and up the blocks
Of steel-blue ice, till he stood again
  By the awful wall of rocks.

Then all at once the monster,
  With a hand so strong and brown,
Doubled him up, and dashed him
  Four hundred feet sheer down!
And still about the ink-black pool,
  Where he lost his life that day,
You may see him spinning round and round,
  Like the wheel of his wife, they say.

And she, poor soul, when she missed him,
  Snapt straight her song in twain,

And never in all her lifetime
  Could join it on again.
For she knew when she brought her cheese-cake
  To end her week of fast,
By the golden rind still broken,
  That her fears were true at last.

THE LAST VOYAGE.

AT shut of day they sat and talked,
  In their old house by the sea ;
The weather-beaten Solomon,
  And his good wife Marsalee.

" The sun looks like a ship," he said,
  " That is nearly come to land ;
That slanting beam, like a plank pushed out
  To take aboard some hand."

And when at length the gold-backed clouds
  Crouched in the dark, from view,
He said, " It will be a stormy night ;
  May the good ship weather through ! "

At last the old wife Marsalee
  Could win no answering word ;
The ship was gone, the plank hauled in,
  And Solomon was aboard.

WORLDLY WISE.

It was the boatman Ronsalee,
  And he sailed through the mists so white,
And two little ladies sat at his knee,
  With their two little heads so bright;
And so they sailed and sailed — all three —
  On the golden coast o' the night.

Young Ronsalee had a handsome face,
  And his great beard made him brown;
And the two little ladies in girlish grace
  They kept their eyelids down —
The one in her silken veil of lace,
  And the one in her woolsey gown.

For one little lady lived in the wood,
  Like a flower that hides from the day;
Her name was Jenny — they called her the good,
  And the name of the other was May;
And her palace window looked on the flood
  Where they softly sailed away.

Long time the balance even stood
  With our Ronsalee that day;
But what was a little house in the wood
  To a palace grand and gay?
So he gave his heart to Jenny the good,
  And his hand he gave to May.

THE HUNTER'S WIFE.

'T WAS all through the roses, so ripe and so red,
And all when the summer was shining her best,
That Lindsey, my lover, rode into the West,
The land of the prairie, a-hunting to go
For the fawn and the pheasant, the dove and the doe —
'T was all through the roses, and roses are dead.

I look from the porch-side and dream, as I must,
Of the time when I pulled the green grape-leaves apart,
As Lindsey, my lover, my sweet, sweetest heart,
Rode into the shadow, and out of my sight —
Ah! never a day-dawn has broke on that night,
    And all the green grape-leaves are dry as the dust.

He sat in his saddle, so bright and so brave —
The dint of his hoof-strokes along the wolf's track
I followed and followed — I could not stay back!
O Lindsey, my lover, my hunter, my friend,
I would I had followed thee on to the end —
    Into wilderness places, ay, into the grave.

In the way of his riding the rough rushes fell,
And the fox in his covert all timidly bayed,
And the eagle rose, flapping his broad wings afraid,
For the gun on his shoulder hung polished and bright,
And the knife at his girdle flashed out like a light,
    And the bit at his bridle, it rung like a bell.

'T was all through the roses, and when the year stood
At the sunset, and shone in the gold-colored leaves,

And thin, like a sickle that hangs among sheaves,
The moon of the autumn looked out of the mist,
The brows of my babes for their father I kissed,
    And kept up a truce with my heart, as I could.

'T was all through the roses, and when they were dead,
And the rain slanted slow from the clouds all the day,
And my dogs in the warmth of my chimney-logs lay;
And while of a-shiver, with horn upon horn,
My cattle crouched under the broad-bladed corn,
    Thou still hast some roof-tree, O lost love! I said.

Hush, darlings, oh, hush! he will come back again
When only a day or a night has gone by!
And I rocked them asleep to the kingfisher's cry,
The starling's wild clatter, the call of the quail,
And the beat upon beat of the pioneer's flail;
    But I promised and pacified, all, all in vain.

At last, when the lonesome lament of the loon
Began to be heard, while the frost, sharp and cold,
Was cutting his harvest of scarlet and gold,
And when in the prairie-grass, fallen and dead,
The wings of the starlings no longer shone red,
    My lullaby fell to a mournfuller tune.

Then fear came upon me, and day after day
I lingered, in visions, his camp-grounds about —
The game-pots were steamless, the fires all were out;
The tent-poles a-tumble, and ready to fall,
That held the rough buffalo-hide for a wall,
    And the black-snake lay under the fagots and hay.

Like dry sands my hearth-stones slid under my feet,
As I sat with just only my door-planks between
My babes and the panther so lithe and so lean,
And with only the blaze of the clearing to scare
The hungry and horrible eyes of the bear, —
    And so came the winter in harness of sleet.

And now, as the wind ploughs the furrows so white
Across the long prairie, I cannot but cry —
My stables are littered with oat-straw and rye,
The breath of my cattle makes warmth in the cold,
My dogs are in kennel, my sheep are in fold,
    But where lies my Lindsey, my lover, to-night?

Again and again from my pillow I start,
And feel down the wolf-skin that covers the beds
Of my darlings, and drag to my bosom their heads,
As under my windows, now to and now fro,
I hear the wild catamount stealthily go —
    The blood all a-curdle and cold in my heart.

Yet sometimes a sweet vision blesses my eyes:
I see a gay huntsman ride over the snow,
And I blush, for the gifts at his girdle I know:
The red combs of cocks, and the antlers as clear
And white as the ivory, are gifts for his dear,
    And I call to my darlings, Awake, and arise!

I call at my peril — the dream groweth dim —
The combs red as roses, the white antlers pass;
And I see but the lift of the long prairie grass,
And hear but the whimper and moan of unrest
From the swollen and snag-slivered streams of the West,
    But there cometh no news, and no tidings of him.

O women who sit while the winter winds rave,
And mourn for the husbands and lovers so low
Beneath the wild drifts of the leaves and the snow, —
Remember, while grief in its fountain thus stirs,
Your burden is lighter to bear than is hers
  Who mourns for her dead that had never a grave.

O women whose hands, when the winter has fled,
Shall pluck off the roses and strew them so deep
O'er the beds where your dearly-beloved ones sleep,
The while in your desolate darkness you pine, —
Remember your sorrow is lighter than mine
  Who know not, nor can know, the place of my dead.

SYLVIA.

LONE among the evening shades,
Brown and purple, red and gray,
Went the tender Sylvia,
Fairest of the rustic maids,
Driving home her pastured cows:
Close along the drooping boughs
Of a black, enchanted grove,
Went she, dreaming dreams of love,
Dreaming dreams about a lover, —
Went she, treading down the clover,
Ivy buds and daisies fair,
And wild violets, unaware, —
Went she, slowly, with her cows,
Treading through the round red clover.
Ah, to see her thoughtful brows,
And her sweet mouth, was to love her!

In the black, enchanted grove
Lived a spirit dressed with clay,
And to see her was to love ;
So he sang a herdsman's lay,
Bringing all her cows that way.

Of their meeting, if they met,
    Not a word the story tells, —
But of days in clouds that set,
    And of winds in gusty swells
Driving madly every way, —
And of cattle gone astray
In the rainy woods ; of skies
Shutting all their golden eyes ;
And of moanings in the air,
That did seem, the story says,
For some lost soul — let us pray
    That it was not Sylvia's.

BALLAD.

FROM THE SCLAVIC.

ALL in the early morning
    The Sclavic maid so fair
Arose at her mother's calling,
    And combed her yellow hair ;

And laced with silken ribbons
    Her bodice of leaf-green,
And tript adown the mountain path
    The frosty reeds between.

And while the rough winds kissed her,
   She knelt at the fountain's brink,
But the ice was frozen all across,
   And her pitcher would not sink.

Ah! then she fell a-weeping,
   And her red mouth trembled white,
For she feared her mother's cruel eyes,
   As well indeed she might.

"Come, sun!" she cried through her sobbing,
   "Come out of the clouds so brown,
And lick the ice with your golden tongue,
   And let my pitcher down!

"O eagle, strong-winged eagle,
   Come out of the skies so blue,
And split the ice with your horny beak,
   And let my pitcher through!"

But the sun, for all her sobbing,
   Came not through the clouds so brown,
To lick the ice with his golden tongue,
   And let her pitcher down.

And the eagle, proudly soaring,
   Came not from his home so blue,
To make a wedge of his horny beak,
   And split the ice in two.

Ah! then in the early morning
   A piteous sight was seen —
Her tears all frozen into pearls,
   Along her bodice green.

For, lo! betwixt the stiff black reeds,
  Adown the mountain path,
She heard her mother calling
  In her foolish woman's wrath:

" Oh, wilful, stubborn daughter,
  Since thou idlest all the day,
I would the winds might beat thee,
  And take thy breath away!

" Yea, beat and break and crush thee,
  Since thou art so high and proud,
And I would the needles of the frost
  Might sew thee in a shroud! "

Alas for the wicked woman,
  Little dreamed she in that hour
That a word may be, for good or ill,
  Omnipotent in power.

And alas for the Sclavic maiden,
  She turned her east and south,
And her heart it fluttered into her throat,
  And fluttered out of her mouth.

The winds they fell to beating her,
  And she knew not where to flee,
And, to 'scape from her mother's cruel eyes,
  She hid in a maple-tree.

And in its time of blooming,
  That tree grew strangely fair —
Its leaves like the maiden's bodice green,
  And its blossoms like her hair.

But still, as the sunshine gilded
  Its head, so brave and high,
There shivered through its branches old
  A dull and dolorous cry.

One day, as it chanced, there rested
  Two lads in its pleasant shade,
And they were the minstrel brothers
  Of the little Sclavic maid.

And, lo ! as they played a merry tune
  They each grew heavy at heart,
And the wood of their viols all at once
  It brake and snapt apart.

Then cried they both : " This maple
  Is the best that e'er we saw.
Oh, would n't it make us fiddle-sticks
  Right silver-sweet to draw ! "

And straight they fetched an axe and set
  Its sharp edge in the wood,
And all in a spout the sap came out,
  And ran as red as blood ;

While all the body of the tree
  It trembled low and high,
And all the tender branches made
  A dull and dolorous cry.

And when it fell beneath their strokes,
  And lay along the land,
The touch of every leaf was like
  Some gentle little hand.

But, ah! the saddest part of all
　My tale is yet to tell:
For when from out the viol strings
　At last the music fell,

The mother's cold and cruel heart
　Grew wild with pain and fear —
She knew it was her daughter's voice
　That sounded in her ear.

And, as the maple-tree had done,
　She fell to rise no more,
But prostrate lay, and so became
　The door-stone of her door.

SECOND SIGHT.

LITTLE lass of Dalnacardoch,
Carding wool of Dalnacardoch,
Oh, the dreams that lie about her,
　Full of light, and over full,
Like the clouds in golden weather,
While she sits and smites together
The two cards that tear the tangles
　From her fleece of heathland wool.

Slyest lass of Dalnacardoch,
Shyest lass of Dalnacardoch!
Oh, I know your pretty secret,
　And ye have no need to speak;
'T is your thoughts about a lover
That are running in and over —

Running sadly in and over
That dear dimple of your cheek.

As the lily in the water
Swims up softly through the water,
Giving forth her folded sweetness
  When the sun is in the skies,
So from out its place of hiding
Comes your heart up at the bidding
Of the bold audacious glances
  That he sends you from his eyes.

In the harvest of the barley
'T was the sheaf of Nichol Marley
That was tied with gay green ribbons
  All untwisted from bright hair,
While the moon, so fair and fickle,
Like a dagger, not a sickle,
Struck down sharply through the mist-cloud,
  Lying swarth-like on the air.

Oh, the broom that waved so yellow
O'er the heathlands, now is sallow,
Oh, the grass as green 's a ribbon,
  Now is withered, wild, and gray ;
And the sheared sheep then incloses,
With their backs as pink as roses,
Loose among the dry black nettles
  And the rough-leaved thistles stray.

Oh, the lass of Dalnacardoch,
Woe, the lass of Dalnacardoch,
Still her gold-dreams lie about her,
  And she lives in sweet belief

That the heath with bloom is shining,
And the grass as green's the twining
Of the fortune-witching ribbon
  Twisted in with Nichol's sheaf.

He is hunting on high Rannoch —
On the heathery moor of Rannoch,
By the brave Loch-Ericht eagle,
  Driving blindly toward his nest;
True to nature, onward, sunward,
With a broken leg dragged downward,
And a clot of wet, red feathers,
  Growing sodden in his breast.

'T is his rifle-shots thick flying,
By the screaming and the crying
Of the patriarchal ravens
  Sailing stately, far and near,
And by faintly outlined doubles
Moistened red along the stubbles,
Where in one bed, both together,
  Death o'ertook them, doe and deer.

Fearless lass of Dalnacardoch,
Tearless lass of Dalnacardoch,
Tease the tangles from the tangles —
  Comb and card your fleeces white
With your heart as light's a feather,
And your dreams like golden weather,
And God save ye, little lassie,
  Save ye from a second sight!

CHARLEY'S DEATH.

THE wind got up moaning, and blew to a breeze ;
  I sat with my face closely pressed on the pane ;
  In a minute or two it began to rain,
And put out the sunset-fire in the trees.

In the clouds' black faces broke out dismay
  That ran of a sudden up half the sky,
  And the team, cutting ruts in the grass, went by,
Heavy and dripping with sweet wet hay.

Clutching the straws out and knitting his brow,
  Walked Arthur beside it, unsteady of limb ;
  I stood up in wonder, for, following him,
Charley was used to be ; — where was he now ?

" 'T is like him," I said, " to be working thus late ! " —
  I said it, but did not believe it was so ;
  He could not have staid in the meadow to mow,
With rain coming down at so dismal a rate.

" He 's bringing the cows home." — I choked at that
    lie :
  They were huddled close by in a tumult and fret, —
  Some pawing the dry dust up out of the wet,
Some looking afield with their heads lifted high.

O'er the run, o'er the hilltop, and on through the gloom
  My vision ran quick as the lightning could dart ;
  All at once the blood shocked and stood still in my
    heart ; —
He was coming as never till then he had come !

Borne 'twixt our four work-hands, I saw through the
    fall
Of the rain, and the shadows so thick and so dim,
They had taken their coats off and spread them on
    him,
And that he was lying out straight, — that was all!

POEMS OF THOUGHT AND FEELING.

PICTURES OF MEMORY.

AMONG the beautiful pictures
  That hang on Memory's wall,
Is one of a dim old forest
  That seemeth best of all :
Not for its gnarled oaks olden,
  Dark with the mistletoe ;
Not for the violets golden
  That sprinkle the vale below ;
Not for the milk-white lilies
  That lean from the fragrant hedge,
Coquetting all day with the sunbeams,
  And stealing their shining edge ;
Not for the vines on the upland
  Where the bright red berries be,
Nor the pinks, nor the pale sweet cowslip,
  It seemeth the best to me.

I once had a little brother,
  With eyes that were dark and deep —
In the lap of that old dim forest
  He lieth in peace asleep :
Light as the down of the thistle,
  Free as the winds that blow,

We roved there the beautiful summers,
The summers of long ago ;
But his feet on the hills grew weary,
And, one of the autumn eves,
I made for my little brother
A bed of the yellow leaves.

Sweetly his pale arms folded
My neck in a meek embrace,
As the light of immortal beauty
Silently covered his face :
And when the arrows of sunset
Lodged in the tree-tops bright,
He fell, in his saint-like beauty,
Asleep by the gates of light.
Therefore, of all the pictures
That hang on Memory's wall,
The one of the old dim forest
Seemeth the best of all.

GRAND–DAME AND CHILD.

THE maple's limbs of yellow flowers
Made spots of sunshine here and there
In the bleak woods ; a merry pair
Of bluebirds, which the April-showers
Had softly called, were come that day ;
Another week would bring the May,
And all the meadow-grass would shine
With strawberries ; and all the trees
Whisper of coming blooms, and bees
Work busy, making golden wine.

The white-haired grand-dame, faint and sick,
  Sits fretful in her chair of oak ;
The clock is nearly on the stroke
Of all the day's best hour, and quick
  The dreamy house will glimmer bright —
No candle needed any more,
  For Miriam's smile is so like light,
The moths fly with her in the door.

The lilies carvèd in her chair
  The grand-dame counts, but cannot tell
If they be three or seven ; the pair
  Of merry bluebirds, singing well,
She does not hear ; nor can she see
  The moonshine, cold and pure and bright,
  Walk like an angel clothed in white,
The path where Miriam should be.

Almost she hears the little feet
  Patter along the path of sands ;
Her eyes are making pictures sweet,
  And every breeze her cheek that fans
Half cheats her to believe, I wis,
It is her pretty grandchild's kiss.

The dainty hood, her fancy too
  Sees hanging on the cabin wall,
And from her modest eyes of blue,
  Fair Miriam putting back the fall
Of her brown hair, and laughing wild —
Her darling merry-hearted child ;
  Then with a step as light and low
  As any wood-birds in the snow,
She goes about her household cares.

"The saints will surely count for prayers
   The duties love doth sweeten so,"
Says the pleased grand-dame ; but, alas !
No feet are pattering on the grass,
No hood is hanging on the wall —
It was a foolish dreaming, all.

The morning-glories winding up
   The rustic pillars of the shed,
Open their dark bells, cup by cup,
   To the June's rainy clouds ; the bed
Of rosemary and meadow-sweet
   Which Miriam kept with so much care,
Is run to weeds, and everywhere
Across the paths her busy feet
   Wore smooth and hard, the grass has grown —
And still the grand-dame sits alone,
Counting the lilies in her chair —
   Her ancient chair of carvèd oak —
And fretful, listening for the stroke
Of the old clock, and for the pair
   Of bluebirds that have long been still ;
   Saying, as o'er the neighboring hill
The shadows gather thick and dumb —
" 'T is time that Miriam were come."

And now the spiders cease to weave,
   And from between the corn's green stems,
   Drawing after her her scarlet hems,
Dew-dappled, the brown-vested Eve
   Slow to his purple pillows drops ;
   His tired team now the plowman stops ;
In the dim woods the axe is still,

And sober, winding round the hill,
   The cows come home. " Come, pretty one,
I 'm watching for you at the door,"
Calls the old grand-dame o'er and o'er,
   " 'T is time the working all were done."

And kindly neighbors come and go,
   But gently piteous ; none have said,
" Your pretty grandchild sleepeth so
   We cannot wake her ; " but instead
Piling the cushions in her chair,
   Carved in many a quaint design
   Of leaves and lilies, nice and fine,
They tell her she must not despair
   To meet her pretty child again —
To see her wear forevermore
   A smile of brighter love than when
The moths flew with her in the door.

TO THE WINDS.

TALK to my heart, O winds —
   Talk to my heart to-night ;
My spirit always finds
   With you a new delight,
Finds always new delight
In your silver talk at night.

Give me your soft embrace
   As you used to long ago,
In your shadowy trysting-place,
   When you seemed to love me so —

When you sweetly kissed me so,
On the green hills long ago.

Come up from your cool bed,
  In the stilly twilight sea,
For the dearest hope lies dead,
  That was ever dear to me ;
Come up from your cool bed,
And we 'll talk about the dead.

Tell me, for oft you go,
  Winds, lovely winds of night,
About the chambers low,
  With sheets so dainty white,
If they sleep through all the night,
In the beds so chill and white :

Talk to me, winds, and say,
  If in the grave be rest ;
For, oh, life's little day
  Is a weary one at best ;
Talk to my heart, and say
  If death will give me rest.

TO THE SPIRIT OF GLADNESS.

UNDERNEATH a dreary sky,
  Spirit glad and free,
Voyaging solemnly am I
  Toward an unknown sea.
Falls the moonlight, sings the breeze,
But thou speakest not in these.

In the summers overflown
  What delights we had !
Now I sit all day alone,
  Weaving ditties sad ;
But thou com'st not for the sake
Of the lonesome rhymes I make.

Faithless spirit, spirit free,
  Where may'st thou be found ?
Where the meadow fountains be
  Raining music round,
And the thistle-burs so blue
Shine the livelong day with dew.

Keep thee, in thy pleasant bowers,
  From my heart and brain ;
Even the summer's lap of flowers
  Could not cool the pain ;
And for pallid cheek and brow
What companionship hast thou ?

Erewhile, when the rainy spring
  Filled the pastures full
Of sweet daisies blossoming
  Out as white as wool ;
We have gathered them, and made
Beds of Beauty in the shade.

Would that I had any friend
  Lovingly to go
To the hollows where they blend
  With the grasses low,
And a pillow soft and white
Make for the approaching night.

THE NEW-YEAR.

LIKE the cry of Despair, where the war-weapons rattle,
Or the moan of a god in some mythical battle,
Rung out o'er the senses of pain and of swooning
Above the death-woe of immortal discrowning,
There came yesternight in the midst of my dreaming
A wail, waking visions of terrible seeming.

The fires of the sunset had burnt from the shadows
Their leashes, and slipt, they ran over the meadows,
Deepening up from the dulness and grayness of ashes,
To the hue of that deep wave the night-time that washes,
Where sorrow's black tresses are gathered up never,
But sweep o'er the red pillows ever and ever.

Thus startled from slumber, I fearfully listened :
The frost had been busy, and phantom-shapes glistened
Along the cold pane where the dead bough was creaking,
When, close in my chamber, I heard a low speaking ;
And I said, " Wherefore comest thou, mystical spirit ?
Have I evil or good at thy hands to inherit ? "

Like a rose-vine entwining some ruinous column,
The sweet and the lovely were over the solemn,
As fell through the silence this cadence, replying :
" Watch with me, O mortal, watch with me, I 'm
        dying ! "
And I answered, " I will, by the blessèd evangel ! "
Unknowing my guest, whether demon or angel.

It seemed, as I sat with the sad darkness holding
Communion, I almost could hear the shroud folding

About the still bosom and smoothly wound tresses
That love might imprison no more with caresses —
The half-smothered sobs, and the orphan-like calling,
With passionate kisses the dust over falling.

" Art thou dead ? " I said ; " thus doth my watch have
    its ending ?
And needest thou not any more my befriending ? "
" Nay, not dead, but fallen, and mortally wounded,"
The death-subdued accent along the dark sounded —
" Claimest thou of me largess ? " — " Yes," said I, " thy
    story,
So number me swiftly the days of thy glory."

Along the wild moorland the wind whistled dreary,
And low as a death-watch my heart beat, a-weary,
As like one beside the hushed portal of Aiden,
Awaiting the accent to soothe or to sadden,
I sat in expectancy, charmèd and holy,
Till thus spake the spirit, serenely and slowly :

" On a bed of dead leaves and a snow-pillow lying,
The winds stooping round him, and, sorrowful, crying,
His beard full of ice, his hands folded from reaping,
My sire, when I woke into life, lay a-sleeping,
And so of my brief reign was given the warning,
Ere yet I beheld the sweet eyes of the morning.

" ' Blow winds of the wilderness,' cried I, ' and cover
With dim dust the pallid corpse under and over,
For through the bright gates of the orient, sweeping,
The heralds of day come — I would not be weeping ; '
And putting away from my lip sorrow's chalice,
I left him beside the blue wall of my palace.

" So, a twelvemonth agone, with my young wing ex-
panded,
On the shores of my kingdom, a monarch I landed ;
Star-lamps were aglow in the cloudy-lined arches,
As I sent the first embassy hours on their marches ;
And day, softly wrapt in a fleece that was golden,
Came up when my council with light first was holden.

" The silvery rings of two moons had their filling,
When the north drew his breath in, so bitterly chilling,
And clad in a robe of red hunter-like splendor,
On a hollow reed piping a madrigal tender,
Through meadow and orchard, came March, his loud
laughter,
Half drowned, in the whine of the winds, crouching
after.

" Next came from the south land, one, fair as a maiden,
Her lap with fresh buds and green sprouting leaves
laden ;
Her slight dewy fingers with daffodils crowded,
Her lip ever smiling, her brow ever clouded ;
But the birds on her flowery wake that came flying,
Beside a thick blossoming hedge found her dying.

" Blown, like a silvery cloud o'er the edges
Of morning, the elder-blooms swayed in the hedges,
The quail whistled out in the stubble, and over
The meadow the bee went in search of the clover ;
When came, with a train of delights for her warders,
The dewy-eyed May, up the green river borders.

" Bright ridges of bees round the full hive were humming,
Away in the thick woods the partridge was drumming ;

The rush of the sickle, the scythe-stroke serener,
Were pleasantly mixed with the song of the gleaner,
When under the shadows of full-blowing roses
The days of the virginal June had their closes.

" When oxen unyoked laid their foreheads together,
And berries were ripe for the schoolboys to gather ;
When sultry heats over the hilltops were winking,
And down in the hollows the streamlets were shrinking ;
When birds hushed their musical glee to a twitter,
Came July, with a mist of gold over her litter.

" Like the slim crescent moon through an amber-cloud
    shining
Above the brown woods when the day is declining,
Among the ripe wheat-shocks the sickle was glowing,
And over the summer dark shadows went blowing,
When, crowned with the oat-flowers, heavy and yellow,
Came August, her cheek with the summer's sun sallow.

" About the next comer deep calmness was lying,
And yet from her presence the wild birds went flying,
As out of the orchards and grape-woven bowers
She gathered the fruit with no sigh for the flowers,
And shook down the nuts on the withering mosses,
Unmindful of all the bright summer-time losses.

" When harvesters home from the cornfield were bring-
    ing
The baskets of ripe ears, with laughter and singing,
What time his past labor the husbandman blesses
In cups of sweet cider, just oozed from the presses,
Beneath the broad forest boughs, saddened in seeming,
And hooded with red leaves, October sat dreaming.

" Winds for the dead flowers mournfully searching,
Tall phantoms that out of the darkness came marching,
Clouds, full of blackness and storms, fleetly flying,
Or on the bleak edges of winter-time lying,
Quenching with chilly rain Autumn's last splendor —
These were the handmaids that came with November.

" Making the gentle kine, sorrowful lowing,
Turn from the tempest so bitterly blowing —
Now lying on slopes, to the southern light slanted,
Now filling the woods with hymns mournfully chanted,
I saw — my steps weakly beginning to falter —
The last Season lay his white gift on the altar.

" Then I knew by the chill through my bosom slow
        stealing,
And the pang at my heart, that my dark doom was
        sealing,
And seeing before me the ever-hushed portal,
I sought to reveal to some pitying mortal,
The while from my vision the life-light was waning,
The gladness and grief of my bright and brief reigning.

" Ah, many a poet I had whose sweet idyls
Made vocal the chambers of births and of bridals,
And many a priest, too, both shaved and unshaven,
To hide in the meal of the world the Word's leaven ;
But still at the church and the merry mirth-making,
With the good and the gay there were hearts that were
        breaking.

" Deeds darker than night and words sharper than dag-
        gers
Have peopled my wilderness places with Hagars ;

The wayfaring man has been often benighted,
Where never a taper for guidance was lighted ;
But over the desolate cloud and the scorning
Has risen the gladness that comes with the morning.

"On the white cheek of beauty the blushes have trembled,
Betraying the heart that would else have dissembled,
When the eloquent whisper of young Love was spoken ;
But oh, when the burial sod has been broken
For dear ones, with hands folded close for the sleeping,
The nights have been dismal with comfortless weeping.

" Thus, mortal, I give to your keeping this story
Of transient dominion — its sadness and glory,
And while my last accents are mournfully spoken,
The sceptre I swayed, in my weak hand is broken,
And darkness unending my gray hair is hooding,
And over, and round me, the midnight is brooding."

The silence fell heavy : my watching was over,
The old year was dead, and though many a lover
He had in his lifetime, not one would there tarry
To mourn at his deathbed — for all must make merry
About the young monarch, some grace to be winning,
With welcome or gift, while his reign was beginning.

FIRE PICTURES.

In the embers all aglow,
  Fancy makes the pictures plain,
As I listen to the snow
  Beating chill against the pane —

The wild December snow
  On the lamp-illumined pane.

Bent downward from his prime,
  Like the ripe fruit from its bough,
As I muse my simple rhyme,
  I can see my father now,
With the warning flowers of time
  Blooming white about his brow.

Sadly flows the willow-tree
  On the hill so dear, yet dread,
Where the resting-places be,
  Of our dear ones that are dead —
Where the mossy headstones be
  Of my early playmates dead.

But despite the dismal snow,
  Blinding all the window o'er,
And the wind that, crouching low,
  Whines against my study-door,
In the embers' twilight glow
  I can see one picture more.

Seeming almost within call,
  'Neath our ancient trysting-tree,
Art thou pictured, source of all
  That was ever dear to me ;
But the wasted embers fall,
  And the night is all I see —

The night with gusts of snow
  Blowing wild against the pane,

And the wind that crouches low,
Crying mournfully in vain,
And the dreams that come and go
Through my memory-haunted brain.

TO THE SPIRIT OF SONG.

COME, sweet spirit, come, I pray,
Thou hast been too long away ;
Come, and in the dreamland light,
Keep with me a tryst to-night.

When the reapers once at morn
Bound the golden stocks of corn,
Shadowy hands, that none could see,
Gleaned along the field with me.

Come, and with thy wings so white
Hide me from a wicked sprite,
That has vexed me with a sign
Which I tremble to divine.

At a black loom sisters three
Saw I weaving.   Can it be,
Thought I, as I saw them crowd
The white shuttles, 't is a shroud ?

Silently the loom they left,
Taking mingled warp and weft,
And, as wild my bosom beat,
Measured me from head to feet.

Liest thou in the drowning brine,
Sweetest, gentlest love of mine,
Tangled softly from my prayer
By some Nereid's shining hair?

Or, when mortal hope withdrew,
Didst thou, faithless, leave me too,
Blowing on thy lovely reed,
Careless how my heart should bleed?

By this sudden chill I know
That it is, it must be so —
Sprite of darkness, sisters three,
Lo, I wait your ministry.

DISSATISFIED.

For me, in all life's desert sand
  No well is made, no tent is spread ;
No father's nor a brother's hand
  Is laid in blessing on my head.
The radiance of my mortal star
  Is crossed with signs of woe to me,
And all my thoughts and wishes are
  Sad wanderers toward eternity.

Stricken, riven helplessly apart
  From all that blest the path I trod ;
Oh, tempt me, tempt me not, my heart,
  To arraign the goodness of my God !
For suffering hath been made sublime,
  And souls, that lived and died alone,

Have left an echo for all time,
  As they went wailing to the throne.

There have been moments when I dared
  Believe life's mystery a breath,
And deem Faith's beauteous bosom bared
  To the betraying arms of Death ;
For the immortal life but mocks
  The soul that feels its ruin dire,
And like a tortured demon rocks
  Upon the cradling waves of fire.
To mine is pressed no loving lip,
  Around me twines no helping arm ;
And like a frail dismasted ship
  I blindly drift before the storm.

TO THE HOPEFUL.

HARK ! for the multitude cry out,
  O watchman, tell us of the night ;
And hear the joyous answering shout,
  The hills are red with light !

Lo ! where the followers of the meek,
  Like Johns, are crying in the wild,
The leopard lays its spotted cheek
  Close to the new-born child.

The gallows-tree with tremor thrills —
  The North to mercy's plea inclines ;
And round about the Southern hills
  Maidens are planting vines.

The star that trembled softly bright,
  Where Mary and the young child lay,
Through ages of unbroken night
  Hath tracked his luminous way.

From the dim shadow of the palm
  The tattooed islander has leant,
Helping to swell the wondrous psalm
  Of love's great armament!

And the wild Arab, swart and grave,
  Looks startled from his tent, and scans
Advancing truth, with shining wave,
  Washing the desert sands.

Forth from the slaver's deadly crypt
  The Ethiop like an athlete springs,
And from her long-worn fetters stript,
  The dark Liberian sings.

But sorrow to and fro must keep
  Its heavings until evil cease,
Like the great cradle of the deep,
  Rocking a storm to peace.

MY BROTHER.

THE beech-wood fire is burning bright —
  'T is wild November weather —
Like that of many a stormy night
  We 've sat and talked together.

Such pretty plans for future years
  We told to one another —
I cannot choose but ask with tears,
  Where are they now, my brother?

Where are they now, the dreams we dreamed,
  That scattered sunshine o'er us,
And where the hills of flowers that seemed
  A little way before us?

The hills with golden tops, and springs,
  Than which no springs were clearer?
Ah me, for all our journeyings
  They are not any nearer!

One, last year, who with sunny eyes
  A watch with me was keeping,
Is gone : across the next hill lies
  The snow upon her sleeping.

And so alone, night after night,
  I keep the fire a-burning,
And trim and make the candle bright,
  And watch for your returning.

The clock ticks slow, the cricket tame
  Is on the hearth-stone crying,
And the old Bible just the same
  Is on the table lying.

The watch-dog whines beside the door,
  My hands forget the knitting —
Oh, shall we ever any more
  Together here be sitting!

Sometimes I wish the winds would sink,
    The cricket hush its humming,
The while I listened, for I think
    I hear a footstep coming.

Just as it used so long ago ;
    My cry of joy I smother —
'T is only fancy cheats me so.
    And never thou, my brother !

BURNS.[1]

HE died : he went from all the praise
  . That fell on ears unheeding,
And scarcely can we read his lays
    For pauses in the reading,
To mourn the buds of poesy
    That never came to blushing ;
For who can choose but sigh, ah me !
    For their untimely crushing !

And when we see, o'er ruins dim,
    The summer roses climbing,
We sadly pause, and think of him,
    The beauty of whose rhyming
Spread sunshine o'er the darkest ill, —
    Alas ! it could not cover
The heart from breaking, that was still
    Through all despairs a lover —

[1] Written on reading in the Letters of Burns: "We have no
flour in the house, and must borrow for a few days."

A lover of the beautiful
  In nature's sweet evangels ;
For his great heart was worshipful
  For men, and for the angels.
The rank with him was not the man,
  He knew no servile bowing ;
And wee things o'er the furrow ran
  Unharmed beside his ploughing.

Lights flowing out of palaces
  Dimmed not the candles burning,
Whereby the glorious mysteries
  Of music he was learning ;
And not with envious looks he eyed
  The morning larks upgoing,
From meadows that were all too wide
  And green for peasant mowing.

For by his cabin-door the grass
  Was pleasant with the daisies ;
And o'er the brae, some bonny lass
  Was happy in his praises.
O Thou who hear'st my simple strain,
  The while I muse his story —
Here knew he all a poet's pain,
  Grant now he have the glory !

THE POET.

Upon a bed of flowery moss,
With moonbeams falling all across —
Moonbeams chilly and faint and dim,
(Sweet eyes I ween do watch for him) —

Lieth his starry dreams among,
The gentlest poet ever sung.

The wood is thick — 't is late in night,
Yet feareth he no evil sprite,
Nor vexing ghost — such things there be
In many a poet's destiny.
Haply some wretched fast or prayer,
Painèd and long, hath charmed the air.

Softer than hymeneal hymns
The fountains, bubbling o'er their rims,
Wash through the vernal reeds, and fill
The hollows : all beside is still,
Save the poet's breathing, low and light.
Watch no more, lady — no more to-night ! —

Heavy his gold locks are with dew,
Yet by the pansies mixed with rue
Bitter and rough, but now that fell
From his shut hand, he sleepeth well.
He sleepeth well, and his dream is bright
Under the moonbeams chilly and white.

The night is dreary, the boy is fair —
Hath he been mated with Despair,
Or crossed in love, that he lies alone
With shadows and moonlight overblown —
Shadows and moonlight chilly and dim ?
And do no sweet eyes watch for him ?

Nay, rather is his soul instead
With immortal thirst disquieted,

That oft like an echo wild and faint
He makes to the hills and the groves his plaint?
That oft the light on his forehead gleams,
So troubled under its crown of dreams?

Watch no more, lady, no more, I pray,
He is wrapt in a lonely power away!
Sweet boy, so sleeping, might it be
That any prayer I said for thee
Could answer win from the spirit shore,
This were it, " Let him wake no more!"

PARTING WITH A POET.

ALL the sweet summer that is gone,
    Two paths I sighed to mark —
One brightly leading up and on,
    One downward to the dark.

No prophecy enwrapt my heart,
    No Vala's gifts were mine ;
Yet knew I that our paths must part —
    The loftier one be thine.

For not a soul inspiredly thrills,
    Whose wing shall not be free
To sweep across the eternal hills,
    Like winds across the sea.

And wheresoe'er thy lot may be,
    As all the past has proved,
Love shall abide and be with thee,
    For genius must be loved.

While I, the heart's vain yearning stilled,
  The heart that vexed me long,
Essay with my poor hands to build
  The silvery walls of song.

Still, through the nights of wild unrest,
  That softer joyance bars,
Winding about my vacant breast
  The tresses of the stars.

While at the base of heights sublime,
  Dim thoughts forevermore
Lie moaning, like the waves of time
  Along the immortal shore.

TO MARY.

OH, will affection's tendrils twine
  About that summer time for aye,
When, midway 'twixt thy home and mine,
  The quiet village churchyard lay ! —
With stars beginning to ascend,
  The night-hawks scooping through the air —
Dost thou remember, O my friend,
  How often we have parted there ?

That summer was a sunlit sea,
  Reflecting neither cloud nor frown,
Yet in its bright wave noiselessly
  Some ventures of the heart went down :
Blest be the one that still outrides
  The silent but tumultuous strife

Of hopes and fears, the heaving tides
  That beat against the shore of life !

The flowers run wild that used to be
  So softly tended by thy hand —
Colors of beauty struck at sea,
  And drifted backward to the land ;
Breathing of havens whence we sailed,
  Visions of lovelight seen and fled,
Swift barks of gladness met and hailed —
  Of beacon fires, and land ahead !

To-night, sweet friend, the light and shade
  Are trembling softly in my heart ;
A hush upon my soul is laid —
  Our paths henceforth must lie apart ;
In the dim chamber where I sit,
  Fears, hopes, and memories rise and blend,
Like cloud wastes with the sunshine lit —
  Only with them art thou my friend !

VISIONS OF LIGHT.

THE moon is rising in beauty,
  The sky is solemn and bright,
And the waters are singing like lovers
  That walk in the valleys at night.

Like the towers of an ancient city,
  That darken against the sky,
Seems the blue mist of the river
  O'er the hilltops far and high.

I see through the gathering darkness
The spire of the village church,
And the pale white tombs, half hidden
By the tasselled willow and birch.

Vain is the golden drifting
Of morning light on the hill ;
No white hand opens the windows
Of those chambers low and still.

But their dwellers were all my kindred,
Whatever their lives might be,
And their sufferings and achievements
Have recorded lessons for me.

Not one of the countless voyagers
Of life's mysterious main
Has laid down his burden of sorrows,
Who hath lived and loved in vain.

From the bards of the elder ages
Fragments of song float by,
Like flowers in the streams of summer,
Or stars in the midnight sky.

Some plumes in the dust are scattered
Where the eagles of Persia flew,
And wisdom is reaped from the furrows
The plow of the Roman drew.

From the white tents of the Crusaders
The phantoms of glory are gone,
But the zeal of the barefooted hermit
In humanity's heart lives on.

Oh! sweet as the bell of the Sabbath
    In the tower of the village church,
Or the fall of the yellow moonbeams
    In the tasselled willow and birch —

Comes a thought of the blessèd issues
    That shall follow our social strife,
When the spirit of love maketh perfect
    The beautiful mission of life.

THE TIME TO BE.

I SIT where the leaves of the maple
    And the gnarled and knotted gum
Are circling and drifting around me,
    And think of the time to come.

For the human heart is the mirror
    Of the things that are near and far ;
Like the wave that reflects in its bosom
    The flower and the distant star.

As change is the order of nature,
    And beauty springs from decay,
So in its destined season
    The false for the true makes way.

The darkening power of evil,
    And discordant jars and crime,
Are the cry preparing the wilderness
    For the flower and the harvest-time.

Though doubtings and weak misgivings
　　May rise to the soul's alarm,
Like the ghosts of the heretic burners,
　　In the province of bold reform.

And now as the summer is fading,
　　And the cold clouds full of rain,
And the net, in the fields of stubble
　　And the briers, is spread in vain —

I catch through the mists of life's river
　　A glimpse of the time to be,
When the chain, from the bondman rusted,
　　Shall leave him erect and free —

On the solid and broad foundation,
　　A common humanity's right,
To cover his branded shoulder
　　With the garment of love from sight.

RESPITE.

Leave me, dear ones, to my slumber,
　　Daylight's faded glow is gone ;
In the red light of the morning
　　I must rise and journey on.

I am weary, oh, how weary !
　　And would rest a little while ;
Let your kind looks be my blessing,
　　And your last " good-night " a smile.

We have journeyed up together,
　Through the pleasant daytime flown ;
Now my feet have pressed life's summit,
　And my pathway lies alone.

And, my dear ones, do not call me,
　Should you haply be awake,
When across the eastern hilltops
　Presently the day shall break.

For while yet the stars are lying
　In the gray lap of the dawn,
On my long and solemn journey
　I shall be awake and gone ;

Far from mortal pain and sorrow,
　And from passion's stormy swell,
Knocking at the golden gateway
　Of the eternal citadel.

Therefore, dear ones, let me slumber —
　Faded is the day and gone ;
And with morning's early splendor
　I must rise and journey on.

LUTHER.

OH, ages, add with reverent light
　New splendors to the name of him
Who fought for conscience a good fight,
　And sung for truth the morning hymn !

Who, when old sanctions, like a flood,
Drove wrathful on, to work his fall,
Put forth his single hand and stood
Sublimer, mightier than they all.

Stood, from all precedent apart,
The double challenge to prefer —
A conflict with his own weak heart,
As well as with the powers that were.

Who spake, and, speaking, clave in twain
The mocking symbols in his way ;
Who prayed, and scoffing tongues grew fain
To pray the prayers they heard him pray.

Who, guided by a righteous aim,
Enkindled with his mortal breath
A beacon, on the cliffs of fame,
That shines across the wastes of death ;

From cell to old cathedral height,
From cowlèd monk to vestal nun,
As through the cloudy realms of night
The fiery seams of daybreak run —

Till in the pilgrim's way, the reeds
Like unto strong red cedars thrive,
And free from wrappings of old creeds,
The corpse of thought stands up alive.

Gone from the watchings of the night,
The wrestling night of lonely prayers ; —
Oh, ages, add your reverent light
To the great glory that he bears !

PERVERSITY.

If thy weak, puny hand might reach away,
And rend out lightnings from the clouds to-day,
At little pains, as, with a candle flame
    Touching the flax upon the distaff here,
Would fill the house with light, it were the same —
A little thing to do. It is the far
Makes half the poet's passion for the star,
    The while he treads the shining dewdrop near.

Of mortal weaknesses I have my share —
    Pining and longing, and the madman's fit
Of groundless hatreds, blindest loves, despair —
    But in this rhymèd musing I have writ
Of an infirmity that is not mine :
My heart's dear idol were not less divine
That no grave gaped between us, black and steep ;
'Though, if it were so, I could oversweep

    Its gulf — all gulfs — though ne'er so widely riven ;
Or from hot desert sands dig out sweet springs ;
For I believe, and I have still believed,
That Love may even fold its milk-white wings
    In the red bosom of hell, nor up to heaven
Measure the distance with one thought aggrieved.

    Why should I tear my flesh, and bruise my feet,
Climbing for roses, when, from where I stand,
Down the green meadow I may reach my hand,
    And pluck them off as well ? — sweet, very sweet
This world which God has made about us lies, —
Shall we reproach him with unthankful eyes ?

THE SPIRIT-HAUNTED.

O'ER the dark woods, surging, solemn,
  Hung the new moon's silver ring ;
And in white and naked beauty,
  Out from Twilight's luminous wing,
Peered the first star of the eve ; —
'T was the time when poets weave
Radiant songs of love's sweet passion,
  In the loom of thought sublime,
And with throbbing, quick pulsations
  Beat the golden web of rhyme.

On a hillside very lonely,
  With the willows' dewy flow
Shutting down like sombre curtains
  Round the silent beds below,
Where the lip from love is bound,
And the forehead napkin-crowned, —
I beheld the spirit-haunted —
  Saw his wild eyes burn like fire,
Saw his thin hands, clasped together,
  Crush the frail strings of his lyre,
As upon a dream of splendor
  His abraded soul was stretched,
And across the heart's sad ruins
  Winged imaginations reached
Toward the glory of the skies —
Toward the love that never dies.

In a tower, shadow-laden,
  With a casement high and dim,

Years agone there dwelt a maiden,
  Loving and beloved by him.
But while singing sweet one day
A bold masker crossed her way.

Then — her bosom softly trembling
  Like a star in morning's light —
Faithless to her mortal lover,
  Fled she forth into the night, —
A great feast for her was spread
In the Kingdom overhead.

Woe, oh woe! for the abandoned;
  Dim his mortal steps must be ;
Death's high-priest his soul has wedded
  Unto immortality ! —
Twilight's purple fall, or morn,
Finds him, leaves him, weary, lorn.

In her cave lies Silence, hungry
  For the beauty of his song ;
Echoes, locked from mortal waking,
  Tremble as he goes along,
And for love of him pale maids
Lean like lilies from the shades.

But the locks of love unwinding
  From his bosom as he may,
Buries he his soul of sorrow
  In the cloud-dissolving day
Of the spirit-peopled shore
Ever, ever, evermore.

ON THE PICTURE OF A MAGDALEN.

To be unpitied, to be weary,
To feel the nights, the daytimes, dreary,
To find nor bread nor wine that 's cheery,
    To live apart,
To be unneighbored among neighbors,
Sharing the burdens and the labors,
Never to have the songs or tabors
    Gladden the heart.

To be a penitent forever,
And yet a sinner — never, never
At peace with the Divine Forgiver —
    Always at prayer,
Longing for Mercy's white pavilion,
Yet all the while a stubborn alien,
Uprising proudly in rebellion,
    Hell, Heaven, to dare.

To feel all thoughts alike unholy,
To count all pleasures but as folly,
To mope in ways of melancholy,
    Nor rest to know ;
To be a gleaner, not a reaper,
A scorner proud, a humble weeper,
And of no heart to be the keeper, —
    This is my woe !

NOBILITY.

HILDA is a lofty lady,
  Very proud is she —
I am but a simple herdsman
  Dwelling by the sea.
Hilda hath a spacious palace,
  Broad and white and high ;
Twenty good dogs guard the portal —
  Never house had I.

Hilda hath a thousand meadows —
  Boundless forest lands ;
She hath men and maids for service —
  I have but my hands.
The sweet summer's ripest roses
  Hilda's cheeks outvie —
Queens have paled to see her beauty —
  But my beard have I.

Hilda from her palace windows
  Looketh down on me,
Keeping with my dove-brown oxen
  By the silver sea.
When her dulcet harp she playeth,
  Wild birds, singing nigh,
Cluster listening by her white hands —
  But my reed have I.

I am but a simple herdsman,
  With nor house nor lands ;

She hath men and maids for service —
I have but my hands.
And yet what are all her crimsons
To my sunset sky —
With my free hands and my manhood
Hilda's peer am I.

WHAT AN ANGEL SAID.

I DREAMED of love ; I thought the air
Was glowing with the smile of God —
An angel told me all the sod
Was beauteous with answered prayer —
I looked, and lo ! the flowers were there.

I could not tell what place to tread,
So thick the yellow violets run ;
Along the brooks, and next the sun
The woods were like a garden-bed ;
And whispering soft, the angel said,

(While in his own he took my hand,)
" Dear soul, thou art not in a dream,
All things are truly what they seem —
Thou art but newly come to land,
Through shallows and across the sand."

I felt the light wings cross my face,
My heavy eyes I felt unclose,
And from my dreaming I arose,
If I had dreamed, and by God's grace,
Saw glory in the angel's place.

TO AN EARLY SWALLOW.

My little bird of the air,
If thou dost know, then tell me the sweet reason
Thou comest alway, duly in thy season,
    To build and pair.
For still we hear thee twittering round the eaves,
Ere yet the attentive cloud of April lowers,
Up from their darkened heath to call the flowers,
    Where, all the rough, hard weather,
    They kept together,
Under their low brown roof of withered leaves.

    And for a moment still
    Thy ever-tuneful bill,
And tell me, and I pray thee tell me true,
If any cruel care thy bosom frets,
The while thou flittest plowlike through the air —
    Thy wings so swift and slim,
    Turned downward, darkly dim,
Like furrows on a ground of violets.

Nay, tell me not, my swallow,
    But have thy pretty way,
And prosperously follow
    The leading of the sunshine all the day.
    Thy virtuous example
Maketh my foolish questions answer ample —
    It is thy large delights keeps open wide
    Thy little mouth; thou hast no pain to hide;
And when thou leavest all the green-topped woods
Pining below, and with melodious floods

Flatterest the heavy clouds, it is, I know,
Because, my bird, thou canst not choose but go
      Higher and ever higher
      Into the purple fire
That lights the morning meadows with heart's-ease,
And sticks the hillsides full of primroses.

      But tell me, my good bird,
If thou canst tune thy tongue to any word,
Wherewith to answer — pray thee tell me this:
      Where gottest thou thy song,
      Still thrilling all day long,
Slivered to fragments by its very bliss !
      Not, as I guess,
      Of any whistling swain,
With cheek as richly russet as the grain
Sown in his furrows ; nor, I further guess,
      Of any shepherdess,
      Whose tender heart did drag
Through the dim hollows of her golden flag
After a faithless love — while far and near,
      The waterfalls, to hear,
Clung by their white arms to the cold, deaf rocks,
      And all the unkempt flocks
      Strayed idly.   Nay, I know,
If ever any love-lorn maid did blow
Of such a pitiful pipe, thou didst not get
In such sad wise thy heart to music set.

      So, lower not down to me
From its high home thy ever-busy wing ;
I know right well thy song was shaped for thee
      By His unwearying power

Who makes the days about the Easter flower
Like gardens round the chamber of a king.
And whether, when the sobering year hath run
His brief course out, and thou away dost hie
To find thy pleasant summer company;
  Or whether, my brown darling of the sun,
When first the South, to welcome up the May,
    Hangs wide her saffron gate,
And thou, from the uprising of the day
Till eventide in shadow round thee closes,
Pourest thy joyance over field and wood,
    As if thy very blood
Were drawn from out the young hearts of the roses —

    'T is all to celebrate,
    And all to praise
The careful kindness of His gracious ways
    Who builds the golden weather
So tenderly about thy houseless brood —
Thy unfledged, homeless brood, and thee together.

    Ah! these are the sweet reasons,
My little swimmer of the seas of air,
Thou comest, goest, duly in thy season;
And furthermore, that all men everywhere
    May learn from thy enjoyment
That that which maketh life most good and fair
    Is heavenly employment.

LOOKING BACK.

I HAVE been looking back to-day
    Upon life's April promise hours,
Its June is with me now, but May
    Left all her blushes in the flowers.

A still and sober gladness reigns
    Where there was hopeful mirth erewhile —
Hardly the soul its wisdom gains —
    Through suffering we learn to smile.

The heart that went out beating wild
    With visions of the bliss to be,
Has come back weary, like a child
    That sits beside the mother's knee.

The vision of a coming bliss —
    A bliss from earth that never springs —
In youth was but the chrysalis
    That time has glorified with wings.

And if I see no longer here
    The splendor of a transient good,
A cloud has left my atmosphere,
    And heaven is shining where it stood.

LIGHTS OF GENIUS.

THESE are the pillars, on whose tops
    The white stars rest like capitals,

Whence every living spark that drops
  Kindles and blazes as it falls ;
And if the archfiend rise to pluck,
  Or stoop to crush their beauty down,
A thousand other sparks are struck,
  That Glory settles in her crown.
The huge ship, with its brassy share,
  Ploughs on to lead their light its course,
And veins of iron cleave the air
  To waft it from its burning source ;
All, from the insect's tiny wings,
  And the small drop of morning dew,
To the wide universe of things,
  The light is shining, burning through :
The light that makes the poet's page
  Of stories beautiful as truth,
And pours upon the locks of age
  The glory of eternal growth.

COMING.

THEY are mustering, they are marching —
  Hark, how their tramping rolls !
They are coming, coming, coming !
  A hundred thousand souls !

From the granite hills, the seaside,
  In solid ranks like walls,
A thousand men to take the place
  Of every man that falls !

Right on across the midnight,
  Right onward, stern and proud,

Their red flags shining as they come
Like morning on a cloud.

Battalion on battalion
The West its bravery pours,
For the colors God's own hand has set
In the bushes at their doors !

In the woods and in the clearings,
Our lovers, brothers, sons,
Our young men and our old men
Are shouldering their guns.

They have heard the bugle blowing —
Heard the thunder of the drum,
And farther than the eye can see
They come, and come, and come !

A LESSON.

" Weep no more, lady, weep no more,
    Thy sorrow is in vain,
For violets plucked, the fairest showers
Will not make grow again."
                    PERCY'S RELIQUES.

IDLY in my house I lay,
    Waiting still for joys unearned,
Till it came about one day
    That a lesson thus I learned.

" Listless lady, will you walk ? "
    Quick I turned my face about —
" All ablush upon one stalk,
    Three sweet roses have come out ! "

Quick I turned ; my gardener stood
　　With his eager eyes on mine ;
" Three," he said, " as red as blood ;
　　Will you see them where they shine ?

" Such sweet things were never born !
　　Lady, will you come and see ? "
Then I answered, with slow scorn :
　　" Bring them hither, from the tree ! "

Off from mine he took his eyes —
　　" I obey your cold commands,
Asking this, for you are wise :
　　Will they bloom in your white hands ? "

Faint in heart, and sick in head,
　　Seeing dark as through a glass, —
" What is that to you ? " I said ;
　　" Go, and bring my will to pass ! "

Down the stair I heard his sighs,
　　Low and low and lower fall ;
" I am dull, and she is wise ;
　　But they will not bloom, for all !

" Earth is hard and earth is brown,
　　And the rains they coldly fall ;
White the hands and soft as down ;
　　But they will not bloom, for all !

" Nature she is very wise,
　　And so faithful to her ways,
That no sinful, selfish sighs
　　Ever change her — God have praise !

" Very wise and very still,
    Never bought and never sold,
At her own sweet time and will
    Giving scarlet, white or gold.

" Never any idle pause,
    Never any noisy stir ;
But if we reject her laws,
    All the worse for us, not her !

" O my roses, fair and bright,"
    Through the garden gate he sighed,
" May it prove that through your blight
    Wisdom shall be justified.

" I would spare you if I could ! "
    Sighing down the garden walk ;
There they shone as red as blood,
    Three together on one stalk.

" Stay ! " I cried, with trembling lip,
    All too late the slow commands ;
Clip ! and then a clip and clip !
    And the flowers were in my hands.

Just a moment, brave and bright,
    Just a moment, ripe and red ;
" Gardener, take them from my sight ! "
    They were drooping, dying, dead.

Strong of heart and sound of head,
    Straight I called my girls and boys :
" Joys that are unearned," I said,
    " Are but mockeries of joys."

And their light and laughing glee,
  As about good tasks I set,
Said as plain as plain could be,
  There be sweet buds waiting yet.

CHASING ECHOES.

Two travellers, when the east was red,
Arose, paid reckoning for their bed,
And, having broken fast with bread
  And meat, set out together.
Of heart and hope they felt no lack ;
So each along the highway's track
Carried his knapsack on his back
  As lightly as a feather.

But when the sun his hot rays sent,
Aside into the fields they went,
And walked on grasses dew-besprent,
  And cool with many a shadow ;
Where robin, leaving his bush astir,
Fluttered up with a sudden whir,
And whistling to each, " Good morning, sir ! "
  Went sailing over the meadow.

At top of the dead tree, solemn and still,
The black crow sat like a thing of ill ;
The red-winged woodpecker struck with bill
  Horny and hard, like a hammer ;
The modest bluebird twittered her song ;
The quails ran over the ground in a throng ;
The steel-blue swallow, with wing so strong,
  Took hold of the air like a swimmer.

And evil seemed to flee with the night,
As upward pushing his horn so bright,
The sun went, leaving a trail of light
   In the mist, like a golden furrow ;
And viewing it all with a shake of the head,
The younger man to the elder said,
" But for the sweat of the brow for bread,
   The world would hold no shadow ! "

So our travellers fell into easy talk,
Half of it earnest, half of it mock,
On methods the terrible fiat to balk ;
   And arguing thus together,
Left the field, unaware, behind ;
And entered a pathless wood so blind,
Where mingled murmur of leaves and wind
   Gave token of stormy weather !

Then to a whisper their loud speech fell —
Over the hillside, down in the dell —
Which was the right road neither could tell,
   And the rainy night was falling.
And now the elder a sad breath drew ;
" We are lost," he said, " and the thing to do
Is just to stand, and call ' Halloo ! '
   And see what comes of calling."

And the younger, answering back with dump
Of gun and knapsack, all in a lump,
Turning to one and another clump,
   Filled the woods with hallooing ;
When, lo ! from the heart of silence rung
A sound that seemed like a silver tongue,

And which both men, with hope high strung,
    Believed to their bitter ruing.

For soon the sky was all a-frown,
The shadows changed from dun to brown,
And pitiless the rain came down,
    And winds wailed, oh, so dreary!
And never even the little spark
Of a friendly candle threw on the dark
Its welcome gleam, the path to mark
    For the feet so worn and weary.

They turned their sad case round and round;
'T was death to sleep on the sodden ground —
And nothing better could there be found
    Than calling out, yet higher;
And as they, breathless, harked once more,
The voice came nearer than before,
As if the woodman had come to the door,
    Or they to his hut were nigher.

And so the twain got heart again,
Saying, "If it rains, why, let it rain!
Some hermit hereabout, 't is plain,
    Is watching for our coming;
How sweet 't will be to see him spread
His board with fruit, and wine and bread,
The while his fire, with mosses fed,
    In rosy warmth is humming!"

Thus by the silver tongue misled,
As best they could they trudged ahead,
To find the supper and find the bed,
    And find the hermit holy;

But what with trees so thickly set,
And what with rain and cold and wet,
And weariness and hunger-fret,
   They made their way but slowly.

At last the winds began to spin
Among the faded leaves and thin ;
And then, as daybreak light poured in,
   The cock-crow, and the rattle
Of falling bars, and pasture-rails
With tinklings blent of pans and pails,
   And low of drowsy cattle.

The night was past, the rain was done,
The sun was like an Easter sun,
And all the tuneful birds begun
   To fill the air with praises.
" Ah," said the friends (in pride's despite),
" That lying echo served us right ;
Men who will sin against the light
   Must reap the thorns, not daisies !

" And we had travelled east and west,
Had had our work-days and our rest,
And gained good gains, but not the best,
   For this was left for learning :
That, after all is done and said,
But the straight way gets men ahead,
And never honey-sweetened bread
   Like honesty of earning ! "

SONG FOR ALL SOULS.

AH, many a night I 've lain awake,
Of the nights when I was young —
Long, long, and long ago —
To listen and listen o'er again
To the lilting lay with the low refrain,
Half sad, half sweet, " Heigh-ho ! "
Float silvery over the silver lake,
With its clear refrain, " Heigh-ho ! "
Till far and near the echoes rung,
Some sad, some sweet, " Heigh-ho ! "
" Blown away like daisy leaves ;
Whirled away like snow;
All gone, dead and gone,
Weary heart, heigh-ho ! "

Ah, many a night I 've lain awake
In the garret rude and low,
To listen to the lilting lay,
Swelling and dying far away,
Save only just the strange refrain,
Half of pleasure and half of pain,
Blown silvery over the silver lake —
Blown soft as moonshine over the streams,
And across my pillow and into my dreams :
" Sweet hearts and friends, heigh-ho !
All gone, dead and gone ;
Whirled away from me,
Like dry leaves in the winter winds,
Or snowflakes in the sea."

Ah, many a night I've lain awake,
And listened with all my heart,
To hear from over the silver lake
The silvery echo start.
Ay, start and tremble, strain o'er strain,
To a wild and wailing call,
Then softly sink to the sad refrain
With a dulcet, dying fall :
" All gone, dead and gone ;
Whirled away from me,
Like flowers of grass along the grass,
Or sea-spray o'er the sea."

And I marvelled as I lay awake,
And the marvel would not go,
Who thus across the silver lake
Should nightly sing and row ;
As if that he the lake had crossed
Till youth and hope and love were lost,
To come no more, no more ;
And he could not choose but sing so low
The lilting lay with the sad refrain,
And to sing it o'er and o'er again :
" Sweet hearts and friends, heigh-ho !
All gone, lost and gone ;
Whirled away from me,
Like dead leaves in the winter wind,
Or sea-spray o'er the sea."

And I did not know, as I lay awake
And listened to that song,
Blown silvery over the silver lake,
That I, and that ere long,

That very rower's mood should take,
And sing the same sad song —
That song so low, so low —
And sing it o'er and o'er again,
From the wild and wailing call,
To the dulcet, dying fall:
" Sweet hearts and friends, heigh-ho!
All gone, lost and gone ;
Whirled away from me,
Like dead leaves in the winter wind,
Or sea-spray o'er the sea."

HUGH THE VOLUNTEER.

Boys, are you all at home to-night?
    Simon, and Seth, and John?
How should the old house be so changed
    If only one is gone !

You know I love you, each and all —
    I need not say I do,
But my heart is just as sad and sick
    As if I had only Hugh.

I am with him in his tent at night —
    His morning drill I share —
In the march, and in the field of fight —
    I am with him everywhere.

I miss his strong and willing hands
    In everything we do —
Another must do double work
    To fill the place of Hugh.

Pray for him night and morn, boys,
  Pray for him all the day —
Let me see, if he lives he will be
  Twenty years old in May.

Ah, then we 'll make the old house ring
  With many a merry sound —
God grant he may be back again
  Before the time comes round.

Ay, back again, all sound and safe,
  To sing a birthday glee,
And make his mother's heart grow young —
  But if he should n't be ;

We 'll keep his place at the table, all
  The same as if he were here —
He is n't the lad to spare himself,
  But there is n't much to fear.

He is n't the lad to spare himself,
  Nor the lad to yield the right —
But would to God this fight were done,
  And our Hugh at home to-night !

TO MY FIRE.

LET me trim and make you fair,
  With a hickory limb or two ;
Ah, I have not anywhere
  Such a cheerful friend as you !
When I come home tired and sad,
Always glowing, always glad.

Memories my soul that rack
  Shrink from your rebuking flame ;
And their ghosts go wavering back
  To the darkness whence they came,
When your embers sing and hum
Of the happy days tó come.

When the future seems to lend
  Scarce a gleam, my life to grace,
Like an old familiar friend
  You look up into my face ;
And my thoughts from vain regret
Turn to what is left me yet.

Many, many a lonesome night
  You have been my confidant,
With your genial look and light
  Comforting my discontent.
All my heart I trust to you —
Never had I friend so true.

When the wind down chimney blows,
  How your bickering blazes spread,
Till each blackened rafter glows
  With your shadows warm and red,
And adown my lowly walls
More than kingly splendor falls.

THREE GOOD SHIPS.

THREE good ships came sailing in,
 Long ago, ay, long ago —
Three good ships came sailing in
 So early in the morning ;
And all the winds to the shore did blow,
And all the sails were as white as snow,
 So early in the morning.

Three good ships so brave and new,
 Long ago, ay, long ago,
Three good ships so brave and new,
 Early in the morning ;
And the sea was smooth and the sky was blue,
And every soul on board was true,
 Early in the morning.

Sailing over the silver sea,
 Long ago, ay, long ago,
Freighted with freight that was all for me,
 Early in the morning ;
And " Hope " and Faith," they were stout and tall,
But " Love " was the best ship of them all,
 Early in the morning.

Three good ships a-sailing in,
 Long ago, ay, long ago,
Three good ships a-sailing in
 Early in the morning ;
But there were breakers to be crossed,
And one of the three good ships was lost,
 Early in the morning.

Two good ships a-sailing in,
　Slow and sad, and sad and slow,
Two good ships a-sailing in
　Through the cloudy morning ;
For air and sky were all a-frown,
And of the two ships one went down,
　In the mournful morning.

Sailing over the solemn sea,
　Through the foam, the cold white foam,
One good ship is left to me,
　Far away from the morning ;
Hope and Love, they both are gone,
But Faith is sailing sadly on
　Toward the eternal morning.

FLAWS.

O SUNSHINE, like a cloth of gold
　Drawn out along the air,
The clouds, or yellow, black, or brown,
A-sailing up, a-sailing down,
　But make you doubly fair !

O grasses, like a queen's gay shawl
　Upon her crowning day,
The border of rough, prickly burs,
And nettles black, and wilding furze,
　Your tenderer tints display.

O bird of ragged quill, and wing
　As speckled as a flower,

Sing, sing your heart up to your throat;
'T is just the one wild, wailing note
That gives your song its power.

Sweetheart of mine — sweetheart of mine,
Whom all my thoughts adore,
Hide your blue eyes, and frown and pout;
It is our little fallings out
That make us love the more!

Whatever things be fine or bright —
Gay grass, or golden air,
Or red of rose, or lily's snow —
It is the *flaw* that makes them so;
All fair would not be fair!

Of better things, it seems to me,
Life's best is but the sign;
Else, in this wicked world, would be
No room for blessèd charity —
No room for love divine.

HOPE.

WHEN all my fields are frozen,
When all my orchards nakèd stand,
I hear a sound that is like the sound
Of a sower, sowing the land.
And all at once the limbs of leaves,
So darkly-dim before,
Shine round me like a thresher's sheaves
When he stands in his threshing-floor.

Awake from troubled slumber,
  In the middle watch o' the night,
I see a hand that is like the hand
  Of a painter, painting the light.
And all at once, with the shadows
  Are threads of silver spun,
And all my room is like the bloom
  Of a garden in the sun.

When pleasures please no longer,
  When the charm of love is lost,
When my dearest hopes before me
  Like chaff in the winds are tost ;
My empty heart forgets its lack,
  And I hear a voice that sings
Like the mother-bird when she calleth back
  Her little ones to her wings.

When the sea of life is darkest,
  When the billows gap with graves,
I hear a step that is like a step
  That is treading on the waves ;
And all at once the clouds are rent,
  And I with my spirit see
That time is but an incident
  Of the great eternity.

TO ANY DESPONDING GENIUS.

TAKE this for granted once for all :
  There is neither *chance* nor *fate*,
And to sit and wait for the sky to fall,
  Is to wait as the foolish wait.

The laurel, longed for, you must *earn* —
It is not of the things men lend,
And though the lesson be hard to learn,
The sooner the better, my friend.

That another's head can have your crown
Is a judgment all untrue,
And to drag this man, or the other down,
Will not in the least raise you !

For, in spite of your demur, or mine,
The gods will still be the gods,
And the spark of genius will outshine
The touchwood, by all odds !

Be careful, careful work to do,
Though at cost of heart, or head —
The praises, even of the Review,
Will hardly stand in stead.

No light that through the ages shines
To worthless work belongs —
Men dig in thoughts as they dig in mines,
For the jewels of their songs.

A fresco painter in ceiling wrought,
With eyelids strained, 't is said,
Till he could but read of the fame so bought,
With the page above his head.

Hold not the world as in debt to you,
When it credits you day by day,
For the light and air, for the rose and dew,
And for all that cheers your way.

And you, in turn, as an honest man,
Are bound, you will understand,
To give back either the best you can,
Or to die, and be out of hand.

COMING AND GOING.

HOARDING and heaping — hoarding and heaping —
And now there are lights, and garlands gay,
For a babe is born in the house to-day,
    And his two blue eyes are sleeping;
And close by the cradle the father stands,
And thinks of his acres of well-sown lands,
And of when the two little dimpled hands
    Will be strong enough for reaping.

Budding and blooming — budding and blooming —
And the winds are playing like flutes on the hills,
And the stones are beaten like drums in the rills,
    And the birds in clouds are coming;
And song and fragrance float in the breeze,
And all the blossoms of all the trees
Are edged with fringes of golden bees
    Sucking and humming — sucking and humming.

Wailing and weeping — wailing and weeping —
And now the lights in the house are low,
And now the roses have ceased to glow,
    And the women watch are keeping;
And close by the coffin the father stands,
And, bitterly moaning, wrings his hands,
And barren of pleasure are all his lands,
    For the babe wakes not from sleeping.

Blighting and blowing — blighting and blowing —
And the stones of the rivulet silent lie,
And the winds in the fading woodlands cry,
  And the birds in clouds are going ;
And the dandelion hides his gold,
And their blue little tents the violets fold,
  And the air is gray with snowing :
So life keeps coming and going.

THE OTHER SIDE OF THE PICTURE.

THEY may talk of old age
  And its pleasures who please,
Of the rosy-cheeked lad on
  The grandfather's knees ;
Of the granddaughter, too,
  With her soft golden hair
Hanging over the back of
  His great easy-chair ;
But I don't quite relish
  My time of the day,
Sitting here in my nightcap
  Rheumatic and gray !
My grandson is surely
  A nice little elf,
But then I would rather
  Be boy for myself !
And I love my granddaughter,
  So sweet and so shy,
But I 'd rather have gold hair
  Than gray, would n't I ?

I can't make it seem any way
  But just queer,
That I should have taken on
  Year after year,
Until my broad shoulders
  Bent under the strain,
And I had to prop up my
  Weak legs with a cane !
And take to soft crusts,
  And meal gruel and milk,
And go in a jacket
  Of wool, not of silk,
And carefully garter
  My fleecy-lined hose,
And keep a sharp eye to
  The end of my nose !
When I think of the time
  We were married, my dear,
It seems to me something
  That happened last year,
And I fairly distrust both
  My sense and my sight,
When I look up and see
  That your head is so white !
And spite all assurance,
  I can't think it 's true
That I should be I, and
  That you should be you !
'T is hard to receive it
  And make it seem fair,
That we should be toddling
  The way that we are ;
But rather as if an
  Exception should be

Made out and extended
To you and to me,
As if we had come to
The close of the day
Without ever having had
Open, fair play!
I know I am wrong here,
But when all is done,
The shadow will not be so sweet
As the sun.
So, let the old people
Talk fine as they please
About lives lived over
In holiday ease;
I say, what is ease worth,
Laid up high and dry,
With a great gouty toe,
And a rheum in the eye?
And think, if 't were all
Just the same to the shelves,
The old folks would rather
Stand up for themselves!
And run in the race with
The sturdy-legged boys,
And share with the gay girls
Their frolicsome joys;
And, bravely defiant
Of all gouty pains,
Tear off the red flannels
And burn up the canes;
And put on the shining
And beautiful gear,
And cease to look querulous,
Crooked, and queer.

But I, after all, am not
  So set at strife
With the wonderful order
  And wisdom of life,
As dare, if I might, to turn
  Up and turn back
The locks, thin and gray,
  To the side, thick and black;
Or boldly to take the
  Responsible part
Of saying, if life were
  To live from the start,
I 'd render up cleaner
  Account of my trust,
Or deal with my neighbor
  More honest and just.
So let us, my darling,
  Give praise to his name,
Who has kept us from slipping
  In pitfalls of shame ;
And, wrapt from the chill
  Of the rough winter weather,
Go down the life hill
  As we came up, together !
And when we no longer
  Can brave the rough storms,
Just sleep in the shelter
  Of each other's arms.

THE TIME OF THE DEW-FALL.

WE sat upon the smooth sea sand,
  And watched the tide flow in and out,
  And knew what it was all about —
Heart held in heart and hand to hand —
  In the time of the morn and the dew-fall.

With faces toward each other leant,
  We saw the green heads of the trees,
  And heard the whispering of the breeze,
And knew what all the sweetness meant,
  In the time of the morn and the dew-fall.

We saw the long gray east o'erblown
  With flowers that wore the look of light,
  And they were lovely in our sight,
And all their secret meanings known,
  In the time of the morn and the dew-fall.

Like the thick coming of a cloud
  We saw the birds, and knew each note —
  Of speckled-wing, and golden-throat,
Or soft and low, or shrill and loud,
  All in the morn and the dew-fall.

We dropped the seed-corn in the ground
  Without a single thought or fear
  About the full, ripe, rounded ear,
When time should bring the harvest round,
  All in the morn and the dew-fall.

Ah, not in vanity or pride,
  But out of love, whence wisdom springs,
  We took the tangled web of things
And stretched it straight from side to side,
  All in the morn and the dew-fall.

Our hearts, alas, no longer beat
  As one, and hand has fallen from hand,
  And I am slow to understand
The things that were so plain and sweet
  In the time of the morn and the dew-fall.

AN EVENING RHYME.

THIS was a goodly day — the sun
  Sunk to his rest in radiant calms ;
  I hear the gray sea singing psalms
The same as he has always done.

The moon in tender beauty clad
  Looks down upon me from the sky —
  What is it ails the time, that I
Should be so sick at heart, so sad !

My baby's little lispings war
  Against it, all in vain — ah me,
  His golden head upon my knee
Seems farther from me than the star !

I feel, alas I know not what
  Of darkness on my senses fall —
  Friends come — the best friend of them all
Comes to me, yet he finds me not ;

Or I find him not, for he seems
  Like other men, nor less nor more —
  Time was with me the dress he wore,
The book he read, was food for dreams.

That time will come again to me —
  For if we would, we cannot break
  The sweet affinities that make
Such poems in our lives — not we.

And this dull mood that seems th' abuse
  Of opportunity, is right;
  Light cannot be defined by light —
The blur, the shadow, have their use;

The failure teaches us to know
  The way of success — strife bringeth strength —
  Pain works itself to peace at length,
The unstable brings the sure, and though

The world within our hearts to-day,
  Like a great emerald in a rim
  Of rubies, straightway groweth dim,
And slippeth from our hearts away;

I hold this truth all truths above —
  Whatever else that firmest stands
  Shall slide together like dry sands —
The truth, the eternity of love!

OLD FRIENDS.

You with fortune's gale that float,
Welcome to my rough-hewn boat !
Pleasant is your sunny crew,
  But, O friends, of rainy weather,
Tenderer love I bear to you,
  We have borne the heat together !

Pleasure's tie a chance may sever,
But the ties of sorrow, never !
And, old friends, though bitter storms
  Part us, in my dreams I gather
Each of you in memory's arms,
  And we sail away together,

Toward that fair and friendly shore
Whither hope has gone before.
For life's promise now is lost —
  Time has cut youth's golden tether,
And we feel the autumn frost
  Falling on our heads together.

But though gloom our voyage enshrouds,
Day breaks brightest in the clouds ;
And though earth be sad and cold,
  Heaven is made of flowery weather,
And as here we 're growing old,
  There, we shall grow young together.

THE SUICIDE.

WHERE the dry, dusty road makes a crook to evade
The clump of sweet maples that offer their shade,
'T is there that the grave of poor Margaret is made.

Where the river you see pushes into the shore,
As if in its bosom some treasure it bore
Belonging to earth, which it fain would restore ;

Ah, there 't was they found her, her arms o'er her head,
As if she had drawn up the waves to o'erspread
Her corpse from all pity, when she should be dead.

Where the grass to the water slopes green, it was there
They shut up her eyes from their wondering stare,
That they wrung out the wet from her garments and
    hair.

I shall say, if the judgment shall call me to speak,
" A kiss might have put out the fire in her cheek
That urged her the last awful refuge to seek."

"MY BOY."

AH, winter days, be not so cold, so cold !
    And if my little houseless boy you see,
Quilt all your iron shadows thick with gold,
    And lap them round him — he is all to me.

Oh, winter winds, if ever, as you blow,
  You find, in some wild place apart from joy,
A shining head, with curls along the snow,
  Soften your rough voice — that will be my boy!

Oh, happy mothers! while you watch at night
  The bright blaze making all the wide room gay,
Keep on some upper floor a little light —
  My poor, lost child may chance to pass that way!

And if, when all without is blind with gloom, —
  Among your boys and girls, alive with joy,
A little white face peer, — make room, make room,
  Between their red cheeks — that will be my boy!

False witnesses to prison may have lied
  My pretty lamb — oh, warden! if you see
One strange to wrong, and ready to divide
  His slice — nay, give it all, why that is he!

Loose from his tender limbs the cruel bands —
  Even though he sinned, shall that my love destroy?
Here to your chains I give my old, rough hands,
  To prison, to death will I, to save my boy!

GROWTH.

THE living stream must flow, and flow,
  And never rest, and never wait,
  But from its bosom, soon or late
Cast the dead corpse. Time even so

Runs on and on, and may not rest,
　But from its bosom casts away
　The cold dead forms of yesterday —
Once best, may not be always best.

That which was but the dream of youth,
　Begot of wildest fantasy,
　To our old age, perhaps, may be
A good and great and gracious truth.

That which was true in time gone by,
　As seen by narrow, ignorant sight,
　May in the longer, clearer light
Of wiser times, become a lie.

I hold this true — who ever wins
　Man's highest stature here below,
　Must grow, and never cease to grow —
For when growth ceases, death begins.

LITTLE THINGS.

SHALL we strike a bargain, Fate?
　And wilt thou to this agree?
Take whatever things are great,
　Leave the little things to me!

Take the eagle, proud and dark,
　Broad of shoulders, strong of wing;
Leave the robin, leave the lark,
　'T is the little birds that sing!

Take the oak-wood, towering up,
  With its top against the skies ;
Leave one little acorn cup,
  Therein all the forest lies !

Take the murmurous fountain-heads,
  Take the river, winding slow ;
But about my garden-beds
  Leave the dewdrop, small and low.

Winding waves are fine to view,
  Sweet the fountain's silver call ;
But the little drop of dew
  Holds the sunshine, after all.

Take the sea, the great wide sea,
  White with many a swelling sail ;
Leave the little stream to me,
  Sliding silent through the vale.

Poesy will find her theme
  In thy grander portion, still,
'T is my little, unpraised stream
  Of the meadow, turns the mill.

Take the palace, all ashine,
  With its lofty halls and towers ;
Let the little house be mine,
  With its door-yard grass and flowers.

Take the lands, the royal lands,
  All with parks and orchards bright ;
Leave to me the little hands,
  Clinging closely morn and night.

Ah, for once be kindly, Fate,
To my harmless plan agree ;
Take whatever things are great,
Leave the little things to me !

BURNS.

TIME, paint him as he was among
His darling daisies at the plow,
With bonnet old and poor, but hung
Right bravely on his honest brow.

Or better, with his plaidie wide
And unashamed of homespun gear,
Turning his weeding clips aside
To save old Scotia's emblem dear.

For idle, all, the strife to vamp
With gauds, great nature's simple plan ;
The rank is but the guinea's stamp,
The gold for a' that is the man.

Ah, paint him as he was, nor seek
His life with alien grace to trim ;
No look of scourging in his cheek,
No saintly chastity for him !

Paint him a lover — in his song
Catching all hearts, his own still light —
Not haggard, as he looked ere long,
Affronted at neglect and slight.

Bravely against the fate foregone,
  Striving some little good to win —
Not in that wave which on and on
  Allured him, till it drew him in.

Paint the great soul that yet with cries
  Must rend the clay, not wear it through,
Making within his wondrous eyes
  Signs of the work it had to do.

Alas, that wayward, wavering strife
  Towards worthier living, but reveal
The war, the mystery of the life
  That other men but half conceal.

Paint all the bonny braes and streams
  That called his inspirations out;
Not the poor skeleton of dreams
  He lived his after-life about.

Ah, Time, be gentle with his fame,
  Nor let his frailties, judgment sway,
For when he seemed the most to blame
  'T was nature having all her way.

'T was love that was his law of right,
  And spite of all he thus defied,
No life has a diviner light
  Than his, upon the heavenly side.

NANNIE.

I can remember when our roof
  Would not keep out the rain ;
We have been very poor, Nannie,
  I wish we were again !

For when the frosty autumn came,
  And all the oaks had bled
Their piteous hearts into the leaves
  Until the woods were red,

I never felt the chill, Nannie,
  And never feared the storm ;
Your love was better than a cloak
  To keep me safe and warm.

And sometimes in the winter days
  I 've almost felt the glow
Of fire-light, as I stooped to write
  Your name upon the snow.

Now all is changed.   The hills are gone
  Where gently every night
The cows were used to stoop their necks
  Beneath your hands so white.

The red rose through the broken pane
  Leans tenderly no more
To see the sunshine's golden rule
  Along the ashen floor.

And you never sit upon my knee,
  And never make me sure
You love me just as well as in
  The days when we were poor.

THE OLD MAN'S WOOING.

COME sit upon my knee, Minie,
  And, darling, do not frown,
You know my hair is thin and white,
  And yours is thick and brown:
So sit upon my knee, Minie,
  And lean your bright head low
Against my cheek, for see, Minie,
  My hair is white as snow.

And sing me that old song, Minie,
  About the summer dead,
Its pleasant tune has all the time
  Been going through my head,
Since when you sang it first, Minie,
  In tones so sweet and clear,
With but a little sky between
  Ourselves and heaven, my dear.

My eyes are going blind, Minie,
  My heart is sad with care,
And you are like a bright young rose,
  That I must never wear.
If you were not so young, Minie,
  And I were not so gray,
I'd ask if you would smile sometimes,
  And make my darkness day.

Oh, when I 'm dead and gone, Minie,
　You must not come to weep,
The lightest sigh you breathed for me
　Would wake me out of sleep :
Would wake me out of death, Minie ;
　Ah, do not tremble so,
You know I cannot love, Minie,
　My hair is white as snow.

CHEER AND WARNING.

HERE 's a rhyme and a cheerful God-speed
　For the weak and the pushed to the wall ;
And here 's for the strong a take heed,
　Lest haply they stumble and fall.

For none are too low and too poor
　For hope to go down to, and none
In th' world's highest places are sure
　Of keeping the heights they have won.

The best man should never pass by
　The worst ; but, to brotherhood true,
Entreat him thus gently, " Lo, I
　Am tempted in all things, as you."

Of one dust all peoples are made,
　One sky doth above them extend,
And whether through sunshine or shade
　Their paths run, they meet at the end.

And whatever his honors may be
  Of riches, or genius, or blood,
God never made any man free
  To find out a separate good.

So, giving to virtue its worth,
  The frail be I slow to decry,
For while there 's a soul on the earth
  That suffers and sins, so do I.

ALL IN ALL.

MORE than we have been, my brother,
We must be to one another,
    In our dark estate.
We are poor, and very lonely —
Love, and one another only,
    We must work and wait.

All the green and dewy splendor,
All the blossoms sweet and tender,
    From the fields are gone.
In the woodland, in the mowing.
At the seedtime, at the ploughing —
    We must work alone.

They are gone that made the brightness —
Gone, who gave our hearts their lightness ;
    And while life shall last,
We no more may turn our faces
Forward to the world's high places —
    Our delights are past.

We must plant bright flowers about them —
We must learn to live without them
  In our dark estate,
And must henceforth be, my brother,
All in all to one another,
  While we work and wait.

CHANGE.

WE had but a humble home,
  With few and simple joys ;
But my father's step was proud and firm,
  And my brothers were laughing boys.

We have much that we longed for then,
  Our hearth is broad and bright ;
But my brothers now are saddened men,
  And my father's hair is white.

MY LITTLE ONE.

AT busy morn — at quiet noon —
  At evening sad and still,
As wayward as the lawless mist
  That wanders where it will,
    She comes — my little one.

I cannot have a dream so wrought
  Of nothings, nor so wild
With fantasies, but she is there,
  My heavenly-human child —
    My glad, gay little one.

She never spake a single word
  Of wisdom, I agree ;
I loved her not for what she was,
  But what she was to me —
  My precious little one.

You might not call her beautiful,
  Nor haply was she so ;
I loved her for the loveliness
  That I alone could know —
  My sweet-souled little one.

I say I loved, but that is wrong ;
  As if the love could change
Because my dove hath got her wings,
  And taken wider range !
  Forgive, my little one.

I still can see her shining curls
  All tremulously fair,
Like fifty yellow butterflies
  A-fluttering in the air —
  My angel little one.

I see her tender mouth, her eyes,
  Her garment softly bright,
Like some fair cloud about the morn
  With roses all alight —
  My deathless little one.

WHAT A WRETCHED WOMAN SAID TO ME.

ALL the broad East was laced with tender rings
    Of widening light ; the Daybreak shone afar ;
Deep in the hollow, 'twixt her fiery wings,
    Fluttered the morning star.

A cloud, that through the time of darkness went
    With wanton winds, now, heavy-hearted, came
And fell upon the sunshine, penitent,
    And burning up with shame.

The grass was wet with dew ; the sheep-fields lay
    Lapping together far as eye could see ;
And the great harvest hung the golden way
    Of Nature's charity.

My house was full of comfort ; I was propped
    With life's delights, all sweet as they could be,
When at my door a wretched woman stopped,
    And, weeping, said to me, —

" Its rose-root in youth's seasonable hours
    Love in thy bosom set, so blest wert thou ;
Hence all the pretty little red-mouthed flowers
    That climb and kiss thee now !

" *I* loved, but *I* must stifle Nature's cries
    With old dry blood, else perish, I was told ;
Hence the young light shrunk up within my eyes ;
    And left them blank and bold.

" I take my deeds, all, bad as they have been, —
  The way was dark, the awful pitfall bare ; —
In my weak hands, up through the fires of sin,
  I hold them for my prayer."

" The thick, tough husk of evil grows about
  Each soul that lives," I mused, "but doth it kill ?
When the tree rots, the imprisoned wedge falls out,
  Rusted, but iron still.

" Shall He who to the daisy has access,
  Reaching it down its little lamp of dew
To light it up through earth, do any less,
  Last and best work, for you ? "

POEMS OF NATURE AND HOME.

WOOD NYMPHS.

Wood nymphs, that do hereabouts
Dwell, and hold your pleasant routes,
When beneath her cloak so white,
Holding close the black-eyed night,
Twilight, sweetly voluble,
Acquaints herself with shadows dull ;
While above your rustic camp,
Hesperus, his pallid lamp
For the coming darkness trims,
From the gnarlèd bark of limbs
Rough and crabbed — slide to view !
I have work for you to do.

To this neighborhood of shade
Came I, the most woful maid
That did ever comfort glean
From the songs of birds, I ween ;
Or from rills through hollow meads,
Washing over beds of reeds,
When, to vex with more annoy,
Found I here this sleeping boy.

I must learn some harmless art,
That will bind to mine his heart.
Never creature of the air
Saw I in a dream so fair.
Wood nymphs, lend your charmèd aid.
Underneath the checkered shade
Of each tangled bough that stirs
To the wind, in shape of burs,
Rough and prickly, or sharp thorn —
Whence the tame ewe, newly shorn,
Stained with crimson, hurries oft,
Bleating toward the distant croft —
Dew of potency is found
That would leave my forehead crowned
With the very chrisms of joy —
The sweet kisses of this boy.
These quaint uses you must know —
Poets wise have writ it so.

When the charm so deftly planned
Shall be wrought, I have in hand
Work your nimble crew to please,
Mixed alone of sweetnesses.
This it is to bring to me
Fairest of all flowers that be —
Oxlips red, and columbines,
Ivies, with blue flowering twines,
Flags that grow by shallow springs,
Purple, pranked with yellow rings ;
Slim ferns, bound in golden sheaves ;
Mandrakes, with the notchèd leaves ;
Pink and crowbind, nor o'erpass
The white daisies in the grass.

Of the daintiest that you pull
I will tie a garland full,
And upon this oaken bough
Dropping coolest shadows now,
Hang it, 'gainst his face to swing,
Till he wakes from slumbering;
Evermore to live and love
In this dim consenting grove.

Shaggy beasts with hungry eyes —
Ugly, spotted dragonflies —
Limber snakes drawn up to rings,
And the thousand hateful things
That are bred in forests drear,
Never shall disturb us here;
For my love and I will see
Only the sweet company
Of the nymphs that round me glide
With the shades of eventide.

Crow of cock, nor belfry chime,
Shall we need to count the time —
Tuneful footfalls in the flowers
Ringing out and in the hours.

CONTENT.

My house is low and small;
But behind a row of trees
I catch the golden fall
Of the sunset in the seas;

And a stone wall hanging white
　With the roses of the May,
Were less pleasant to my sight
　Than the fading of to-day.
From a brook a heifer drinks
　In a field of pasture ground,
With wild violets and pinks
　For a border all around.

My house is small and low ;
　But the willow by the door
Doth a cool deep shadow throw
　In the summer on my floor ;
And in long and rainy nights,
　When the limbs of leaves are bare,
I can see the window lights
　Of the homesteads otherwhere.

My house is small and low ;
　But with pictures such as these —
Of the sunset, and the row
　Of illuminated trees,
And the heifer as she drinks
　From the field of meadowed ground,
With the violets and pinks
　For a border all around, —
Let me never, foolish, pray
　For a vision wider spread,
But contented, only say,
　Give me, Lord, my daily bread.

TO THE EVENING ZEPHYR.

I SIT where the wild bee is humming,
  And listen in vain for your song ;
I 've waited before for your coming,
  But never, oh, never so long.

How oft, with the blue sky above us,
  And waves breaking light on the shore,
You, knowing they would not reprove us,
  Have kissed me a thousand times o'er !

So sweet were your dewy embraces,
  Your falsehood, oh, who could believe !
Some phantom your fondness effaces —
  You could not have aimed to deceive.

You told not your love for me ever,
  But all the bright stars in the skies,
Though striving to do so, could never
  Have numbered one half of your sighs.

Alone in the gathering shadows,
  Still waiting, sweet zephyr, for you,
I look for the waves of the meadows,
  And the phantoms that trail o'er the blue.

The blossoms that waited to greet me,
  With heat of the noontide opprest,
Now flutter so lightly to meet me,
  You 're coming, I know, from the West.

Alas, if you find me thus pouting,
'T is only my love that alarms ;
Forgive, then, I pray you, my doubting,
And take me once more to your arms !

THE EMIGRANTS.

Don't you remember how oft you have said,
Darling Coralin May,
" When the hawthorns are blossoming we shall wed,
And then to the prairie away ! "
And now, all over the hills they peep,
Milkwhite, out of the spray,
And sadly you turn to the past and weep,
Darling Coralin May.

When the cricket chirped in the hickory blaze,
You cheerily sung, you know, —
" Oh for the sunnier summer days,
And the time when we shall go ! "
The corn-blades now are unfolding bright,
While busily calls the crow ;
And clovers are opening red and white,
And the time has come to go —

To go to the cabin our love has planned,
On the prairie green and gay,
In the blushing light of the sunset land,
Darling Coralin May.
" How happy our lives will be," you said, —
Don't you remember the day ? —
" When our hands shall be, as our hearts are, wed ! "
Darling Coralin May.

" How sweet," you said, " when my work is o'er,
    And your axe yet ringing clear,
To sit and watch at the lonely door
    Of our home in the prairie, dear."
The rose is ripe by the window now,
    And the cool spring flowing near ;
But shadows fall on the heart and brow
    From the home we are leaving here.

OF HOME.

My heart made pictures all to-day
Of the old homestead far away.
It is the middle of the May,
And the moon is shining full and bright —
The middle of May, and the middle of night.

Darkly against the southern wall
Three cherry-trees, so smooth and tall,
Their shadows cast — we planted all,
One morning in March that is long gone by, —
My brother Carolan and I.

I hear the old clock tick and tick
In the small parlor, see the thick
Unfeathered wings of bats, that stick
To moonlit windows, see the mouse,
Noiseless, peering about the house.

I 'm going up the winding stairs,
I 'm counting all the vacant chairs,
And sadly saying, " They were theirs, —

The brothers and sisters who no more
Go in and out at the homestead door."

I hear my sweet-voiced mother say,
" Leave, children, leave all work to-day,
And go into the fields and play."
And the birds are singing where'er we go —
How beautiful, to be dreaming so !

And yet, while I am dreaming on,
I know my playmates all are gone ;
That none the hope of our childhood keep,
That some are weary, and some asleep,
And that I from the homestead am far away
This middle of night, in the middle of May.

THE RECLAIMING OF THE ANGEL.

OH smiling land of the sunset,
How my heart to thy beauty thrills —
Veiled dimly to-day with the shadow
Of the greenest of all thy hills !
Where daisies lean to the sunshine,
And the winds a-ploughing go,
And break into shining furrows
The mists in the vale below ;
Where the willows hang out their tassels,
With the dews all white and cold,
Strung over their wands so limber,
Like pearls upon cords of gold ;
Where in milky hedges of hawthorn
The red-winged thrushes sing,

And the wild vine, bright and flaunting,
  Twines many a scarlet ring ;
Where, under the ripened billows
  Of the silver-flowing rye,
We ran in and out with the zephyrs —
  My sunny-haired brother and I.

Oh, when the green kirtle of May time
  Again over the hill-tops is blown,
I shall walk the wild paths of the forest,
  And climb the steep headlands alone —
Pausing not where the slopes of the meadows
  Are yellow with cowslip beds,
Nor where, by the wall of the garden,
  The hollyhocks lift their bright heads.
In hollows that dimple the hillsides,
  Our feet till the sunset had been,
Where pinks with their spikes of red blossoms
  Hedged beds of blue violets in,
While to the warm lip of the sunbeam
  The cheek of the blush rose inclined,
And the pansy's soft bosom was flushed with
  The murmurous love of the wind.

But when 'neath the heavy tresses
  That swept o'er the dying day,
The star of the eve like a lover
  Was hiding his blushes away,
As we came to a mournful river
  That flowed to a lovely shore,
" Oh, sister," he said, " I am weary —
  I cannot go back any more ! "
And seeing that round about him
  The wings of the angel shone —

I parted the locks from his forehead,
And kissed him and left him alone.

OLD STORIES.

No beautiful star will twinkle
  To-night through my window-pane,
As I list to the mournful falling
  Of the leaves and the autumn rain.

High up in his leafy covert
  The squirrel a shelter hath ;
And the tall grass hides the rabbit,
  Asleep in the churchyard path.

On the hills is a voice of wailing
  For the pale dead flowers again,
That sounds like the heavy trailing
  Of robes in a funeral train.

Oh, if there were one who loved me — •
  A kindly and gray-haired sire,
To sit and rehearse old stories
  To-night by my cabin fire —

The winds as they would might rattle
  The pane, or the trees so tall —
In the tale of a stirring battle
  My heart would forget them all.

Or if, by the embers dying,
  We talked of the past, the while,

I should see bright spirits flying
  From the pyramids and the Nile.

Echoes from harps long silent
  Would troop through the aisles of time,
And rest on the soul like sunshine,
  If we talked of the bards sublime.

But, hark ! did a phantom call me,
  Or was it the wind went by ?
Wild are my thoughts and restless,
  But they have no power to fly.

In place of the cricket humming,
  And the moth by the candle's light,
I hear but the deathwatch drumming —
  I 've heard it the livelong night.

Oh for a friend who loved me —
  Oh for a gray-haired sire,
To sit with a quaint old story
  . To-night by my cabin fire !

THE ORPHAN GIRL.

MY heart shall rest where greenly flow
  The willows o'er the meadow —
The fever of this burning brow
  Be cooled beneath their shadow.
When summer birds go singing by,
  And sweet rain wakes the blossom,
My weary hands shall folded lie
  Upon a peaceful bosom.

When, Nature, shall the night begin
    That morning ne'er displaces,
And I be calmly folded in
    Thy long and still embraces?
Dearer than to the Arab maid,
    When sands are hotly glowing,
The deep well and the tented shade,
    Were peace of thy bestowing.

THE GRANDMOTHER.

She says she has left the world behind,
    But the world is not forgot,
And says she keeps as strong in her mind
    As she ever was, God wot.
Only the things about her change
    Too fast for her to see,
And all is wide, and vast, and strange —
Ah! foolishly awry, and strange,
    And not as it used to be!

She says the boys are kept from school
    To mind her, without call;
'T is pity if she cannot rule
    Herself, who has ruled them all!
She will not have them stand and wait,
    She can climb the stile alone,
Only the path is not so straight,
So smooth and pleasureful and straight,
    As it was in the years agone!

She says her old eyes keep their sight,
    And, up the farm and down,

She knows when the buckwheat-field is white,
    And the barley-field is brown.
She takes her little trembling share,
    When the harvest song is sung,
Only the ears are not so fair —
Ah ! not so large and fine and fair
    As they were when she was young.

She says when the tune for the dance is set
    Her feet grow almost light,
And her heart would still be dancing yet
    When the winds play up at night ;
Only for this, she says : they pass
    No more like a dancer's tread,
But as if they blew across the grass —
The long, wild, waving, tear-wet grass —
    That grows above her dead.

NOONDAY AT HARVEST.

THE middle of day, and the middle of June —
    No breath of air is blowing,
And the still and sultry heats of noon
    Glint hot along the mowing.

Now echoes from the distant horn
    Come shrilling through the meadows,
Among the reapers reaping corn,
    And the shadows reaping shadows.

Now boldly out of the hills they start —
    Now farther fade, and thinner,

And the farmer slowly mounts his cart,
And slowly drives to dinner.

Now out of the stubble's crispy beds,
And down to the marshy hollow,
While tossing their jackets over their heads,
The sunburnt reapers follow,

In hats of straw, and blue shirt-sleeves,
And with herculean shoulders —
A picture they that needs must please
The eyes of all beholders.

With head dropt low, the sober gray
Betwixt the ruts steers surely,
And a little girl on a wisp of hay
By her father sits demurely ;

Trimming her locks of tawny gold
With leaves of rose and cedar,
While her little brother, ten years old,
Sits sideways on the leader.

Loose dangle down his dusty feet,
His tongue like a crow is cawing,
And he keeps his balance in his seat
By even-timed see-sawing.

Two cows that pasture in the road,
With never an eye to mind them,
Are stealing mouthfuls out the load
That is coming up behind them.

Here, over the steep bank where they pass,
An old gray stone is cropping,
All round about it the tender grass
In luminous fringes dropping.

And there a water cuts the land
Betwixt the fields and fallows,
And silvery over the silver sand
Lies all in warm, soft shallows.

The merry horn no longer sounds,
The winds a hush are keeping,
And the echoes whisper back like hounds,
And fall in the hills a-sleeping.

And never a cricket makes his call,
Nor wild bird shows a feather,
As men and children, shadows and all,
Move slowly home together.

MOTHER AND CHILD.

Within her rustic woodland bower,
Like some warm-hearted, tender flower,
    With young buds all around her,
She kept, in her gracious and glad content,
And never a dream nor fancy went
    From the tendrilled twigs that bound her.

The house was full of the pleasant noise
Of gay, glad girls and sturdy boys,
    Each with a heart like a blossom ;

They were seven — five ranged between
The head that was touching sweet sixteen
 And the babe on the mother's bosom.

In hopeful toil the day went by,
And when the tired sun built in the sky
 His great, red, cloudy bower,
She gathered her buds about her knee —
The sturdy three and the gentle three —
 This motherly woodland flower.

And when the glory died in the west,
And the birds were all in the sleepy nest,
 She would sit in the twilight shadow,
And think how her baby should grow so fine,
And make her place in the world to shine
 As the lily maketh the meadow.

Years came and went, and the pleasant noise
Was hushed in the house, and the girls and boys
 Came now no more about her ;
As the bird went home to the drowsy nest,
And the sun to his cloudy bower in the west,
 They had learned to do without her !

The little children that used to be —
The comely three and the sturdy three —
 Young men and beautiful maidens,
And each had chosen out of the heart,
And gone to be in a bower apart,
 And to dress them separate Edens.

And the mother's thoughts went wearily
Across the prairie, and over the sea,

And through the wintry weather,
About the streets, o'er the desert sand,
To take them once again by the hand,
And to gather them all together.

But alway, as the sun went down,
And the gold and scarlet fell to brown,
And the brown to deeper shadow,
Her babe made all the house as bright
As the lily, with her leaves of light,
Maketh her place in the meadow.

She could not grow from the loving arms,
Nor go to meet the wide world's storms
Away from the lowly portals :
For Death, in the broidered slip and cap,
Had left her to lie in the mother's lap,
In her babyhood immortal.

LONGINGS.

I LONG, how I long for some dim little nook,
With the leaves of the wild open rose for my book,
And to read there the sweet things, and things that are
        true,
Which the Lord's hand has written in sunshine and
        dew.

And I long, my old mother, to lie on thy breast,
With never a thought to o'erlap the deep rest,
My warm to thy cold heart, my face to thy face —
A loyal and royal and restful embrace.

I long so to whisper myself to the trees,
And to sing out my nature, as sings the free breeze,
And to make the waste places o'erflow with my strains,
As the meadows' green cisterns o'erflow with the rains.

I loug with great longing acquainted to be
With the hill-top, the mountain, the terrible sea ;
To cry the wild cry of the raven, above,
And to 'plain with the turtle the dole of my love.

I long from my feet to unfasten the shoes,
And my hair from its combs, and its fillets to loose,
And deep in the arms of the water to tread,
Till the leaves of the lilies are over my head.

Ay, under the lilies to languish and swim —
All the world like a dream that is distant and dim —
No conscience to goad me, no cloud to o'ercast,
No hope for the future, no sigh for the past.

O just for a day, for one day to be free
From all that I have been, from all I can be ;
To feel, like a curtain, forgetfulness fall,
And shield me away from myself most of all.

I long for this day stricken out and apart
From my friend, and my neighbor, my home and my
    heart,
And to find, with the swallow, some dear little nest,
When the crimson is fading all out of the west.

A dear little nest, such as only can stand
In visions, and not on the sea or the land,

Where never that guest, that no other can see,
Should sit at the hearth-side, a terror to me.

LO! THE SPRING RAIN!

DRIP-A-DROP! drip! drop!
O soft and soaking rain!
And paint all over the fairy's cup
The red on the golden grain,
And draw the green through the long white leaves
Of the frozen grass again.

Drip-a-drop out of the skies,
And winds blow east and west,
The lily lids are over her eyes,
And ye cannot break her rest;
All safe from wind and rain she lies,
With her hands across her breast!

Drip-a-drop, fast or slow,
For your showers, or more or less,
Will never stain through her grassy roof
To the folds of her bridal dress —
Will never dampen the curl from the curls
That her pallid cheek caress.

Drip-a-drop, call to the Eve
To shut up the daisy's eye,
And to teach the rose her leaves to close
Where the sweets compacted lie,
That she at the break of the day may wake,
And all outblush the sky.

Drip-a-drop all to the Morn —
  Arise, disshadow the hills,
And send the larks from your nesting lap,
  To wake the sun with their trills,
And shake the damps of dew from the lamps
  Of the glorious daffodils.

Drop! drip, drop! drip, drop!
  Till you empty each sable cloud;
For there never was sleep so still and deep
  As the sleep of the folding shroud,
That only breaks when Gabriel wakes
  The dead with his trump so loud.

PLANTING SONG.

Up, my brown eyes! up, my brown eyes!
  Get your white necks under the yoke —
Up, up, for the day has broke.
Red and yellow, yellow and red,
Like roses blown in a daffodil bed —
  Up, my brown eyes, under the yoke!

On, my brown eyes! on, my brown eyes!
  Bend your white necks low to your work —
Early, early, early and late,
Stretch out the traces stiff and straight,
  And plough up the furrows moist and dark —
  Down with your white necks, down to your work!

Go, my brown eyes! go, my brown eyes!
  White necks all of the yoke unworn —

Out, out, out of the traces —
Up, up, up with your faces !
And come, little maidens, and plant the corn !
Yellow, yellow, e'en as the morn !

Rest, my brown eyes ! rest, my brown eyes —
Free of the traces, night and morn !
Light as the dew-fall, light as the rain,
Patter back, little maids, again ;
Back to the meadows you sowed with corn ;
Feet so waxen, strong-limbed oxen,
Rest in the shade of the broad-leaved corn !

MILKMAID'S MARRIAGE SONG.

Come up, my speckle-face !
Come, my fair speckle-face !
Come, for the morning is bright as can be ;
Leave the grass, dewy wet —
Leave the dear violet —
Come, my good speckle, you 're going with me !

Out of the woody land,
Up through the meadow land,
Down by the flax-field, and past the gay corn ;
Come, ere the rising sun
Over yon cloud so dun
On the high eastern hill pushes his horn ;

Past the green barley ridge,
Over the shallow bridge,
On through the clover as red as a rose ;

We must be far away,
Ere the blue eye of day,
Opening in sunshine, in shadow shall close.

Come, little speckle-face,
Come from your hiding-place ;
You must be combed till your coat is like silk —
Oh, but you'd proudly come
If you could know for whom
You shall hereafter give pails full of milk !

Softly as marriage bells,
Through the low dipping dells
Brings the sweet water that runs to the sea ;
Lift, lift your eyes so brown —
How can you keep them down,
When, little speckle, you 're going with me ?

Never the buttercups
Shone with such pearly drops,
Never the meadow-lark sung out so gay ;
Come from your hiding-place,
Speckle-face, speckle-face,
I 'm to be married — be married to-day !

MAYING.

In the sweet time of May,
When fields and woods are gay,
And large and little flowers are all a-blooming,
I think that thou must find
This true, if thou but mind :
Pleasure is either past, or else a-coming.

When merry birds do crowd
The branches, singing loud —
The black, the bluebird — he of scarlet feather —
And tender, brown-eyed doves,
Make dole to tell their loves,
And winds and waters talk and laugh together ;

When bees about their hives
Are working for their lives,
When with his shadow every leaf is dancing,
While from the land, the sea
For very joy doth be
Retiring now, and now again advancing ;

When not a cloud be spied
The blue of heaven to hide,
And not a lamb of all the flock be straying,
I think if thou art fair,
Thou still must needs declare
'T is not our birthright here to go a-Maying.

THE SNOW-FLOWER.

THE fields were all one field of snow,
The hedge was like a silver wall ;
And when the March began to blow,
And clouds to fill, and rain to fall,
I wept that they should spoil it all.

At first the flakes with flurrying whirl
Hid from my eyes the rivulet,
Lying crooked, like a seam of pearl,

Along some royal coverlet —
I stood, as I remember yet,

With cheeks close-pressed against the pane,
  And saw the hedge's hidden brown
Come out beneath the fretting rain ;
  And then I saw the wall go down —
  My silver wall, and all was brown.

And then, where all had been so white,
  As still the rain slid slant and slow,
Bushes and briers came out in sight,
  And spikes of reeds began to show,
  And then the knot-grass, black and low.

One day, when March was at the close,
  The mild air balm, the sky serene,
The fields that had been fields of snows,
  And, after, withered wastes, were seen
  With here and there some tender green ;

That day my heart came sudden up
  With pleasure that was almost pain —
Being in the fields, I found a cup,
  Pure white, with just a blood-red vein
  Dashed round the edges, by the rain.

The rain, which I that wild March hour
  So foolishly had wept to see,
Had shaped the snow into a flower,
  And thus had brought it back to me
  Sweeter than only snow, could be.

THE TWO MOWERS.

I KNOW not what brings back to-day
A scene of the long ago,
When, all betwixt the blue and the gray,
Two mowers came to mow.

About the scythes that cut their path
The dewdrops fell in showers,
And every long and luminous swath
They swung, was mixed with flowers.

Here ivies sweet and tufted crows
Lie low beneath their tread ;
And there the slender neck of a rose
Without her royal head.

Swish ! swish ! and neither heeds nor spares
The pansy freaked with jet,
Nor she that sad embroidery wears,
Nor the milky violet.

Swish ! then a pause, and then another swath,
And a zigzag line is seen ;
And in betwixt them, on the path,
A turf of sheltering green.

We children could not keep away,
But ran with skip and bound,
To find on her nest of sticks and clay
A bird so safe and sound.

Her back as smooth and brown as a mouse,
  And her wing of a ruddy glow,
Like the roof and hearthstone of the house
  Whence the mowers came to mow.

How fixed the day in memory stands!
  And the time of the day, for then,
We that had called them only *hands*
  Began to call them *men* !

We made our hands with raking rough —
  And the winds they kissed us brown ;
And the shaggy beards grew fair enough
  Before the sun was down.

For we knew that deep in the hearts of both
  True love had been the guest,
That made them cut the zigzag swath,
  And spare the lowly nest.

PLEA TO OCTOBER.

LITTLE 't is I ask of thee,
  Season fine and fair,
Lying betwixt the roses lost
And the falling of the frost —
  Little for my share.

Fortune has been hard with me ;
  Thou hast wealth to spare.
Thus my plea, the whole day long:
Shall I call it just a song,
  Or shall I call it prayer ?

What thou wilt, thou may'st withhold,
    Till we shall agree.
Lo! thou mak'st the winds that blow
'Twixt the sunflower and the snow
    To be sweet with me.

Keep the daffodilly's gold,
    Keep the corn and wine;
But some green and grassy nook,
Where to lie and read my book,
    Leave, I pray, for mine.

Oh, be kind, be kind to me;
    Nor let rough winds blow,
Putting out, with rainy nights,
All the twinkling meadow-lights,
    Burning down so low.

Hearts have failed me all the way
    Toward the night's dread fall;
Grant *that* hour, for mercy's sake,
Love enough to keep awake,
    Sweetest eyes of all.

I contented am to be
    Neither fine nor fair;
Lo! thou rightest me this wrong —
Slight it not for just a song,
    But grant it for a prayer.

Friendship may but last a day;
    Passion is a spell
Transient as the whirlwind's breath;

Grant me love as strong as death —
Ay, indestructible !

A PASSING WISH.

OH, for the life of a gipsy !
A strong-arm, barefoot girl ;
And to have the wind for a waiting-maid
To keep my hair in curl ;
To bring me scent of the violet,
And the red rose, and the pine ;
And at night to spread my grassy bed —
Ah ! would n't it be divine ?

Oh, for the life of a gipsy !
So gloriously free !
Through the world to roam, and to find a home
'Neath every greenwood tree ;
To milk my cow in the meadow,
Wherever she chanced to stand ;
And to have my cornfields planted
By every lad in the land !

Oh, for the life of a gipsy !
With the dew to fringe my gown :
And to have the sun for a sweetheart
To come and kiss me brown ;
To take each little chubby-cheek
That I chose, and call her mine,
And teach her to tramp from camp to camp —
Ah ! would n't it be divine ?

Oh, for the life of a gipsy !
  To lie in the lazy shades ;
And to predict sweet fairings
  To all the village maids ;
To give them caps of pretty flowers,
  And shawls of wool so white,
And troops of lovers to sing them songs
  At their window-panes at night !

Oh, for the life of a gipsy !
  To hunt the hare for play ;
And to take my trap on my shoulder
  And hie away and away —
Away to the tents by the water,
  When the stars begin to shine —
To my glad wild crew, with hearts so true —
  Ah ! would n't it be divine ?

Oh, for the life of a gipsy !
  To be up at the dawning gray ;
And to have my dog, like my shadow,
  Beside me all the day ;
To have a hat of plaited straw,
  And a cloak of scarlet dye,
And shoot like a light through the glens at night,
  And make the owlets cry !

Oh, for the life of a gipsy !
  To roam the wild woods through ;
To have the wind for a waiting-maid,
  And the sun for a sweetheart true ;
To say to my restless conscience,
  Be still ; you are no more mine !

And to hold my heart beneath my art—
Ah ! would n't it be divine ?

A YEAR AGO.

THE sun across the hill
  Is gazing bright and bold,
But the valley with the frost in her lap,
  Chaste and chilly cold ;

All in her sheets of mist,
  From morn to evening lies,
Unconscious of the bold, bright face
  Of her lover in the skies !

Spirits of coming flowers
  The sense wellnigh deceives ;
The rose awaiting to be dressed
  In her dainty body of leaves ;

The hollyhock and pink,
  For their cups of brown and red,
And the lily for a holy veil
  To lap about her head.

The fisher sings by the sea,
  As he mends his broken net,
And all with golden drops of light
  Are the rainy shadows set.

In a cloud of whitest dreams,
  But a little year ago,

Like a tender Alpine flower
Nestling under the snow,

The lady of my heart
Was with me all day long,
And the tears came out of her happy eyes
To praise the fisher's song.

Her song is sweeter now
Than the fisher's by the sea,
And the rose in her dainty body of leaves
Is not so fair as she !

THE GRAVE OF THE SETTLER'S BOY.

THE hill is bleak and bare enough,
    Thistles are all the flowers it owns ;
Round it the road runs zigzag, rough
    With miry ruts and loose, gray stones.

Ay, bleak and bare and cheerless, save
    One quiet spot that scarce is seen,
And there, about a little grave,
    The turf is smooth, and low and green.

For, seeing that lone grave, sometimes
    The teamster checks his whistling gay,
And blocks his heavy wheel, and climbs
    The fence, and pulls the weeds away.

There kindly nature paints the shade
    With insects, as with tenderest dies ;

There fox and hare, all unafraid,
  Look straight into the hunter's eyes.

For while he thinks of suns gone down,
  Of hopes long lost, of long-lost care,
His trusty rifle, bright and brown,
  Slips from his shoulder, unaware.

All things are solemn ; 'gainst the sky,
  The wood, a mass of shadow flows,
And high above the shoals of rye,
  Her long, red arms the wild-brier throws.

The birds scarce sing there even at morn,
  But as the long, slow hours go past,
With golden bills and bills of horn,
  Peck the black stubs, until at last,

Leaving the world to deeper gloom,
  The sunshine from the landscape goes,
And o'er the yet rejoicing bloom
  The moon her hoarded pallor snows.

PRESENCE.

THE wild, sweet water, as it flows, —
  The winds, that kiss me as they pass, —
The starry shadow of the rose,
  Sitting beside her on the grass, —

The daffodilly, trying to bless
  With better light the beauteous air, —

The lily, wearing the white dress
Of sanctuary, to be more fair, —

The lithe-armed, dainty-fingered brier,
That in the woods, so dim and drear,
Lights up betimes her tender fire
To soothe the homesick pioneer, —

The moth, his brown sails balancing
Along the stubble crisp and dry, —
The ground-flower, with a blood-red ring
On either hand, — the pewit's cry, —

The friendly robin's gracious note, —
The hills, with crimson weeds o'errun, —
The althea, with her crimson coat
Tricked out to please the wearied sun, —

The dandelion, whose golden share
Is set before the rustic's plow, —
The hum of insects in the air, —
The blooming bush, — the withered bough, —

The coming on of eve, — the springs
Of daybreak, soft and silver-bright, —
The frost that, with rough, rugged wings,
Blows down the cankered buds, — the white

Long drifts of winter snow, — the heat
Of August, falling still and wide, —
Broad cornfields, — one chance stalk of wheat,
Standing with bright head hung aside,—

All things, my darling, all things seem
  In some strange way to speak of thee ;
Nothing is half so much a dream,
  Nothing so much reality.

My soul to thine is dutiful,
  In all its pleasure, all its care ;
O most beloved! most beautiful!
  I miss, and find thee everywhere!

CRADLE SONG.

ALL the air is white with snowing,
  Cold and white — cold and white ;
Wide and wild the winds are blowing,
  Blowing, blowing wide and wild.
Sweet little child, sweet little child,
  Sleep, sleep, sleep, little child :
Earth is dark, but heaven is bright —
  Sleep, sleep till the morning light :
Some must watch, and some must weep,
And some, little baby, some may sleep :
  So, good-night, sleep till light ;
  Lullaby, lullaby, and good-night!

Folded hands on the baby bosom,
  Cheek and mouth rose-red, rose-sweet ;
And like a bee's wing in a blossom,
  Beat, beat, beat, and beat ;
So the heart keeps going, going,
While the winds in the bitter snowing
  Meet and cross — cross and meet —

Heaping high, with many an eddy,
Bars of stainless chalcedony
All in curves about the door,
Where shall fall no more, no more,
Longed-for steps, so light, so light.
Little one, sleep till the moon is low,
Sleep, and rock, and take your rest;
Winter clouds will snow and snow,
And the winds blow east, and the winds blow west;
Some must come, and some must go,
And the earth be dark, and the heavens be bright:
   Never fear, baby dear,
Wrong things lose themselves in right;
   Never fear, mother is here,
Lullaby, lullaby, and good-night.

O good saint, that thus emboldenest
   Eyes bereaved to see, to-night,
Cheek the rosiest, hair the goldenest,
   Ever gladdened the mother sight.
Blessed art thou to hide the willow,
   Waiting and weeping over the dead,
With the softest, silkenest pillow
   Ever illumined hair o'erspread.
Never had cradle such a cover;
   All my house with light it fills;
Over and under, under and over,
   'Broidered leaves of the daffodils;
All away from the winter weather,
   Baby, wrapt in your 'broideries bright,
Sleep, nor watch any more for father —
Father will not come home to-night.

Angels now are round about him,
  In the heavenly home on high ;
We must learn to do without him —
  Some must live, and some must die,
  Baby, sweetest ever was born,
  Shut little blue eyes, sleep till morn :
  Rock and sleep and wait for the light,
  Father will not come home to-night.

Winter is wild, but winter closes ;
The snow in the nest of the bird will lie,
And the bird must have its little cry ;
Yet the saddest day doth swiftly run,
Up o'er the black cloud shines the sun,
And when the reign of the frost is done
The May will come with roses, roses —
Green-leaved grass and red-leaved roses —
Roses, roses, roses, roses,
Roses red, and lilies white.
Sleep, little baby, sleep, sleep ;
Some must watch, and some must weep ;
Sweetly sleep till the morning light,
Lullaby, lullaby, and good-night.

A LAST WISH.

[UNFINISHED.]

GIVE me to see, though only in a dream,
Though only in an unsubstantial dream,
The dear old cradle lined with leaves of moss,
And daily changed from cradle into cross,
What time athwart its dull brown wood, a beam

Slid from the gold deeps of the sunset shore,
Making the blur of twilight white and fair,
Like lilies quivering in the summer air;
And my low pillow like a rose full-blown.

Oh, give mine eyes to see once more, once more,
My longing eyes to see, this one time more,
   The shadows trembling with the wings of bats,
And dandelions dragging to the door,
And speckling all the grass about the door,
   With the thick spreading of their starry mats.

Give me to see, I pray and can but pray,
Oh, give me but to see to-day, to-day,
The little brown-walled house where I was born,
The gray old barn, the cattle-shed close by,
The well-sweep, with its angle sharp and high;
The flax field, like a patch of fallen sky;
The millet harvest, colored like the corn,
Like to the ripe ears of the new husked corn.

And give mine eyes to see among the rest
This rustic picture, in among the rest,
For there and only there it doth belong,
I, at fourteen, and in my Sunday best,
Reading with voice unsteady my first song,
The rugged verses of my first rude song.

POEMS OF GRIEF AND CONSOLATION.

LYRA: A LAMENT.

MAIDENS, whose tresses shine,
Crowned with daffodil and eglantine,
Or from their stringèd buds of brier roses,
Bright as the vermeil closes
Of April twilights after sobbing rains,
Fall down in rippled skeins
And golden tangles low
About your bosoms, dainty as new snow ;
While the warm shadows blow in softest gales
    Fair hawthorn-flowers and cherry-blossoms white
Against your kirtles, like the froth from pails
    O'er-brimmed with milk at night,
When lowing heifers bury their sleek flanks
In winrows of sweet hay or clover banks, —
Come near and hear, I pray,
My plainèd roundelay.

Where creeping vines o'errun the sunny leas,
Sadly, sweet souls, I watch your shining bands,
Filling with stainèd hands
    Your leafy cups with lush red strawberries ;
Or deep in murmurous glooms,
In yellow mosses full of starry blooms,

Sunken at ease — each busied as she likes,
  Or stripping from the grass the beaded dews,
Or picking jagged leaves from the slim spikes
  Of tender pinks — with warbled interfuse
Of poesy divine,
  That haply long ago
Some wretched borderer of the realm of woe
Wrought to a dulcet line ; —
  If in your lovely years
There be a sorrow that may touch with tears
The eyelids piteously, they must be shed
FOR LYRA — DEAD.

The mantle of the May
  Was blown almost within the Summer's reach,
And all the orchard trees,
  Apple and pear and peach,
Were full of yellow bees,
  Flown from their hives away.
The callow dove upon the dusty beam
  Fluttered its little wings in streaks of light,
  And the gray swallow twittered full in sight ;
Harmless the unyoked team
  Browsed from the budding elms, and thrilling lays
  Made musical prophecies of brighter days ;
And all went jocundly. I could but say,
Ah ! well-a-day ! —
What time Spring thaws the wold,
And in the dead leaves come up sprouts of gold,
And green and ribby blue, that after hours
Encrown with flowers ;
Heavily lies my heart
From all delights apart,

Even as an echo hungry for the wind,
When fail the silver-kissing waves to unbind
The music bedded in the drowsy strings
    Of the sea's golden shells —
That, sometimes, with their honeyed murmurings
    Fill all its underswells ; —
For o'er the sunshine fell a shadow wide
When Lyra died.

When sober Autumn, with his mist-bound brows,
Sits drearily beneath the fading boughs,
    And the rain, chilly cold,
    Wrings from his beard of gold,
And as some comfort for his lonesome hours,
Hides in his bosom stalks of withered flowers,—
I think about what leaves are drooping round
    A smoothly shapen mound,
    And if the wild wind cries
Where Lyra lies.

Sweet shepherds softly blow
Ditties most sad and low —
Piping on hollow reeds to your pent sheep —
    Calm be my Lyra's sleep,
Unvexed with dream of the rough briers that pull
From his strayed lambs the wool !
    O star, that tremblest dim
    Upon the welkin's rim,
Send with thy milky shadows from above
Tidings about my love ;
    If that some envious wave
    Made his untimely grave,
Or if, so softening half my wild regrets,
Some coverlid of bluest violets

Was softly put aside,
What time he died !
Nay, come not, piteous maids,
Out of the murmurous shades ;
But keep your tresses crownèd as you may
With eglantine and daffodillies gay,
And with the dews of myrtles wash your cheeks,
When flamy streaks,
Uprunning the gray orient, tell of morn —
While I, forlorn,
Pour all my heart in tears and plaints, instead,
FOR LYRA — DEAD.

IN ILLNESS.

No harsh complaint nor rude unmannered woe,
Shall jar discordant in the dulcet flow
Of music, raining through the chestnut wings
    Of the wild plaining dove,
The while I touch my lyre's late shattered strings,
    Mourning about my love.

Now in the field of sunset, Twilight gray,
Sad for the dying day,
With wisps of shadows binds the sheaves of gold,
And Night comes shepherding his starry fold
Along the shady bottom of the sky.
Alas, that I
Sunken among life's faded ruins lie —
My senses from their natural uses bound !
    What thing is likest to my wretched plight ? —
A barley grain cast into stony ground,
    That may not quicken up into the light.

Erewhile I dreamed about the hills of home
Whereon I used to roam ;
　　Of silver-leavèd larch,
And willows hung with tassels, when like bells
Tinkle the thawing runnel's brimming swells ;
　　And softly filling in the front of March
The new moon lies,
Watching for harebells, and the buds that ease
Hearts lovelorn, and the spotted adder's tongue,
Dead heapèd leaves among —
The verdurous season's cloud of witnesses ;
　　Of how the daisy shines
White, i' the knotty and close nibbled grass ;
　　Of thickets full of prickly eglantines,
And the slim spice-wood and red sassafras,
Stealing between whose boughs the twinkling heats
Suck up the exhalèd sweets
From dew-embalmèd beds of primroses,
That all unpressèd lie,
Save of enamored airs, right daintily,
　　And golden-ringèd bees ;
Of atmospheres of hymns,
　　When wings go beating up the blue sublime
From hedgerows sweet with vermeil-sprouting limbs,
　　In April's showery time,
When lilacs come, and straggling flag-flowers, bright
As any summer light
　　Ere yet the plowman's steers
Browse through the meadows, from the traces free,
Or steel-blue swallows twitter merrily,
With slant wings shaving close the level ground,
Where with his new-washed ewes thick huddled round,
　　The careful herdsman plies the busy shears.

But this was in life's May,
Ere Lyra was away;
And this fond seeming now no longer seems —
Aching and drowsy pains keep down my dreams ; —
    Even as a dreary wind
Within some hollow, black with poison flowers,
    Swoons into silence, dies the hope that lined
My lowly chamber with illumined wings,
    In life's enchanted hours,
When, tender oxlips mixed through yellow strings
Of mullein-stars, with myrtles interfused,
Pulled out of pastures green, I gayly used
To braid up with my hair.   Ah, well-a-day !
Haply the blue eyes of another May,
Open from rosy lids, I shall not see
For the white shroud-folds.   If it thus must be,
Oh, friends who near me keep
To watch or weep,
When you shall see the coming of the night
Comfort me with the light
Of Lyra's love,
And pray the saints above
To pity me, if it be sin to know
Heaven here below.

LAST SONG.

THE beetle from the furrow goes,
    The bird is on the sheltering limb,
And in the twilight's pallid close
    Sits the gray evening, hushed and dim.

In the blue west the sun is down,
  And soft the fountain washes o'er
Green limes and hyacinths so brown
  As never fountain washed before.

I scarce can hear the curlew call,
  I scarce can feel the night-wind's breath ;
I only see the shadows fall,
  I only feel this chill is death.

At morn the bird will leave the bough,
  The beetle o'er the furrow run,
But with the darkness falling now,
  The morning for my eyes is done.

Piping his ditty low and soft,
  If shepherd chance to cross the wold,
Bound homeward from the flowery croft,
  And the white tendance of his fold,

And find me lying fast asleep,
  Be inspiration round him thrown,
That he may dig my grave down deep,
  Where never any sunshine shone.

WEARINESS.

GENTLE, gentle sisters twain,
I am sad with toil and pain,
Hoping, struggling, all in vain,
And would be with you again.

Sick and weary, let me go
To our homestead, old and low,
Where the cool, fresh breezes blow —
There I shall be well, I know.

Violets, gold and white and blue,
Sprout up sweetly through the dew —
Lilacs now are budding too —
Oh, I pine to be with you!

I am lonely and unblest —
I am weary, and would rest
Where all things are brightest, best,
In the lovely, lovely West.

KINDNESS.

IN the dull shadows of long hopeless strife
    I talked with sorrow — round about me lay
The broken plans and promises of life, —
    When first thy kindness crossed my friendless way.

Then felt I, hushed with wonder and sweet awe,
    As with his weary banners round him furled
Felt ocean's wanderer, when first he saw
    The pale-lipt billows kissing a new world.

The joy, the rapture of that glad surprise,
    Haply some heart may know that inly grieves,
Some sad Ruth bowing from love-speaking eyes
    Her trembling bosom over alien sheaves.

ULALIE.

THE crimson of the maple-trees
  Is lighted by the moon's soft glow ;
Oh, nights like this, and things like these,
  Bring back a dream of long ago.
For on an eve as sweet as this —
  Upon this bank — beneath this tree —
My lips, in love's impassioned kiss,
  Met those of Ulalie.

Softly as now the dewdrops burned
  In the flushed bosoms of the flowers ;
Backward almost seems to have turned
  The golden axis of the hours,
Till, cold as ocean's beaten surf,
  Beneath these trailing boughs, I see
The white cross and the faded turf
  Above lost Ulalie.

MY PLAYMATE.

I LITTLE care to write her praise,
  In truth, I little care that she
Should seem as pure in all her ways,
  To others, as she seems to me.

At morn a sparrow's note we heard,
  His shadow fell across her bed,
She smiled and listened to the bird ;
  And when the evening twilight red

Fell with the dew, he came again,
 And perching on the nearest bough,
Higher and wilder sang the strain —
 She did not smile to hear him now.

Many and many years, the light
 Thin moonbeams, sheets for her have spread;
And scented clovers, red and white,
 Have made the fringes of her bed.

Small care for sitting in the sun
 Have I — small care to war with fate :
The wine and wormwood are as one,
 Since thou art dead, my pretty mate.

LELIA.

GONE from us hast thou, in thy girlish hours,
 What time the tenderest blooms of summer cease ;
In thy young bosom bearing life's sweet flowers
 To the good city of eternal peace.

In the soft stops of silver singing rain,
 Faint be the falling of the pale red light
O'er thy meek slumber, wrapt away from pain
 In the fair robes of dainty bridal white.

Seven nights the stars have wandered through the blue,
 Since thou to larger, holier life wert born ;
And day as often, sandaled with gray dew,
 Has trodden out the golden fires of morn.

The wearying tumult of unending strife,
  The jars that through the heart discordant ring,
Drive the dim current of our mortal life
  Against the shore where reigns unending spring.

And though I mourn for Lelia, she who died
  When all the tenderest blossoms ceased to be,
Her being's broken wave has multiplied
  The stars that shine across eternity.

DYING.

My Love, I love but only thee,
  Yet of a truth I must avow
That I have taken an enemy
  Closer in my embrace, than thou.

And if thou comest home some day,
  And find'st the household door shut up,
Be not disconsolate, I pray,
  Because of that one bitter cup ;

But think of all the pleasant years
  Our paths did gently downward slope,
And of the land where fall no tears,
  And live in memory and hope.

In memory of the sacred hours
  When still from heaven some gracious gleam
Ran like the tender hues through flowers,
  Making of all our lives a dream.

In hope of that celestial birth
　From death to life, apart from woe ;
Of love, that to the love of earth
　Is as the sunshine to the snow.

Spring, ay, the summer too, is gone,
　And autumn shadows darken all ;
Why should I care to linger on
　Till the wild storms of winter fall !

KILLVALY.

O THE sweet waters, the silvery waters —
　O the gay grass where together we strayed !
Killvaly, Killvaly ! wild, woody Killvaly,
　O for a day, with my love, in thy shade !

O for a touch of the dear little fingers !
　O for a kiss of the mouth of my maid !
Killvaly, Killvaly ! glorious Killvaly,
　O for the silent consent of thy shade !

O the glad whir of the wings that flew o'er us,
　Downy with linings of ruby and fawn ;
Killvaly, Killvaly ! musical Killvaly,
　O for a day of the days that are gone !

O the kind zephyr, my sweet, sweet accomplice,
　That drowned me almost in the waves of her hair ;
Killvaly, Killvaly ! generous Killvaly,
　How couldst thou yield me a treasure so rare !

O the ripe flush of the royal red roses
I gathered, and gave to my fine little maid ;
Killvaly, Killvaly ! cold, cruel Killvaly,
How couldst thou hide that bright head in thy shade !

What to me now are the dulcetest pleasures ?
What is the world since my pretty one died ?
Killvaly, Killvaly !· calm, quiet Killvaly,
Take me, and lull me to sleep by her side.

SORROW.

ALL the long weary day
When I my tune would play,
He maketh sad stops in my sweetest reed ;
And when the daylight ceases
He breaketh up my sleep to little pieces,
And thereupon doth feed.

Alway at my spare feast,
Ere yet the meat I taste,
He cometh, and beside my board doth sit,
And giveth me such looks
As though that he were drawing with sharp hooks
The marrow out of it.

I may no longer use
Such colors as I choose —
Scarlet or lively green to be my gowns,
For still he letteth fall
His salt and bitter tears on one and all,
Fading my reds to browns.

Long whiles I stay apart
From my most sweet sweetheart,
Because of eyelids drooping in disgrace,
For whatsoe'er I say,
He maketh me to stammer such a way,
As shames me to his face.

The littlest room of all
My house, is not so small,
But there he maketh space and doth abide;
O friends, for pity's sake,
Out of your love a secret chamber make,
And therein let me hide.

For all the weary day
When I my tune would play,
He maketh sad stops in my sweetest reed ;
And when the daylight ceases
He breaketh up my sleep to little pieces,
And thereupon doth feed.

TRACKS.

My lost love, your spirit such quietude brings,
  I know that you live, and are well, as I know
  By the tracks of the birds that I see in the snow,
That songs must be somewhere, that somewhere are
    wings.

Lost, yet you were never *all* lost for a day ;
  I know you are gone to your higher estate,
  And sitting low down in the shadows, I wait
Till I too am ripe to be gathered away.

Never lost, never lost! yet, my dear little friend,
   I miss the glad light of your wonderful eyes ;
   And something I miss from the earth and the skies,
That will not, and cannot come back, to the end.

Our paths through the fields seem to be as strange ways ;
   I wish that some night I could dream a sweet dream,
   Wherein the old nights and the old days would seem
Like the old happy nights and the happy old days.

I wish you could leave the good angels above !
   I wish I could have you, just one fleeting hour,
   To hold in my bosom, my sweet little flower,
And tell you the height and the depth of my love.

Sometimes such a doubt from the last darkness springs ;
   My heart turneth sick, and my faith falleth low,
   But when the faint bird-tracks appear in the snow,
I trust and believe in the songs and the wings.

A MOTHER'S SOLACE.

My little darling seems to me
Lying here dead upon my knee :
I know it is not so — that I
Am dead as much as she can die.

Her hair in many a curl that lies,
Would grow no nearer to her eyes
That any sight of mine could know,
Though I kept her always lying so.

Her hands would seem like a snowy cross,
One on the other, and I her loss
Would mourn with tears, though while they fell
I knew she was alive and well.

So lay this clay that seems to be
My little darling, from my knee :
The life she lives is too divine
To be interpreted to mine.

My senses shut me in their cell —
She is outside, alive and well, —
I am sinful, she is sinless, I
Am dying — she has ceased to die.

The love that made her thus to be
Is more than mine is, therefore she
Needs me not, or I need not her —
Love, so loving her, could not err.

SPRING.

Patches of snow may still be seen,
  And the boughs are black and bare,
But the grass will soon be growing green,
  For the spring is in the air.

The wintry silence seems to take
  Almost the shape of sound,
As if the flowery folk were awake
  In their beds beneath the ground.

The clouds that overhung the hills
  All winter, cold and white,
Have taken the hue of the daffodils,
  For the spring is in the light.

O mourners, as the fields grow fair,
  Let all your fears depart,
For He who wakes the spring-time there
  Can waken it in the heart.

The hopes you mourn as dead, but sleep,
  And will come to life like the flowers ;
The Lord hath taken, and he can keep,
  For his love is more than ours.

When winter cometh, fear no ill,
  For his care is never done,
And the heart of man it draweth him still
  As the dewdrop draws the sun.

OVER THE SHIPS THE WHITE MISTS LIE.

OVER the ships the white mists lie,
  And the sea is cold and gray ;
The moon has taken her place in the sky,
  But her face is turned away.

The half of her lovely light is gone,
  And the sea is cold and gray,
But the ships are sailing on and on
  To their haven in the bay.

They cut the mist, they stem the gale,
　And, till their ports be won,
Sail to the land of morn, and sail
　To the land of the setting sun.

My lover is sailing away from me,
　Sailing night and day,
And wherever I look I seem to see
　The sea-mist, cold and gray.

But I know the while my heart is tossed,
　And the mists of sorrow fall,
"That better 't is to have loved and lost
　Than not to have loved at all."

TO A PICTURE.

Is this all? all? my rose-red lips,
　Where, where are your gentle sighs?
You have only one of your thousand lights,
　My beautiful, beautiful eyes!

The same sweet brow and dazzling hair —
　On the cheek the same warm glow —
Ah, come and be folded in mine again,
　My dear little hands of snow!

O cruel death, wilt thou not yield
　To the might of love like ours?
I have seen the bleak cold earth in the rain
　Blaze wild and red with flowers!

Still, still.   If ever I did you wrong
   That your tender love concealed,
Break this silence, life of my life,
   And say that my wound is healed!

See, see! I am on my knees!   No flush
   In the cheek? in the pulse, no start?
O come from the canvas and make me live —
   Come, come to me, heart of my heart!

One sign, my little white hands! one word,
   My rose-red mouth! though it kill —
Change, change, my darling, your smile to a frown —
   Be anything, but so still.

POEMS OF LOVE.

TELLING FORTUNES.

Two tall, twin lilies from afar,
  Their fair heads toward her softly bowed,
As with her sweet cheek, like a star
    That pillows on some sunset cloud,
      She, in the shadow of the hills,
      Lay low among the daffodils.

Even her silence seemed to speak
  What dullest ear might understand,
As with her hair drawn down her cheek,
    And shining in her milk-white hand,
      She pulled the clovers from the mould,
      And by their leaves her fortune told.

Sometimes from mouth to brow she smiled
  With all a woman's sweetest grace,
But changing to a pouting child
    Within a little moment's space,
      Would toss her clover-flowers about,
      As if she did the world misdoubt.

Now she would look, and now would list
  Till dewdrops fringed her silken gown.

And bars of scarlet crossed the mist,
And the low sun went dimly down.
Then all the frowns would change to fears,
That filled the eyes with sad, soft tears.

At length the moon rose, yellowing o'er
The banks of sea-fog, cold and white,
And up the black sands of the shore
The tide crawled slow. " O cruel night,
Leave me," she cries, " of all the sky,
One star, to tell my fortune by ! "

Hush ! hark ! and round her milk-white hand
She hath reeled the smiling locks so fast ;
She is on her feet — she hath reached the sand —
She is in her lover's arms at last !
The clovers strown like ashes round,
All the sweet fortune being found.

PAUL.

CROSSING the stubble, where, erewhile,
The golden-headed wheat had been,
I saw, and knew him by his smile.
Night, sad with rain, was flowing in.

I drew the curtains, soft and warm,
And when the room was full of light,
We sat — half listening to the storm,
Half talking — all the dreary night.

From their wet sheds, we heard the moan
Our oxen made, — a pretty pair, —

And heard the dead leaves often blown
  In gusty eddies, here and there.

The dull-eyed spider ran along
  The smoky rafters ; the gray mouse
Crossed the bare floor ; and his wild song
  The cricket made through all the house.

Twisting the brown hair into rings,
  Above his meditative eyes,
I counted all the long-gone springs
  That we had sown with flowers ; his sighs

Came thick and fast, as well they might ;
  But when I said, how on, and on,
For his sake, I had kept them bright —
  The slow, reproachful smile was gone.

And seeing that my spoken truth
  Glowed in my silent looks, the same,
All the proud beauty of his youth
  Back on his faded manhood came.

About my neck he clasped his arm,
  As in affection's morning prime,
And said how blest he was — that storm
  Was sweeter than the summer-time !

But when I kissed him back, and said —
  The embers never cast a gleam
Through our low cabin, half so red,
  Sleep vanished — all had been a dream.

THE TRYST.

THE moss is withered, the moss is brown
  Under the dreary cedarn bowers,
And fleet winds running the valleys down
  Cover with dead leaves the sleeping flowers.

White as a lily the moonlight lies
  Under the gray oak's ample boughs ;
In the time of June 't were a paradise
  For gentle lovers to make their vows.

In the middle of night when the wolf is dumb,
  Like a sweet star rising out of the sea,
They say that a damsel at times will come,
  And brighten the chilly light under the tree.

And a blessed angel from out the sky
  Cometh her lonely watch to requite ;
But not for my soul's sweet sake would I
  Pray under its shadow alone at night.

A boy by the tarn on the mountain side
  Was cruelly murdered long ago,
Where oft a spectre is seen to glide
  And wander wearily to and fro.

The night was sweet like an April night,
  When misty softness the blue air fills,
And the freckled adder's tongue makes bright
  The sleepy hollows among the hills.

When, startled up from the hush that broods
  Beauteously o'er the midnight time,
The gust ran wailing along the woods
  Like one who seeth an awful crime.

The tree is withered, the tree is lost,
  Where he gathered the ashen berries red,
As meekly the dismal woods he crossed —
  The tree is withered, the boy is dead.

Now nightly, with footsteps slow and soft,
  A damsel goes thither, but not in joy ;
Put thy arms round her, good angel aloft,
  If she be the love of the murdered boy.

For still she comes, as the daylight fades,
  Her tryst to keep near the cedarn bowers.
Bear with her gently, tenderly, maids,
  Whose hopes are open like summer flowers.

DEATH'S FERRYMAN.

BOATMAN, thrice I 've called thee o'er,
Waiting on life's solemn shore,
Tracing, in the silver sand,
Letters, till thy boat should land.

Drifting out alone, with thee,
Toward the clime I cannot see,
Read to me the strange device
Graven on thy wand of ice ;

Push the curls of golden hue
From thine eyes of starlit dew,
And behold me where I stand,
Beckoning thy boat to land.

Where the river mist, so pale,
Trembles like a bridal veil,
O'er yon lowly drooping tree,
One that loves me waits for me.

Hear, still boatman, hear my call !
Last year, with the leaflet's fall,
Resting her pale hand in mine,
Crossed she in that boat of thine.

When the corn shall cease to grow,
And the rye-field's sea-like flow
At the reaper's feet is laid,
(Crossing, spoke the gentle maid,)

Dearest love, another year
Thou shalt meet this boatman here —
The white fingers of despair
Playing with his shining hair.

From this silver-sanded shore,
Beckon him to row thee o'er ;
Where yon solemn shadows be,
I shall wait thee — come and see !

— There ! the white sails float and flow,
One in heaven and one below ;
And I hear a low voice cry,
Ferryman of Death am I.

JUSTIFIED.

COME up, my heart, come from thy hiding-place ;
Stern Memory grows importunate to make
Hard accusation ; and if that I be
Not grossly misadvised, thou 'rt much to blame.
  Was 't thou, that on a certain April night,
When sweetnesses were breaking all the buds,
And the red creeping vines of strawberries
Hung out their dainty blossoms toward the sun —
When first the dandelion from his cell
Came, like a miser dragging up his gold,
And making envious the poor traveller,
And the wild brook — thou wottest how it ran,
Betwixt the stubbly oat-field and the slope
Where, free from needless shepherding, that night
The sheep went cropping thistle-leaves, and I .
For the soft tinkling of their silver bells
Staid listening, so I said, and said again,
To be unto my conscience justified —
Was 't thou that tempted me to let the dew
Of midnight straiten all my pretty curls,
And woo the bat-like clinging damps to come
And bleach the morning blushes from my cheeks ?
Ah, me ! how many years since that same night
Have come and gone, nor brought a fellow to it !
Thou need'st not shake so, guilty prisoner,
For though those white hairs round my forehead teach
A judgment cold and passionless, and though
The hand that writes is palsy-touched, withal,
I cannot wrong so deeply, grievously,
The glorifying beauty of the world,
As to declare that thou art all condemned !

Yet stay, I pray thee : make some sweet excuse
To that staid saintly dame, Austerity ;
For she and I have been a thousand times
At variance about her sober rule.
Once, when I left my gleaning in the wheat,
(The time was June, sunset within an hour,)
And underneath a hedge, that rained down flowers
Of hawthorn and wild roses in my lap,
Sat idling with young Jocelyn, till that
The shadows of the mowers, stretching out
Like threatening ghosts, did cut our pastime off,
She rated me so mercilessly hard
That I was fain with fables to make peace.
I said that I was tired, and that a bird,
Soft-singing in the hedge, drew me that way ;
And then I said I looked for catydids,
(It was three months before their chirping time,)
And that 't was pleasant to look thence and see
The sunshine topping all the wide-leaved corn,
And the young apples on the orchard boughs
With the betraying red upon their cheeks.
What other most improbable conceits
I told to her, I now remember not !
But I remember that her frowning brows
So chid me to confusion that I said
It was not *Jocelyn* that kept me there !
She smiled, and we since then are enemies.
Silent? thou hast no eloquence to win
Her cold regard upon my waywardness.
Well, be it so ! and though the great wide world
Stare blank that I do soften judgment so,
Thou stand'st acquitted, yea, and justified.

JULIET TO ROMEO.

NAY, sweet, one moment more, thy lips, mayhap,
   Will soothe this heavy aching in my brows —
Stay, while the twilight in the dusky boughs
Sits smiling with the moon upon her lap !

And dost thou kiss me to be free to go ?
   How royally the purple shadows sway
   Across the gorgeous chamber of dead day ;
Now pr'ythee, stay, while they are shining so.

That kiss has made me better — I shall be
   Quite well anon — nay, gentle Romeo,
   I hear the vesper-chanting, soft and low —
When the last echo dies thou shalt be free.

Could that have been the owlet's cry ?   The light
   Is scarcely faded from the hill-tops yet,
   'T is not a half hour since the sun was set ;
Wait, dear one, for the dim concealing night.

The bell is striking ; hark ! 't is only nine,
   I counted truly, love, it was not ten —
   Would you be falsest of all faithless men,
And leave me in the lonely night to pine ?

I hear the watch-dog baying at the moon,
   And hear the noisy cock crow loud and long —
   He cannot cheat me with his shrilly song —
I know the midnight has not come so soon.

What ruddy streaks are running up the sky —
Is that the lark that past the turret flies !
Ah me, 't is morning's golden-lidded eyes
Peeping above the hills ; so, sweet, good-by !

PARTING AND MEETING.

LIKE music in a reed, the light
Was shut up in the dim, wild night ;
And 'twixt the black boughs fell the snowing —
The black March boughs together blowing,
Till hill and valley all were white.

The windows of the old house glowed
With the dry hickory, burning brightly,
As in the old house burned it nightly ;
So little cared they that it snowed —
The two my rhyme is of. If tears
Or shadows filled the eyes, else lit
With sunshine it were best unwrit,
And all about sweet hopes and fears
Were best unsaid, too. Tares will grow
In spite of the most careful sowing ;
We find them in the time of mowing,
Instead of flowers, we all do know.

So it were better that I write
No whit about the lady's sighing ;
'T were better said she had been tying,
To make it pretty for the night,
Buds, white and scarlet, in her hair ; —
And that the ribbon she would wear

Had sadly vexed her — not a hue,
Purple nor carmine that would do ;
Or that the cowslips of the May,
    Her little hand had freely given —
    Nay, more, the sweetest star of heaven —
To gain a rose the more that day
For her sad cheek : so foolish runs
In all of us the blood of youth
    Ere wintry frosts or summer suns
Bleach fancy's fabrics, and the truth
    Of sober senses turns aside
    The images once deified.

    It was a time of parting dread —
For middle night the cock was crowing,
The black March boughs together blowing,
    The lady mourning to be dead ;
And idly pulling down the flowers,
    Tied prettily about her hair —
    Alas, she had but little care
For any bliss of future hours !
That parting made the world all dim
    To her, whichever way she saw ;
I know not what it was to him —
    Haply but as the gusty flaw
That went before the buds — if so,
Hers was a doubly piteous woe !
And years are gone, or fast or slow,
    And many a love has had its making
    Since these two parted, at the breaking
Of daylight, whiter than the snow.

Again 't is March : the lady's brows
    Are circled with another light

Than that of burning hickory boughs,
  Which lit the house that parting night.
And they have met: the eyes so sweet
  In the old time again she sees —
  Hears the same voice — and yet for these
Her heart has not an added beat.

  If there be tremblings now, or sighs,
They are not hers; she feels no sorrow
That he will be away to-morrow,
  Nor joy that bridal mornings rise
Out of his smiling — she is free!
  Oh, give her pity, give her tears!
By one great wave of passion's sea,
  Drifted alike from hopes and fears.

THE EVENING WALK.

" MOTHER, see my cottage bonnet!
    Never was it bleached so white;
I have put fresh ribbons on it,
    And three roses, for to-night.
Think you, mother, they will fade
For a half hour in the shade? "

'T was the coaxing Adelaide
    Thus who said, the bonnet tying
Close about her golden hair.
    Waiting not for a replying
To her question, she must wear
    The new ribbons and the flowers —
None would see them — 't was her mood;
On the hillside near the wood
    She would be the next two hours.

" If you want me, mother dear —
Call, I shall be sure to hear."
So said joyous Adelaide —
Pretty, self-deceiving maid.

Many times before that day
She had gone the selfsame way,
Singing, skipping here and there,
Where a daisy bloomed, or where
Patches of bright grasses lay.
She would pout if you should say
Sweeter music twilight cheers
Than the birds make, and with tears
Tell you, it is not the truth
She has ever seen a youth
Driving cattle any night
Down a meadow full in sight —
Down a meadow thick with flowers,
Driving cattle, brown and white,
    Slowly towards a shallow well,
Hedged with lilies all around,
    Brighter than the speckled shell
Of the " sweet beast " Hermés found.

What deceitful hearts are ours !
    For 'tis true, say all she can,
    That the farm-boy, Corolan,
Drives at night his cattle so —
Silent sometimes drives them, slow —
Sometimes trilling songs of glee —
    Treading very near the shade
Where, unconscious, it may be,
    Sits the blushing Adelaide.

The huge leader of the flock,
  Often with a golden strand,
Made of oat-straw, gayly bound
His black forehead round and round,
  Close to Corolan doth walk,
Gently guided by his hand.

  Haply 't is but for the pleasing
Of his own eyes he doth make
The gold cordage, and for sake
Of the green and flowery dells
His white oxen wear the bells,
  And the song may be for easing
A young heart that loves the flowing
  Of soft sounds in solitudes,
And the lonesome echoes going
  Like lost poets through the woods.
Or all haply, happens so —
  For the maiden says with tears,
  " On the white necks of the steers
Silver bells make music low
When the pastured cattle go
Toward the spring — but not a sound
Sweeter, ever echoes round " —
  So it cannot be she hears !
And if thither Corolan strays,
She has seen him not, she says ;
And if eyes so bold and bright
  As you hint of, pierced the shade,
She would not be night by night
  On the hillside.
                    Adelaide
Surely would not so declare

If she saw young Corolan there.
So we will not wrong the maid
Guessing why the cottage bonnet
Had fresh flowers and ribbons on it.
Or for what the hillside shade
Pleased her — beauteous Adelaide.

WHEN MY LOVE AND I LIE DEAD.

WHEN my love and I lie dead,
Both together on one bed,
Shall it first be truly said,
" Fate was kindly : they are wed ! "

When they come the shroud to make,
Some sweet soul shall say, " Awake
From your long white sleep, and take
Feast of kisses for love's sake."

And though we nor see nor hear —
Safe from sorrow — safe from fear,
Both together on one bier,
We shall feel each other near.

O my lover, O my friend,
This I know will be the end —
Only when our ashes blend
Will our heavy fortunes mend.

MULBERRY HILL.

OH, sweet was the eve when I came from the mill,
Adown the green windings of Mulberry hill :
My heart like a bird with his throat all in tune,
That sings in the beautiful bosom of June.

For there, at her spinning, beneath a broad tree,
By a rivulet shining and blue as the sea,
I first saw my Mary — her tiny feet bare,
And the buds of the sumach among her black hair.

They called me a bold enough youth, and I would
Have kept the name honestly earned, if I could ;
But somehow, the song I had whistled was hushed,
And, spite of my manhood, I felt that I blushed.

I would tell you, but words cannot paint my delight,
When she gave the red buds for a garland of white,
When her cheeks with soft blushes — but no, 't is in vain !
Enough that I loved, and she loved me again.

Three summers have come and gone by with their
 charms,
And a cherub of purity smiles in my arms,
With lips like the rosebud and locks softly light
As the flax which my Mary was spinning that night.

And in the dark shadows of Mulberry hill,
By the grass-covered road where I came from the mill,
And the rivulet shining and blue as the sea,
My Mary lies sleeping beneath the broad tree.

A RUSTIC PLAINT.

SINCE thou, my dove, didst level thy wild wings
  To goodlier shelter than my cabin makes,
  I work with heavy hands, as one who breaks
The flax to spin a shroud of.   April rings

With silvery showers, smiles light the face of May,
  The thistle's prickly leaves are lined with wool,
  And their gray tops of purple burs set full;
Quails through the stubble run.   From day to day

Through these good seasons I have sadly mused,
  The very stars, thou knowest, sweet, for what,
  Draw their red flames together, standing not
About the mossy gables as they used.

No more I dread the winds, though ne'er so rough;
  . Better the withered bole should prostrate lie ; —
  Only the ravens in its black limbs cry,
And better birds will find green boughs enough.

THE LOVER'S VISION.

THE mist o'er the dark woods
  Hangs whiter than snow,
And the dead leaves keep surging
  And moaning below !
What treads through their dim aisles ?
  Now answer me fair —
'T is not the bat's flabby wing
  Beating the air !

A sweet vision rises,
　Though dimly defined,
And a hand on my forehead
　Lies cold as the wind !
I clasp the white bosom,
　No heart beats beneath ;
From the lips, once so lovely,
　Forth issues no breath.

The red moon was climbing
　The rough rocks behind,
And the dead leaves kept moaning,
　As now, in the wind ;
The white stars were shining
　Through cloud-rifts above,
When first in these dim woods
　I told her my love.

Half fond, half reproachful,
　She gazed in my face,
And, shrinking, she suffered
　My fervid embrace :
And speaking not, lingered
　With love's bashful art,
Till the light of her dark eyes
　Burned down to my heart !

Like the leaf of the lily
　When autumn is chill,
The little hand trembled
　That now is so still ;
And I knew the sweet passion,
　Her lips only sighed

In the hush of her chamber —
The night that she died !

O'er the shroud of the pale one
  I made then a vow
To kiss back the crimson
  Of life to her brow,
If she from the still grave
  Would come, as she hath,
And walk at the midnight
  This lone forest path.

The cloud-rifts are closing,
  The white stars are gone,
But the hushed step of Darkness
  Moves solemnly on.
I call the dead maiden,
  But win no reply —
She has gone, and forever, —
  Would I too could die.

YOUNG LOVE.

LIFE hath its memories lovely,
  That over the heart are blown,
As over the face of the autumn
  The light of the summer flown ;
Rising out of the mist so chilling,
  That oft life's sky enshrouds,
Like a new moon sweetly filling
  Among the twilight clouds.

And among them comes, how often,
  Young love's unresting wraith,
To lift lost hope out of ruins
  To the gladness of perfect faith ;
Drifting out of the past as lightly
  As winds of the May-time flow,
And lifting the shadows brightly,
  As the daffodil lifts the snow.

THISBE.

SUNSET's pale arrows shivering near and far ! —
  A little gray bird on an oaken tree,
Pouring its tender plaint, and eve's lone star
  Resting its silver rim upon the sea !

In dismallest abandonment she lies —
  The undone Thisbe, witless of the night,
Locking the sweet time from her mournful eyes
  With her thin fingers, a most piteous sight.

O'er her soft cheek the sprouting grasses lean,
  And the round moon's gray, melancholy light
Creeps through the darkness, all unfelt, unseen,
  And folds her tender limbs from the chill night.

Pressing your cold hands over rushy springs,
  And making your chaste beds in beaded dew,
About her, Nereids, draw your magic rings,
  And wreathe her golden-budded hopes anew.

For by the tumult of thick-coming sighs,
  The aspect wan that hath no mortal name,

I know the wilful god of the blind eyes
Hath sped a love-shaft with too true an aim.

ROWAN RAMSEY.

ROWAN RAMSEY, she is plain —
  Plain as you would plainness call;
Just her girlish golden hair
Round her brow and bosom fair,
  For adornment, that is all !

Rowan Ramsey, she is vain
  Of her girlish golden hair,
And her feet, if she but stir,
Dance about in spite of her,
  Just to show how small they are !

Rowan Ramsey, she is neat —
  Stocking, petticoat of snow,
And her hair, like veil of lace,
Slippeth fitly to the place
  Of her sleeve, so loose and low.

Rowan Ramsey, she is sweet;
  Nature's child, as you will see ;
Never any bramble-bud,
Born a mile deep in the wood,
  Grew to blossom pure as she.

Rowan Ramsey's smiles do flow
  O'er her chaste, religious frown ;
And no little saintly nun,

At her 'broidery in the sun,
Droppeth eyelid lowlier down.

Rowan Ramsey, she is low,
High in goodness is her part;
When we stand up to be wed,
You shall see her golden head
Shining level with my heart.

Rowan Ramsey, she is small —
Never smaller maid appeared
Outside of a fairy bower ;
I could hide her like a flower,
Underneath my grisly beard.

Rowan Ramsey, she is all
Just as I would have her be ;
Golden hair, and gown so simple,
Brow and bosom, smile and dimple,
Sweet as ever sweet can be !

THE OLD MAN WHO WOULD A-WOOING GO.

MISTRESS lady-lark, mistress lady-lark,
Fly up, fly out of the furrow !
And strip your two round shoulders stark,
For I your wings would borrow.
Ere the east has got a rosy mark,
I must bid my love good-morrow.

Mistress violet, mistress violet,
I want your tender and true eyes !

For mine are as cold and as black as jet,
  And I want your heavenly blue eyes !
Modest violet, maiden violet,
  Pray, can I borrow your blue eyes ?

Mistress nightingale, mistress nightingale,
  I want to borrow your fair tongue,
For I have to sing a sweeter tale
  Than ever you in the air sung ;
Melodious mistress nightingale,
  Be still, and lend me your fair tongue !

Master redbreast, robin redbreast,
  Whose note has so oft my day cheered,
You wear the color my love loves best —
  Will you lend it to a graybeard ?
Oh, stay, my little man, stay in your nest,
  And make me brave for a graybeard !

Master golden-bill, master golden-bill,
  Come speak, and tell me whether
You will lend, to make me a quill,
  A hollow silver feather ?
A letter with love I have to fill —
  Say, shall we write together ?

PICTURES IN THE FIRE.

THE hickory coals were glowing bright
  Upon the hearth so broad and wide,
And I was sitting in their light,
  And Elsie by my side.

The tangles of her cloudy hair
  She pushed aside, and just to see
More plainly where the pictures were
  She leaned upon my knee.

A rustic boy, with bare, brown feet,
  Right where the coals were deepest red,
Binding up roses among wheat,
  She saw, so plain, she said.

And then to make me see him too,
  About my neck, with witching grace,
She put her arm, and softly drew
  My face against her face.

Ah, is it strange I said I found
  A picture that was very sweet,
But not a rustic boy that bound
  Roses among his wheat !

Dear Elsie, in her modest tire,
  I painted then with bashful art,
And said I saw her in the fire
  A-burning in my heart.

And is it strange if new delight
  Shook out to flowers our budding souls ?
The while we sat and watched that night
  For pictures in the coals.

MARGARET.

MARGARET sat in her chamber,
Her gilded and garnished chamber,
And she made to her heart low bushes,
   As we sing a babe to rest,
And she sighed betwixt her blushes,
Oh, where is my own true lover,
My beautiful, beautiful lover,
My beautiful soldier and lover,
   My bravest and my best!

He is coming, she sang, he is coming!
My soldier and lover is coming!
My dreams they were wild with warning;
   Poor heart, beat not so low.
See, see! 't is the broad, bright morning!
And where are the damp, dim meadows,
The blighted and bloomless meadows,
Where a shadow, leading shadows,
   All night I saw him go!

So Margaret sat in her chamber,
Alone in her lofty chamber,
With its crimson carpets glowing,
   And curtains blue as the sky;
And she kept her tears from flowing,
And her fears from wild awaking,
And her heart from outright breaking
With the little song she was making,
   " O my lover, he could not die!"

Again and again she found him,
With upturned faces around him,
Yet sang she over and over
    The lullaby song, so sweet :
" He is coming, my soldier and lover !
O roses, burst into blooming,
And bees, be goldenly humming,
To grace and gladden his coming,
    Whenever the hour shall beat ! "

SPINNING.

PUT on the bands ! begin, begin !
My wheel to-day of itself will spin —
    The wool is as white as the daisies ;
Before the first lark flew at the sky,
Lem, my lover, went whistling by,
    And my cheek yet burns and blazes
    Like a rose the sunshine praises.

Every bird has its throat in tune,
The air is sweet as the middle June,
    And my beautiful morning-glory,
Before it was time for the day to break,
Opened her blue eyes wide awake
    To hear the wind's light story,
    The wooing wind's light story.

My cows, their foreheads as soft as silk,
Leaned to my hands when I went to milk,
    And gave me pails-full, and over ;
And the doves that pecked at the dewy grass,

Cooed and fluttered to see me pass,
And the bee on the top of the clover
Shone with his gold all over.

My busy wheel, run fast, run fast!
You will bring the shadows straight at last,
Aslant from the meadow willows ;
Then fast, and faster, and faster yet,
Till the Day shall turn a somerset
Clear into her cloudy pillows,
And the stars go to bed in the billows.

And when the moon comes up in the skies,
And the flowers are shutting their sleepy eyes,
And the bee creeps under the clover —
Oh, then the light will be out in the mill,
And a step will be hurrying down the hill,
And that will be Lem, my lover!
My dear, my darling lover.

Then turn by spindle, and off slip band,
And idle wheel, at the wall-side stand,
And, heart, make tenderest hushes;
What though I yet have my gown to spin,
He'll kiss my shoulders and hide them in
Ripples of rose-red blushes —
And I shall be dressed with blushes.

MY ENEMY.

Ay, love did make my love of all things fair —
He combed and combed, as fine as threads of silk,

The leaves of daffodillies for her hair —
  Her little hands compressed of curds of milk,
And set her in my path, and made her be,
From morn to eve, my sweetest enemy.

He laid the leaves of roses in and out
  From cheek to mouth, to dazzle me with light —
Round shoulder, throat, I dare not write about,
  Or guess what place he got so pure a white ;
But they were all composed to make her be
My pretty plague — my sweetest enemy.

He stole the music of the nightingale —
  Of all best birds, the world of birds among,
And made such melodies as cannot fail
  Of deadly work, to lie upon her tongue —
Built her a casement in the wall whence she
Might spread a snare of songs — sweet enemy.

Her eyes ! To know how I should name her eyes
  Drives me about the world like one distraught —
An ever tender infinite surprise
  Veiled, even as by their lids, with every thought
Shaped by my clumsy wits to make you see
How that she is my sweetest enemy.

I have no refuge from her any more.
  If toward the house of sleep I take my flight,
'T is her white hand that turneth back the door,
  Her arms that entertain me all the night,
So that her fatal charms do make her be,
Even in dreams, my sweetest enemy.

THE SAILOR'S CHILD.

OVER the hilltops, over the mountains,
Over the stretches of long, bright lea,
There is a dear little, dim little island,
Lying asleep in the arms of the sea.

Shoulder to shoulder, and never aweary,
Roll in the sea-waters, day after day,
Fringing this dear little, dim little island
All with a wreath of the softest spray.

Birds, with wings that are lined with colors,
Made of the hues of the morns and eves,
Slip and slide like the summer sunshine
In and out through the dancing leaves.

Over the reaches of green sea-waters,
Over the spray-fringe, white as snow,
Winds that are laden rich with spices,
Go and come, and come and go.

Wrapt in a veil that is sown with blossoms,
Pink and ivy, apple and rose ;
Singing loud with the lark at daybreak,
Low with the dove at the even-close —

Waits and watches a sailor's daughter,
Who, when the skies of the midnight frown,
Charms the demons that love the darkness,
And saves the ships that would else go down.

Waits and watches a sailor's daughter,
   Fair as the fairest maidens be,
All in this dear little, dim little island,
   Lying asleep in the arms of the sea.

Once this maid had a loyal lover,
   Born and rocked on the cradling waves,
Now he lies with their foam for a cover,
   Low on the bed of the' coral caves.

THE LOVER'S MAY-SONG.

As after the winter
   So wild and so dread,
One waits by the lily
   Fast froze in the bed
Of the garden, for some
   Little leaf to appear,
   So I wait, by my dear.

Now soft airs are thawing
   The icicles down
From the eaves, and the swallows
   So bright and so brown,
Ere long in their places
   Will twitter and sing,
   Bill to bill — wing to wing.

The low-cornel up through
   The dead leaves will shoot,
And turn her whole heart
   Into scarlet-hued fruit,

As the sun her white bosom
Makes quick with a kiss —
Think, my darling, of this !

And think of the dear little
   Rose-colored things,
That will lie all atremble
   Like butterfly wings,
Because of their joy in
   The beds of the moss,
   And, my love, be not cross.

And think of the May-star,
   That wears, like a queen,
Her pearls in a setting
   Of emerald green —
How she gathers her tenderness
   Out of the snow,
   And you cannot say no.

And think of the cool-wort,
   So timid and sweet,
How she cometh almost
   In the face of the sleet,
The grace of her healing
   On sick hearts to press,
   And you needs must say yes.

LOVE'S SPURNING.

COME row in my painted boat, Jane,
There 's something I would say —

'T is all about your marrying me,
   And having your own way.

The beanfields wrong your little hands,
   Your feet are cold in the dew,
But if you will keep the ring of gold
   That I have brought for you;

No time of merriment shall fall
   But that you shall be there —
Your shoulders wrapt in a shawl of lace,
   And an ivory comb in your hair.

Row on in your painted boat, and leave
   My beanfields in disgrace —
My sweetheart's arm around my neck
   Is better than all your lace!

No ivory comb want I, nor ring,
   Nor painted boat, so brave,
And the way that pleases him is all
   The way that I care to have.

THE RIVALS.

You need not stay by my bed, Tommy,
   My wants are all gone by,
And something 's got in my head, Tommy,
   That makes me wish to die.

You need not kiss my face, Tommy,
   Nor keep your hand on my brow,

For see in my eyes the shadow lies,
  Of another lover, now.

Jennie is out at the gate, Tommy —
  How fair she looks to-day !
My forehead is burning up, Tommy,
  You must take your hand away !

She wears your rose in her hair, Tommy —
  'T is not so sweet as her breath,
Nay, do not kiss my mouth, Tommy,
  I 'm almost choked to death !

She is coming up this way, Tommy —
  I hear her footstep fall ; —
Straighten me, sweet, from head to feet,
  And turn me toward the wall.

I am saying foolish things, Tommy,
  I am sick and crazed, you know,
But mind, 't is all myself, Tommy,
  Not you, that makes me so.

I wish I had better words, Tommy,
  To thank you while I live,
For being so true, that I to you
  Have nothing to forgive.

Don't fret when I am dead, Tommy, —
  'T is sweeter thus to part,
Than to be upon my feet, Tommy,
  If Jennie had your heart.

HEART-BROKEN.

SHE sat beneath a willow-tree —
The enamored air scarce dared to stir ;
The bird sang for her, and the bee
Seemed as he worked to work for her.
Ah, never was maiden so fair,
And the corn was in the milk,
And its tassel of bright silk
Lying loose on the wind like her hair.

Out of the woods a hunter came —
His bugle to the cadence swung,
As artfully he wove her name
In the soft ditty that he sung.
And a shudder filled all the green place,
And the cloud that was at dawn
Like the white wing of a swan,
Grew black, and o'ershadowed her face.

Beneath the willow-tree so low,
She lay — her hands upon her breast,
All cold and white like winter snow
Within the last year's empty nest.
And the song of the hunter was still,
And the blackbird on the thorn
Whistled hoarsely, and the corn
Rustled withered and dry on the hill.

ONCE FOR ALL.

'T WAS in the bright morning of life and of love,
And earth in her springtime was smiling and gay,
   I walked with my lady
   A lane green and shady,
And all overblown with the rose-leaves of May, —
   With pale and with bright leaves,
   With red and with white leaves, —
O'erblown and o'erstrown with the roses of May.

The sun up the east rode serenely and slow,
And swung back the silver-barred gates of the day ;
   'T was all so ideal
   That nothing seemed real,
And which was the substance we hardly could say,
   Ourselves, or our shadows,
   As down the green meadows
We walked, through the leaves of the roses of May !

All sounds were so sweet, so celestially sweet,
We scarce could dissever the grave from the gay.
   O blending confusions,
   O darling illusions,
That filled up our hearts to o'erflowing that day !
   Not we, but our shadows,
   Along the green meadows,
Seemed brushing the dew from the daisies away.

Like butterfly wings caught with butterfly wings,
My fancies in speech fluttered this and that way,

As, deep among mazes
Of golden-eyed daisies,
I said, " Will you love me a little to-day ?
'T is only a minute
Can have heaven in it ;
Lady and lady-love, what do you say ? "

Her spirit stood calm, poised like butterfly wings,
And her eyes stabbed me through with a still, steady ray,
As turning serenely,
And standing so queenly,
She said, " Love a *little ?* and just for a *day !*
Why, sir, the rough bramble
With scorn stands a-tremble,
And blushes up scarlet to hear what you say ! "

Then, soft as the melting of frost into mist,
Her taunt to a tender reproach fell away ;
" Is love an adorning,
To pluck of a morning,"
She said, " and to wear like a rose of the May ?
Love lost is loved never —
Loved once is loved ever —
The joy of eternity, not of a day ! "

'T was all in the heyday of life, long ago,
And the gold and the black hair are both growing gray,
And through the rough weather
We walk on together,
For the wife of the years is my lady of May ;
And still she says, ever,
" Loved *once* is loved *never*,"
And I answer, " Eternity — that is love's day ! "

TRUE LOVE.

THERE is true love, and yet you may
　Have lingering doubts about it ;
I 'll tell the truth, and simply say
　That life 's a blank without it.
There is a love both true and strong,
　A love that falters never ;
It lives on faith, and suffers wrong,
　But lives and loves forever.
Such love is found but once on earth —
　The heart cannot repel it ;
From whence it comes, or why its birth,
　The tongue may never tell it.
This love is mine, in spite of all,
　This love I fondly cherish ;
The earth may sink, the skies may fall,
　This love will never perish.
It is a love that cannot die,
　But, like the soul, immortal,
And with it cleaves the starry sky
　And passes through the portal.
This is the love that comes to stay —
　All other loves are fleeting ;
And when they come, just turn away —
　It is but Cupid cheating.

THE FATAL ARROW.

My father had a fair-haired harvester ; —
   I gleaned behind him in the barley-land ;
   And there he put a red rose in my hand :
Oh, cruel, killing leaves those rose-leaves were !

He sang to me a little love-lorn lay,
   Learned of some bird ; and while his sickle swept
   Athwart the shining stalks, my wild heart kept
Beating the tune up with him all the way.

One time we rested by a limpid stream,
   O'er which the loose-tongued willows whispered low ;
   Ah, blessed hour ! so long and long ago,
It cometh back upon me like a dream.

And there he told me, blushing soft, — ah me ! —
   Of one that he could love, — so young, so fair,
   Like mine the color of her eyes and hair :
O foolish heart ! I thought that I was she !

Full flowed his manly beard ; his eyes so brown
   Made sweet confession with their tender look ;
   A thousand times I kissed him in the brook,
Across the flowers, — with bashful eyelids down.

And even yet I cannot hear the stir
   Of willows by a water but I stop,
   And down the warm waves all their length I drop
My empty arms, to find my harvester.

In all his speech there was no word to mend ;
  Whate'er he said, or right or wrong, was best,
  Until at last an *arrow* pierced my breast,
Tipt with a fatal point, — he called me *friend !*

Still next my heart the fading rose I wore,
  But all so sad ; full well I knew, God wot,
  That I had been in love and he had not,
And in the barley-field I gleaned no more.

RELIGIOUS POEMS AND HYMNS.

THE HANDMAID.

WHY rests a shadow on her woman's heart?
  In life's more girlish hours it was not so;
Ill hath she learned to hide with harmless art
  The soundings of the plummet-line of woe!

Oh, what a world of tenderness looks through
  The melting sapphire of her mournful eyes!
Less softly moist are violets full of dew,
  And the delicious color of the skies.

Serenely amid worship doth she move,
  Counting its passionate tenderness as dross;
And tempering the pleadings of earth's love,
  In the still, solemn shadows of the cross.

It is not that her heart is cold or vain,
  That thus she moves through many worshipers;
No step is lighter by the couch of pain,
  No hand on fever's brow lies soft as hers.

From the loose flowing of her amber hair
  The summer flowers we long ago unknit,

As something between joyance and despair
Came in the chamber of her soul to sit.

In her white cheek the crimson burns as faint
As red doth in some cold star's chastened beam ;
The tender meekness of the pitying saint
Lends all her life the beauty of a dream.

Thus doth she move among us day by day,
Loving and loved ; but passion cannot move
The young heart that has wrapped itself away
In the soft mantle of a Saviour's love !

ASPIRATIONS.

THE temples, palaces, and towers
Of the old time, I may not see ;
Nor 'neath my reverent tread, thy flowers
Bend meekly down, Gethsemane !

By Jordan's wave I may not stand,
Nor climb the hills of Galilee ;
Nor break, with my poor, sinful hand,
The emblems of apostasy.

Nor pitch my tent 'neath Salem's sky,
As faith's impassioned fervor bids ;
Nor hear the wild bird's startled cry
From Egypt's awful pyramids.

I have not stood, and may not stand,
Where Hermon's dews the blossoms feed ;

Nor where the flint-sparks light the sand
Beneath the Arab lancer's steed.

Woe for the dark thread in my lot,
That still hath kept my feet away
From pressing toward the hallowed spot,
Where Mary and the young child lay.

But the unhooded soul may track,
Even as it will, the dark or light,
From noontide's sunny splendors, back
To the dead grandeur of old night.

And even I, by visions led,
The Arctic wastes of snow may stem ;
The Tartars' black tents view, or tread
Thy gardens, O Jerusalem !

O'er Judah's hills may travel slow,
Or ponder Kedron's brook beside,
Or pluck the reeds that overgrow
The tomb which held the Crucified.

And does not He, who planned the bliss
Above us, hear the praise that springs
From every dust-pent chrysalis
That feels the stirring of its wings ?

SICK AND IN PRISON.

WILDLY falls the night around me,
Chains I cannot break have bound me,

Spirits unrebuked, undriven
From before me, darken heaven ;
Creeds bewilder, and the saying
Unfelt prayers, makes need of praying.

In this bitter anguish lying,
Only thou wilt hear my crying —
Thou, whose hands wash white the erring
As the wool is at the shearing ;
Not with dulcimer or psalter,
But with tears, I seek thy altar.

Feet that trod the mount so weary,
Eyes that pitying looked on Mary,
Hands that brought the Father's blessing,
Heads of little children pressing,
Voice that said, " Behold thy brother,"
Lo, I seek ye and none other.

Look, O gentlest eyes of pity,
Out of Zion, the glorious city ;
Speak, O voice of mercy, sweetly ;
Hide me, hands of love, completely ;
Sick, in prison, lying lonely,
Ye can lift me up, ye only.

In my hot brow soothe the aching,
In my sad heart stay the breaking,
On my lips the murmur trembling,
Change to praises undissembling ;
Make me wise as the evangels,
Clothe me with the wings of angels.

Power that made the few loaves many,
Power that blessed the wine at Cana,
Power that said to Lazarus, " Waken ! "
Leave, O leave me not forsaken !
Sick and hungry, and in prison,
Save me, Crucified and Risen !

LONGINGS.

I AM weary of the mystery
Of life and death, and long to see
Into the great Eternity :

The locked hands loose, the feet untied,
The blank eyes re-illuminèd,
The senseless ashes deified.

For as the ages come and go,
The tides of being ever flow,
From light to darkness, ending so.

A little gladness for the birth,
For youth a little soberer mirth,
For age, a looking toward the earth ; —

A listening for the spirit's call,
A reaching up the smooth, steep wall
Of the close grave — and this is all.

Hoping, we find that hope is vain ;
Are pleased, and pleasure ends in pain ;
Loving, we win no love again.

We bring our sorrow, a wild weight,
Praying inexorable fate
To comfort us, and when we wait —

Winning no answer to the quest,
Madly with angels we contest,
Asking if that which is, is best.

So life wears out, and so the din
Goes on, and other lives begin
The same as though we had not been.

True, here and there in time's dead mould
There stands some obelisk of gold,
For which, God knoweth, peace was sold.

For they must meet their fellows' frown,
And wear on throbbing brows the crown,
O'er whom death's curtain shuts not down.

Others for fame may do and dare,
For me it seems enough to bear
The ills of being while we are:

Without the strife, to leave behind
A name with laurels intertwined,
To be of evil tongues maligned.

And had I power to choose, to-day,
Some good to help me on my way,
I truly think that I would say —

" O thou who gavest me mortal breath,
And hold'st me here 'twixt life and death,
Double the measure of my faith ! "

DEVOTION.

WITHIN a silver wave of cloud
  The yellow sunset light was stayed,
As on the daisied turf she bowed :
  I saw and loved her as she prayed —
Thy holy will on earth be done,
As in the heavens, all-hallowed One !

No evil word her lip had learned ;
  Her heart with love was overfull ;
No scarlet sinfulness had turned
  Her garment from the look of wool :
Give us, O Lord, our daily bread ;
Keep us and guide us home, she said.

No violet, with head so low,
  Were sweetly meek as she in prayer ;
Nor rising from the April snow
  A daffodilly, half so fair
As her uprising from the sod,
Fresh from communion with her God.

LIGHT AND LOVE.

LIGHT waits for us in heaven : Inspiring thought !
That when the darkness all is overpast,

The beauty which the Lamb of God has bought
   Shall flow about our savèd souls at last,
And wrap them from all night-time and all woe :
   The Spirit and the Word assure us so.

Love lives for us in heaven : Oh, not so sweet
   Is the May dew which mountain flowers inclose,
Nor golden raining of the winnowed wheat,
   Nor blushing out of the brown earth, of rose,
Or whitest lily, as, beyond time's wars,
   The silvery rising of these two twin stars!

A PRAYER.

FORGIVE me, God! forgive thy child, I pray,
   And if I sin, thy holy spirit move
My heart to better moods : I cannot say,
   Disjoin my human heart from human love!

If, in the rainy woods, the traveller sees,
   Through some black gap, a splendor fair and white,
Shining beneath the wild rough-rinded trees,
   His steps turn thither.   Through the infinite

Of darkness that would else be, as we pass
   From silence into silence, round our way,
Love shineth so.   Doth not the mower stay
   His scythe, if that a bird be in the grass?

If God be love, then love is likest God,
   And our low natures the divineness mocks,
If when we hear the blest " Arise and walk,"
   We turn our faces back against the sod.

The plowman, tired, among the furrowed corn,
    Leans on the ox's shoulder ; done with play,
Childhood among the daisies drops away
    Into the lap of sleep, and dreams till morn.

It is as if, when angels had their birth,⁻
    The one with heaviest glory on its wings,
Dropt from its proper sphere into the earth,
    Where, piteous of our mortal needs, it sings.

Sings sweeter melodies than winds do make,
    Playing their dulcimers for the young May ;
Blessed forever ! if sometimes I take
    Their beauty round my heart — forgive, I pray !

WORSHIP.

I HAVE no seasons and no times
    To think of heaven ; sometimes at night
I go upon a stair of rhymes,
    And find the journey very bright :
And for some accidental good,
Wrought by me, saints have near me stood.

I do not think my heart is hard
    Beyond the common heart of men,
And yet sometimes the best award
    Smites on it like a stone ; and then
A sunbeam, that may brightly stray
In at my window, makes me pray.

The flower I 've chánced on, in some nook
    Giving its wild heart to the bee,

Has taught me meekness, like a book
  Of written preaching ; and to see
A cornfield ripe, an orchard red,
Has made me bow with shame my head.

Of stated rite and formula,
  A formal use the meaning wears ;
When mostly in God's works I see
  And feel his love, I make my prayers,
And by the peace that comes, I know
My worship is accepted so.

THE WAY.

I CANNOT plainly see the way,
  So dark the grave is : but I know
If I do truly work and pray,
  Some good will brighten out of woe.

For the same hand that doth unbind
  The winter winds, sends sweetest showers,
And the poor rustic laughs to find
  His April meadows full of flowers.

I said I could not see the way,
  And yet what need is there to see,
More than to do what good I may,
  And trust the great strength over me ?

Why should my spirit pine, and lean
  From its clay house ; or restless, bow,
Asking the shadows if they mean
  To darken always, dim as now ?

Why should I vainly seek to solve
Free will, necessity, the pall ?
I feel — I know — that God is love,
And knowing this, I know it all.

HYMN.

Bow, angels, from your glorious state
If e'er on earth you trod,
And lead me through the golden gate
Of prayer, unto my God.

I long to gather from the Word
The meaning, full and clear,
To build unto my gracious Lord
A tabernacle here.

Against my face the tempests beat,
The snows are falling chill,
When shall I hear the voice so sweet,
Commanding, Peace, be still !

The angels said, God giveth you
His love — what more is ours ?
Even as the cisterns of the dew
O'erflow upon the flowers,

His grace descends ; and, as of old,
He walks with men apart,
Keeping the promise, as foretold,
With all the pure in heart.

A PRAYER.

My weary head hath lain a weary year
On these hot pillows, and most fearful fears
Have made my eyes acquainted with such tears
    As lie to utter sadness very near.

No coverlid, with borders like the spring
When roses come, and up and down o'erspread
With golden lilies, maketh fair my bed,
    But only darkness is my covering.

No daybreak gladness cometh with the day —
No pictured saint, so sweet and so divine,
Maketh the corners of my room to shine
    When evening falleth round me, cold and gray.

Steps, eager once, have taken a listless fall —
And eyes that seemed to give me tender grace
Have found their pleasure in another face —
    Only its echo answers back my call.

Some dread enchantment, all against my will,
Hath wrought this cruel charm against my life,
And vain are all my struggles, vain my strife —
    Hear me, my Master, hear and help me still!

Thou, who to light immortal life didst bring,
Rising from death, to walk and talk with men,
And teach the lesson, all unlearned till then —
    The gain of loss and cross and suffering —

Let not my sinful soul forsaken be !
This is my prayer all night, and all the day,
What is there I have heavier need to say ?
My very hopes are only mine through Thee !

Brother and friend, the dear familiar face,
The eyes beloved — let each and all depart —
Nor shall I yet be sad, or sick of heart,
So Thou but have, and hold me in Thy grace.

GOING DOWN.

WHEN, like the sinking sun, the year goes down
From the delighting of her flowery day ;
While mists crawl coldly on, and leaves grow brown,
And all the golden glory dies away ;

When we do see the monstrous might of death
In all that lately did so sweetly shine, —
Then do we lean our ear down close to faith,
And ask for evidence of things divine.

Ask for a glimpse of that substantial land
Where no sad eyes are turned upon the past ;
Where the loose footing of this mortal sand
Is builded to a rock that standeth fast.

Where even the memory of fear is o'er,
Where no rough wind nor rising cloud alarms,
And where our darlings never, never more
Shall flee away like shadows from our arms.

For through the mournful fading of the wood,
  And through the sickly flowers that cease to please,
It slowly cometh to be understood
  That somewhere there are better things than these.

But if there were continuance of delights,
  The rock beneath us in the stead of sands,
Ah ! should we seek to climb the rugged heights
  Whereon the everlasting city stands !

Then fade, O flowery wreath that summer weaves,
  And pleasant greenness, vanish from our sight,
Since through the thinning of the earthly leaves
  There breaketh in upon us heavenly light.

DEATHLESS FLOWERS.

I TELL you God is good, as well as just,
  And some few flowers in every heart are sown,
Their black and crumpled leaves show but as dust,
  Sometimes in the hard soil — sometimes o'ergrown
With wild, unfriendly weeds, they hidden lie
From the warm sunshine, but they do not die.

Pressed from a natural quickening by the might
  Of sin, or circumstance, through the evil days,
They find their way at last into the light,
  Weakly and pale, giving their little praise
Of modest beauty, and with grace most sweet
Making the garden of the Lord complete.

A VISION.

ONCE kneeling with my soul alone,
　　When all was dark as dark may be,
A great light round about me shone,
　　And God the Spirit came to me.

Along my garden, where there grew
　　Sharp thistles at the daylight's close,
In the clear morning, wet with dew,
　　Came up the cedar and the rose.

Ambition, pride — how dwarfed and vain!
　　And from my forehead, bowed in prayer,
Fell off the burning crown of pain,
　　And God the Son was with me there.

No more with sinful sorrow bowed,
　　How pleasant seemed the Christian strife!
The angel coming in the cloud
　　Had brightened all the hills of life.

I saw the bruisèd serpent go
　　From Eden, lately darkly dim ;
Man to his ancient stature grow,
　　And God the Father talk with him.

Was some great inspiration there
　　That o'er me never more shall be ?
Or could I make my life as fair
　　As in that vision, Holy Three ?

SHAPING INFLUENCES.

Lead me, O my guardian angel,
  So I pray, and ever pray,
Where the light winds sing their lightest,
Where the bright things bloom their brightest,
  And the flowery fields of May
  Stretch away, and still away!

Lead and leave me, O my angel,
  Where the wild birds, day by day,
Chirp and sing their light love-stories,
All among the golden glories
  Of the flowery fields of May,
  Stretched away, and still away!

Where the rose doth wear her blushes
  Like a garment, and the fair
And modest violets sit together,
Weaving in the mild May weather
  Purples, out of dew and air,
  Fit for any queen to wear.

But, my angel, my good angel,
  This much more I have to say —
O'er the blooming and the singing,
O'er the weaving and the winging,
  Grant to live with me, I pray,
  In these flowery fields of May;

Friends to love with love that only
  Lives of men and women sway —

Over and above the hushes
Of all birds, above the blushes
  Of the reddest rose in May —
  And yet once again I pray,

That when thou shalt give them to me,
  Alway, heart in heart to beat,
They shall make all flowery places
Fairer for their smiling faces,
  And whatever things are sweet —
  Brighter, better, more complete.

Not for time and sense, O angel,
  Dare I thus entreat of thee
Into flowery fields to take me —
'T is the things I see that make me
  For the things I cannot see —
  For the long eternity.

HYMN.

WHEN earthly pleasures fade and flee,
  When clouds of care obscure the light,
Uplift thine eyes, O man, and see
  The long sweet day beyond the night.

When summer's soft delights are gone,
  And flowers are closed in icy walls,
Think of the beauteous hills whereon
  The frost of winter never falls.

When the fierce tempest mows a path
  Of dreadful darkness through the land,
Remember, thou of little faith,
  Who holds the whirlwind in His hand.

When pestilence infects the air,
  And the beloved lies smitten sore,
Think of the heavenly country where
  The inhabitants are sick no more.

And when thy good days all are run
  Even to the last low fluttering breath,
Know, sinking soul, that pain is done,
  That dying is the death of death.

LIGHT AND DARKNESS.

THE sun is shining bright, so bright,
  And the bee to the rose is humming,
But the day is hurrying down to the night,
  And the cloud and the storm are coming ;
So, little bee, hum sweetly on,
For the day of the rose will soon be gone.

The leaves are green, so green in the wood,
  And the bird is wildly winging
His way in the air, for he maketh good
  His little time of singing ;
Right on, my pretty one, right on !
For the light o' the summer will soon be gone.

The blood is bright in the young man's heart,
　And his footstep gayly roameth,
But he and his pleasure soon must part,
　For the enemy surely cometh :
So, light young heart, beat lightly on,
Ere the time for the dreaming of dreams be gone.

The frost it falls on the brightest tress,
　And sweetness is mixed with sadness,
But the maiden seweth her bridal dress,
　And maketh her veil with gladness ;
And whether the rain or the sunshine fall,
The holy heaven is over it all.

The body lies in a lowly bed,
　And the darkness is its cover,
But the soul shall safe through the night be fed,
　And the Lord shall be her lover ;
For He who promised us life shall keep
His promises, whether we wake or sleep.

CHRISTMAS EVE.

No flowers were left in the meadows;
　All empty and cold was the nest;
And the sun, in a white, cold bank of light,
　Was going down in the west.

'T was the day before the Christmas ;
　And with young hearts all astir,
Now turning the reel and now the wheel,
　And making the spindle whir,

We two were alone in the garret —
My playmate Harley and I ;
But the light sped fast, and we ceased at last
From making the spindle fly.

Yet still through the darkening window
(You might cover it all with your hands)
We could see the wood, where the schoolhouse stood,
With its border of level lands.

We could tell the elms from the walnuts,
And the oaks from all the rest,
As covered with snow and row after row
They shimmered against the west.

We could see the barn with great square door,
And the stacks that beyond it rose,
The open sheds full of skeleton sleds,
And harrows and plows and hoes.

We could see the horns of the cattle
As they tossed o'er the hay-filled racks,
Where together they fed with head over head,
And saddles of snow on their backs.

Like pillars of salt in the garden,
We could see the hives of the bees,
And hear the wind's song as it hurried along
To waltz with the tops of the trees.

We could see o'er the roofs of the village
The old St. Xavier's shine,
The Paternity, and the Holy Three,
With its steeple tall and fine.

And my playmate Harley questioned :
" Can there be three Gods above ?
Then how shall we pray, and who shall say
    Which one is the God of Love ? "

And hand in hand from the window,
    As sunk the sun from the earth,
We crossed the room, now dim with gloom,
    And kneeling beside the hearth,

We gathered the faded embers
    All out of their ashen bed,
And blew and blew, on our knees, we two,
    Till the flame shot up, blood-red.

"Now, then," said my playmate Harley,
    " I will find it out for myself ! "
And he gave a look to the old, old Book
    That lay on the dusty shelf.

And so, one over the other,
    He piled up chair upon chair,
Then up he stept and on he crept
    To the top of the trembling stair.

Then down with the Book on his shoulder,
    And back to the fire he came,
And so, eager-eyed, he held it wide
    With page aslant to the flame.

Leaf after leaf of the yellow leaves
    He turned them o'er so fast,
Till at length he said, with uplifted head : —
    " I have found it out at last

"In the prayer which the Lord and Master
　　Has taught us all to say ;
For surely He, if He prayed to three,
　　Would have taught us so to pray !

"And I don't care now if the steeples
　　Be three, or six, or seven ! " —
And he read so loud it was almost proud —
　　" Our Father who art in Heaven."

And there in the dim old garret,
　　While the winds the rafters shook,
And with head bent low to the firelight glow,
　　And our two cheeks, over the Book,

Like a rose that is growing double, —
　　We read, in an under-breath,
Of the holy morn when Christ was born,
　　And of all his life and death.

How He gave himself our ransom,
　　And drank to the very brim
The bitter cup, to lift us up,
　　The whole great world, to Him.

And full and sweet was the comfort
　　Of the faith that there and then
To our hearts we took, as we closed the Book
　　With an all unbreathed Amen.

And many and many a Christmas
　　Has come and gone with its light,
And all the years, through smiles or tears,
　　We have kept the old faith bright.

HIDDEN THINGS.

THE lily she has gone to bed,
  And the little meadow-mouse
Has thatched the roof above her head,
  And carpeted her house
All soft and warm, because she knows
The clouds will shortly bring the snows.

That solemn bird that loves so well
  To be superbly dressed,
Has taken his gorgeous chasuble
  And left an empty nest ;
He knows, the lily being gone,
That winter will come whistling on.

The partridge now has ceased to drum,
  And the bee, so sweet and brown,
Has left the barley-fields, and come
  To her humming-house in town ;
Her honeyed joys aforetime planned,
And all these things I understand.

But I neither understand nor know,
  Though I strive with all my care,
When I do see the winter snow
  A-gathering on my hair ;
And see my youth quite fled away,
Why I do wish, nay, long to stay !

I know that only virtues thrive,
  And know that folly hath no praise ;

Yet, as the foolish women live,
  I live, nor seek to mend my ways.
This is the mystery that I call
The hardest, saddest of them all.

I know that I must shortly lie
  In the cold silence of the grave,
And I believe He reigns on high
  Who died, and rose, and lives to save;
Yea, I believe, yet cry in grief,
Help, Lord, help thou mine unbelief!

HERE AND THERE.

Down in the darkness, deep in the darkness,
  All in the blind, black night;
Near to the morning, clear to the morning,
  All in the glad, gold light!

Down in the daisies, deep in the daisies,
  Under the daisies to lie;
Over the stork's wing, over the lark's wing,
  Over the moon and the sky!

Tears in the daisies, drowning the daisies,
  Blight that no bloom can remove;
Praises and praises, and evermore praises,
  Gladness, and glory, and love!

Broken and bruisèd, and heart-sick and sin-sick,
  Crying for mercy and grace;
Rising and risen and out of our prison,
  Spirits with face unto face!

Longing and looking, and thirsting and fainting,
  Deserts to left and to right ;
Coolness of shadows, and greenness of meadows,
  And fountains of living delight !

Hearts that are aching, and hearts that are breaking,
  Like waves on a rocky-bound shore ;
Footsteps of lightness, and faces of brightness,
  And sickness and sighing no more !

Wanderers, wayfarers, desolate orphans,
  Deaf to the Shepherd's soft call ;
Gathered together by God, our good Father,
  Blessèd forever, o'er all !

HEAVEN OUR HOME.

THE fields with flowers a-blowing,
  They all behind us lie —
Our autumn, it draweth nigh ;
But oh, my friends, we are going
  To the summer hills on high !

We are vexed with wars and warring —
  Our strifes with our days increase,
  But there cometh a swift release —
For oh, my friends, we are nearing
  The life of eternal peace !

Our roof-tree drops asunder —
  Our floor-planks slide like sands —
  In our doors the darkness stands ;

But oh, my friends, there is splendor
In the house not made with hands !

We know no full completeness ; —
In the sky of the day most clear
Some shadow is sure to appear;
But oh, my friends, there is sweetness
In the days of the endless year.

The winds are beating and blowing —
The frost on our heads is white —
We are drawing near to the night ;
But oh, my friends, we are going
To the morning land of light !

In spite of the fast possession,
Our thoughts they flutter and flee,
Like wild birds out to sea —
For we long to know the fashion
Of the life that is to be.

Our golden gains we are losing,
Our hopes are dim with dust,
But oh, my friends, we trust
What seemeth lost is for using
Where there is nor moth nor rust.

Our life is a twice-told story
That charm no longer lends ;
But oh, my friends, my friends,
We are coming close to the glory
That never fades nor ends.

We stand of our strength forsaken,
  And sick unto death, in sooth,
  But this we know of a truth,
That out of the dust we shall waken,
  To a life of immortal youth.

The winter brings rough weather,
  And into the chill and the gloom
  We go, and we never come ;
But oh, my friends, we shall gather
  Together in Heaven — our home.

POEMS FOR CHILDREN.

A CHRISTMAS STORY.

'Tis Christmas Eve, and by the firelight dim,
  His blue eyes hidden by his fallen hair,
My little brother — mirth is not for him —
  Whispers, How poor we are !

Come, dear one, rest upon my knee your head,
  And push away those curls of golden glow,
And I will tell a Christmas tale I read
  A long, long time ago.

'T is of a little orphan boy like you,
  Who had on earth no friend his feet to guide
Into the path of virtue, straight and true,
  And so he turned aside.

The parlor fires, with genial warmth aglow,
  Threw over him their waves of mocking light,
Once as he idly wandered to and fro,
  In the unfriendly night.

The while a thousand little girls and boys,
  With look of pride, or half averted eye,

Their hands and arms o'erbrimmed with Christmas toys,
Passed and repassed him by.

Chilled into half-forgetfulness of wrong,
And tempted by the splendors of the time,
And roughly jostled by the hurrying throng,
Trembling, he talked with crime.

And when the Tempter once had found the way,
And thought's still threshold, half-forbidden, crossed,
His steps went darkly downward day by day,
Till he at last was lost.

So lost, that once from a delirious dream,
As consciousness began his soul to stir,
Around him fell the morning's checkered beam —
He was a prisoner.

Then wailed he in the frenzy of wild pain,
Then wept he till his eyes with tears were dim,
But who would kindly answer back again
A prisoner-boy like him?

And so his cheek grew thin and paled away,
But not a loving hand was stretched to save;
And the snow covered the next Christmas-day
His lonesome little grave.

Nay, gentle brother, do not weep, I pray,
You have no sins like his to be forgiven,
And kneeling down together, we can say,
Father, who art in Heaven.

So shall the blessèd presence of content
  Brighten our home of toil and poverty,
And the dear consciousness of time well spent
  Our Christmas portion be.

FAINT PRAISE.

OUR Tabby she is very wise,
  And also very nice,
But I must say that I despise
  Her way of eating mice :
For if I was a cat
I would n't do that !

She lies with head so low and meek
  Between her paws of silk,
But then she has a thievish trick
  Of lapping at the milk ;
And if I was a cat
I would n't do that !

'T is well enough to know your strength ;
  But she abuses power,
And worries at a mouse the length
  Sometimes of half an hour.
Now if I was a cat
I would n't do that !

Her coat is modest, sober gray,
  Set off with jetty spots,
But then she has a sloven way
  Of rubbing on the pots ;

And if I was a cat
I would n't do that !

The fur is soft upon her breast
  As froth upon the pail,
But then to match against the rest
  She has an ugly tail ;
And if I was a cat
I would n't have that !

THREE MILLERS.

THERE once were three millers,
  A long time ago,
And one was named Peter,
  One John, and one Joe.

They all lived together,
  And worked just as one,
But the mill was owned wholly
  By Joseph and John.

" The world is before us —
  Our way is to win,"
Said Peter, who owned but
  The beard on his chin.

" And I mean, for my part,
  With God's help and grace,
To hold to my manhood,
  And stick to my place."

The mill was a good mill,
  And all the folks round,
Who were farmers, brought thither
  Their grain to be ground.

So 't was not uncommon
  To see at the door
Three carts and six oxen —
  There sometimes were more.

And all through the autumn,
  At night and at morn,
The mill-door was garnished
  With bags full of corn, —

While bushels of millet,
  Of rye, and of wheat,
Gave token of plenty,
  To have and to eat.

But Joseph took all this
  Good fortune for ill,
And sold out to Peter
  His share in the mill.

'T was slow work and weary
  To grind for his bread ;
He would go where the gold
  Grew on bushes, he said.

" You had better stay with us,"
  Said Peter ; but no,
" I will gather my gold from
  The bushes," says Joe.

So Peter wrought on with
  A resolute will,
Though there were by two hands
  The less in the mill.

And still the mill prospered,
  And all the folks said,
" These sturdy young fellows
  Are getting ahead ! "

Then John fell a-moping,
  And saying, " Don't care ! "
And offered to sell out
  To Peter *his* share.

" I hate the hard mill work,"
  He says, " and will go
And gather my gold from
  The bushes, with Joe ! "

Then Peter, half angry,
  Half sorrowful, said,
" Well, don't you come back here
  A-begging for bread ! "

" Not I ! " answered John ;
  " I may come back to *lend*."
But Peter said, " Work, sir,
  Is best in the end ! "

So John, after Joe, turned
  His back on the mill,
And Peter wrought on
  As before, with a will.

And when he was lonesome,
And when he was sad,
He would say that his work
Was the best friend he had.

Some said he was foolish,
Some said he was wise;
Some thought of the bushes,
With tears in their eyes.

But when twenty years, like
The mill-wheel, had turned,
And a snug little fortune
Our Peter had earned, —

All comers said, shaking
Him hard by the hand,
That there was n't a gold-bearing
Bush in the land !

One night, when the wind blew
As hard as could be,
And a terrible moaning
Came up from the sea, —

As he sat by the chimney,
And read the good Book,
There came such a knocking,
The door fairly shook.

Then straight little Peter
Got out of his bed —
The curls, bright as meal-dust,
All over his head, —

And stood at his father's knee
    Sucking his thumb,
With blue eyes wide open
    To see who had come, —

While the mother upon the
    Hot coals left her cake,
And opened the door wide
    For charity's sake.

Then spoke a low voice,
    All a-tremble with fear,
" Can you tell if one Peter,
    A miller, live near ?

" We are poor men, half frozen,
    And starving for bread."
" My brothers ! " cried Peter ;
    " Alive, and not dead ! "

For, wasted and hungry,
    And coated with snow,
His loving eyes knew them
    For John and for Joe.

And the wife, all in tears,
    Took her cake from the coals,
Smoking hot, saying, " Eat,
    And be welcome, dear souls."

Then Peter, one cheek to the
    Bright little face
That was leaned to his own,
    Asked a blessing of grace.

And shamed the two who sat
At his feast, as they told
Of the long, fruitless search
For the bushes of gold ; —

Of the years they had wasted,
The hopes they had spent,
And come back a thousand
Times worse than they went!

" Nay, brothers, take courage,"
Says Peter, at length ;
" The weakness repented,
We turn into strength.

" Ourselves, not our stars,
Make our fates, in the end,
And hence it is never
Too late to amend."

GRANDFATHER'S PICTURE.

" Why, here 's grandfather ! and the snow
A foot deep on the ground !
Still younger than the youngest of
His children, I 'll be bound.
Rash, after nightfall, even for you,
To face out such a squall.
Now was n't it, dear grandfather ? "
" Tut, tut ! boy, not at all ! "

" Why, when we kept your birthday last,
'T was Christmas, seems to me,

Nearly a year ago ; and then
 You passed for seventy-three !
The air is blind, and I should judge
 That where the ground is flat,
The drifts are gathered two feet deep — ”
 “ Ay, sir ; and what of that ?

“ When I was young as you are now,
 ’T was just our dear delight
To take our guns and dogs, and tree
 A bear on such a night !
I know once Johnny Horn and I —
 You mind old Johnny Horn ? ”
“ Oh, no ; I ’ve heard you say he died
 The year that I was born.”

“ Ay, ay ; I have n’t seen his face
 These dozen years, I know — ”
“ These dozen years ? I ’m thirty-five ! ”
 “ Well, well, boy, let it go !
I meant to tell about the bear
 We killed. But never mind :
Folks don’t care any more, it seems,
 To stop and look behind.”

“ I do, you know, dear grandfather ;
 But here ’s your chair, — sit down
And tell us what ’s the news at home ;
 Or have you been to town
With Uncle Sam, or Benjamin,
 To see the sights ? ” — “ Why, no !
Besides, sir, I could go alone,
 If I should choose to go !

" The town — what care I for the town ?
　They 've got no shows, I doubt,
　Worth going after ; none, at least,
　That I can't do without."
" But, grandfather, they've got that witch —
　You know the one I mean ? "
" Of Endor ?　Poh, poh !　what is she
　To witches I have seen !

" There was your grandmother — all tongues
　Were ringing with her praise
The night she danced with me — you 've got
　No dancers nowadays ;
And there was Betsy Byar — a neck
　As graceful as a swan ;
And Mistress Motley — who was 't said
　That she was dead and gone ? "

" But, grandfather, about the shows !
　They talk of four or five
New cherubs in the Academy,
　That seem almost alive ! "
" And what o' that ?　I 'll venture now
　That since the sun was down
I've seen as fine a picture
　As the finest in the town."

" What was it, grandfather ? " — " Why, this :
　Upon my way to-night
I stopt at Benjamin's, to see
　That everything was right.
And there, his little girl upon
　His knee, sat Ben, and read,

His chin propt up above the page
Upon her golden head.

" And upright in the cradle, all
   As quiet as a lamb,
The baby, with his wide eyes toward
   The shadow on the jamb ;
While Jerry down among his books,
   Along the floor lay flat,
One hand upon the open page,
   And one upon the cat.

" The logs were heapt, and on the hearth,
   As bright as bright could be,
The teakettle was humming to
   The tune of coming tea :
And wife and mother filled the while
   The house with her repose —
The brown bands round her face like rings
   Of bees about a rose.

" It seemed to me the very clock
   Perceived the scene was fair,
And counted off the minutes just
   As slowly as she dare.
The moaning of the homeless wind,
   The snowflakes, as they drove
In clouds across the panes, enhanced
   The warmth, the light, the love.

" A pretty story, to be sure,
   If I must scour the land

For pictures, having such an one
  A stone's throw from my hand ! "
" I think you 're right, dear grandfather :
  I have n't seen the one
  That outshines this of yours — " — " What 's more,
  You never will, my son ! "

PHŒBE CARY.

A BALLAD OF CALDEN WATER.

FORWARD and back, from shore to shore,
  All day the boat hath wended ;
But now old Andrew drops his oar,
  As if his task were ended.

" The clouds are gathering black," he said,
  " The pine-tree wildly tossing ;
The traveller must be sore bestead
  Who seeks to-night the crossing."

He looks, and sees from vale or hill
  No 'lated horseman riding ;
But what is this, so white and still,
  Adown the pathway gliding !

He fears to meet some spirit pale,
  Or wraith from out the water ;
He sees the " Daisy of the Dale,"
  The proud Lord Gowen's daughter.

Ah ! many a time that timid dove,
  Swift from her shadow flying,

Hath braved the darkness, all for love,
To Calden water hying.

And many a time before to-night
Hath Andrew rowed her over,
When softly through the waning light
She stole to meet her lover.

But that was in the days gone by ; —
Alas ! the old sad story —
'T was ere he heard the bugle-cry,
And turned from love to glory.

'T was when her foot came down the hill
As light as snowflake falling ;
While over Calden water, still,
She heard her lover calling.

She heard him singing, clear and low,
" The flower of love lies bleeding ; "
The very echoes long ago
Have ceased their tender pleading.

And he who sang that sweet refrain
Is sleeping where they found him, —
Upon the trampled battle-plain,
With his silent comrades round him.

While she — for months within the vale
Have tender maids been sighing,
Because the " Daisy of the Dale,"
Its sweetest flower, was dying.

And Andrew, rowing many a night,
  Hath sadly mused about her ;
While from her chamber, high, the light
  Streamed o'er the Calden water.

What marvel that he clasps his hands,
  And prays the saints to guide him,
As, crossing now the cold wet sands,
  She takes her seat beside him.

She speaks no word of sweet command,
  The proud Lord Gowen's daughter ; —
She signs him with her flower-like hand
  To cross the Calden water.

Trembling old Andrew takes the oar,
  Silent he rows her over ;
Silent she steps upon the shore
  Where once she met her lover.

There is no sound of mortal tread,
  Or mortal voice to greet her,
But noiselessly, as from the dead,
  Her lover glides to meet her.

One moment they each other fold
  In clasp of love undying ;
The next but shadows, deep and cold,
  Upon the shore are lying.

And see ! the darkness grows more drear —
  The pine more wildly tossing,
And backward to the shore in fear
  Old Andrew swift is crossing.

He drops his oar, he leaves his boat,
  He heeds nor fiend nor mortal ;
He 's crossed the castle's bridge and moat,
  He stands within the portal.

Still on, as one who has no power
  Of pausing or of turning,
He mounts unto the very tower,
  Where yet the light is burning.

And there he sees a snow-white bed,
  And sees, with eyes affrighted,
Set at the feet and at the head
  The waxen candles lighted.

Upon a lovely, piteous sight
  As e'er was seen, he gazes : —
A maiden in her dead-clothes white,
  And all bestrewn with daisies !

THE YOUNG MARTYR.

STILL of one among the saints,
  Who for Christ in days of old
Suffered blessèd martyrdom,
  Is this holy legend told.

Proud upon·his royal throne,
  In our Lord's first century,
Sat the Roman Emperor,
  Clothed in purple majesty.

Naught he lacks of pomp and state,
Armèd guards behind him stand ;
And his courtiers, row on row,
Circle him on either hand.

Cold and pitiless anear
Frowns the heathen god of stone ;
And a single Christian youth
Standeth at his feet alone.

Just a boy, a fair-haired child,
In whose eyes you yet can see
All the loving trust he learned,
Praying at his mother's knee.

Martyrs true, his brothers died,
Last of five alone he stands ; —
Five, who rather bow to death,
Than to idols made with hands.

Oft the king has doomed to die
Men and maidens, age and youth ;
But his heart for this fair boy
Moveth with a tender ruth.

So he beckoneth him anear ; —
" Thou art brave and proud," he saith ;
" I would spare thee if I might,
But I fear the people's wrath.

" I will let this royal ring
Careless drop from out my hand ;
Thou shalt stoop and bow the knee,
But to lift it from the sand :

" Yet the gazing crowd will think
  Thou hast bowed the head to give
Homage to our country's god ; —
  Thus shalt thou be free, and live."

Brave the martyr met his eye,
  Proudly standing in his place,
And the light that cometh down
  Out of heaven, was in his face.

" He who made me seeth all," —
  So the Christian answered then, —
" Shall I fear the eye of God
  Less than thou the eye of men ? "

SUSKA.

TRESSES black as her own raven,
  With a sheen like softest silk,
Has the Polish maiden Suska,
  And her throat is white as milk.
Once of all the village beauties
  Had she the merriest glance ;
And her little foot was quickest
  And lightest in the dance.

Now she sits without her cottage,
  Very still and very meek,
With the tears from her dark lashes
  Dropping slowly to her cheek.
Little birds are happy courting
  In the pear-tree overhead ;

And its fragrant, tender blossoms
Are all about her shed.

Suska does not hear the linnets
That are courting in the pear ;
Nor feel the drift of blossoms
Snowing down upon her hair.
And she heeds not Karl, the raven,
Turning on his perch so high,
Though he keep his eye upon her,
Like a cautious, cunning spy.

" O my Pravo ! " weeps the maiden,
" He will never come again.
And alas, 't was my unkindness
Drove him to the battle-plain! "
" *Haughty Suska !* " cries the raven, —
It was Pravo taught him so,
When his cruel little mistress
To his suit had answered, No.

" Hush ! he will not die," sobs Suska ;
" He was born for victory;
But he 'll find another sweetheart,
And he 'll never think of me ;
Some pale girl with golden tresses
Will snare him by her charms,
And I 'd rather mourn him buried
Than in a rival's arms ! "

Close the raven looks, as counting
Every hot and bitter tear ;

While his harsh cry, "*naughty Suska!*"
    Falls upon the maiden's ear.
Blushing both for shame and anger,
    Suska bows her poor head down,
And she sees not how the neighbors
    All are hurrying towards the town.

She does not hear the bugle,
    Blending with the drum's loud beat;
Nor the homeward tramp of soldiers,
    Coming down the village street;
Nor see the close ranks broken,
    And a manly form draw nigh:
But she hears the voice of Pravo,
    And she answers with a cry.

There he stands once more beside her,
    Proud of mien, and proud of face,
All his bosom crossed with orders,
    And his coat bedecked with lace.
" Glory is the only mistress
    I have wooed," he cries, " save you,
Is it yes or no, dear Suska?
    Answer me, and answer true."

Clear she lifts her eyes one moment,
    Then she lets her bright head rest,
Sure the fairest decoration,
    On the soldier's manly breast.
And again in mocking accents,
    As if shocked by what he spies,
Haughty Suska! naughty Suska!"
    Cunning Karl, the raven, cries.

No more anger, shame, or blushing,
But in Suska's look and tone
Is the sweet serene contentment
Of a heart that knows its own.
And as Pravo bends above her,
All his face with joy is pale,
As the flowers that fall and hide them
In a soft white bridal veil.

PROEM.

FOR NATIONAL TEMPERANCE OFFERING, 1850.

KNOWING how all who live are bound together
By the sweet ties of one humanity,
How all are fellow-pilgrims journeying thither
Where shines the city of eternity ;

And seeing that he to whom no brother lendeth
A helping hand to bear his weight of ill,
Oft falters on the pathway which ascendeth
Up the beautiful summit of life's hill ;

And turns to follow by-paths and forbidden,
Winding and winding back from virtue's goal,
Till, where the seir-cryts of the world lie hidden,
Lost and bewildered walks the human soul ;

We who have yet with sin maintained resistance,
And tempted, have not wholly turned aside,

Would come with love, with counsel, and assistance,
　To all whose spirits are more sorely tried.

If there be any who would turn and perish,
　Because no friend has whispered words of cheer,
Any whom yet no heart has learned to cherish,
　To us their sufferings and their hopes are dear.

If there be any faltering, and no longer
　Equal to life's most toilsome marches found, —
Oh lean on us, until your feet, grown stronger,
　Are firmly planted on a vantage ground.

And then, forsaken one, who darkly weepest
　Over a lost one gone from virtue's track,
For thee, even where sin's shafts are sunken deepest,
　We will go fearlessly and lead him back.

Yea, we will save him, even though the hisses
　Of baffled demons mock us as we come ; —
Love's lip is sweeter than the wine-cup's kisses,
　Love's smile is brighter than the wine-cup's foam.

And daily thus to bless our efforts, bringing
　Some soul that turned or might have turned to death,
We shall go up life's hill together, singing
　The sweetly solemn hymns of love and faith.

And from its summit viewing, but not sadly,
　The peaceful valley where shall end our strife,
We will walk downward willingly and gladly
　To the last bivouac on the plains of life.

For, knowing death is but the door of heaven,
  We shall press joyfully to meet the hour ;
Not with the lock-step like cringing felons driven
  Under the gateway of their prison-tower !

THE RECHABITES.

THEY came and brought the Rechabites, who dwelt in
    tents of old,
To chambers dark with tapestry, and cunning work and
    gold ;
And set before them pots of wine, and cups than man-
    tled high,
But when they tempted them to drink, they answered
    fearlessly,
And said : " Our father Jonadab, the son of Rechab,
    spake,
Commanding us to drink no wine forever, for his sake ;
And therefore we will taste not of the cup you bring us
    now,
For our children's children to the end shall keep our
    father's vow."
And the Lord who heard the Rechabites, and loves a
    faithful heart,
Pronounced a blessing on their tribe that never shall
    depart.
Thus we will taste not of the wine, and though the
    streams should dry,
Yet the living God who made us will hear his children
    cry ;
For Moses smote the solid rock, and lo ! a fountain
    smiled,
And Hagar in the wilderness drew water for her child ;

And the beautiful and innocent of all earth's living
    things
Drink nothing but the crystal wave that gushes from
    her springs ;
The birds that feed upon the hills, seek where the foun-
    tains burst,
And the hart beside the water brooks, stoops down to
    slake his thirst ;
The herb that feels the summer rain on the mountain
    smiles anew,
And the blossoms with their golden cups drink only of
    the dew ;
And we will drink the clear cold stream, and taste of
    naught beside,
And He who blessed the Rechabites, the Lord will be
    our guide.

A GREAT SECRET.

My friend, here 's a secret
    By which you may thrive :
I am fifty years old,
    And my wife 's forty-five —

A queen among beauties,
    The wedding-guests said,
When we went to the church
    With the priest, and were wed.

That 's thirty long years past ;
    And I can avow,
She was no more a beauty
    To me, then, than now !

For never the scath of a
Petulant frown
Has ploughed with its furrows
Her young roses down.

And still, like a girl, when
Her praises I speak,
Her heart fairly blushes
Itself through her cheek.

Her smile is more tender
For being less bright ;
And the little bit powder
That makes her hair white,

And all the soft patience
That shows through her face,
In my eyes, are only
Like grace upon grace.

For still we are lovers,
As I am alive,
Though I, sir, am fifty,
And she's forty-five !

And here 's half the secret
I meant to unfold :
She don't know, my friend,
Not the least, how to scold !

Nor does she get pettish,
And sulk to a pout ;
So, since we fell *in* love,
We never fell *out !*

And here 's the full secret
That saves us from strife :
I kept her a *sweetheart*
In making her *wife !*

And if you but wed on
My pattern, you 'll thrive,
For I, sir, am fifty,
My wife, forty-five!

HELPLESS.

You never said a word to me
That was cruel, under the sun ;
It is n't the things you do, darling,
But the things you leave undone.

If you could but know a wish or want,
You would grant it joyfully ;
Ah! that is the worst of all, darling,
That you cannot know nor see.

For favors free alone are sweet,
Not those that we must seek ;
If you loved as I love you, darling,
I would not need to speak.

But to-day I am helpless as a child
That must be led along ;
Then put your hand in mine, darling,
And make me brave and strong.

There 's a heavy care upon my mind,
　A trouble on my brain ;
Now gently stroke my hair, darling,
　And take away the pain.

I feel a weight within my breast,
　As if all had gone amiss ;
Oh kiss me with your lips, darling,
　And fill my heart with bliss.

Enough ! no deeper joy than this
　For souls below is given ;
Now take me in your arms, darling,
　And lift me up to heaven !

THE SOFT NO.

YOUNG Kitty sat knitting.　" My darling," I said,
　" I have had a most beautiful dream !
Shall I tell it ? "　She gave a slight shake of the head,
　And answered : " *I 'm turning the seam !* "

I reached for the mesh, speckled soft like a pink,
　That she held in her fingers so small ;
But she answered : " I can't leave my work — only
　　think —
I am knitting a sock for a doll ! "

" Don't tease me so, Kitty, my dear little one —
　You are dying to hear, I 'll be bound ! "
" Just wait," she said, smiling as bright as the sun,
　" Just wait till I 've knitted a round."

I waited impatient, and then I drew near,
    And, pushing the curls from her brow,
I said : " Are you ready, my Kitty, my dear ? "
    She answered : " *I 'm narrowing now !* "

Still nearer I drew — put my arm round her waist —
    And, breaking of silence the seal,
Repeated : " Dear Kitty ! why, what is your haste ? "
    She answered : " I 'm setting the heel ! "

I smiled and I frowned — I looked up at the clock —
    At the coals 'neath the forestick aglow,
And then at dear Kitty — she held up the sock,
    Saying : " Would you put white in the toe ? "

" You *shall* hear me, Kitty, you dearest of girls,
    And then, if you will, you may scoff ! "
She shook loose the hand I had laid on her curls,
    As she said : " I 'm just *binding off !* "

" I dreamed of a cottage embowered with trees,
    And under the bluest of skies " —
She checked me with — " Sit farther off, if you please,
    My needles will get in your eyes ! "

" I dreamed you were there, like a rose at my door,
    And that love, Kitty, *love,* made us rich ! "
" I told you to sit farther off once before ! "
    She answered ; " I 'm dropping a stitch ! "

She knitted the last, and had broken the thread,
    When I cried : " Am I only a friend ?
Or may I be lover ? " She quietly said :
    " Pray wait till I 've fastened the end ! "

" Will you marry me ? "   Here the worst came to the
worst,
There was nothing to do but to go ;
For I learned at the last, what I might have known
first,
It was all her soft way to say, No !

HYMN

FOR THE DEDICATION OF THE CHURCH OF THE STRANGERS IN NEW YORK CITY.

COME down, O Lord, and with us live !
For here, with tender, earnest call,
The Gospel thou didst freely give,
We freely offer unto all.

Come with such power and saving grace,
That we shall cry with one accord,
" How sweet and awful is this place,
This sacred temple of the Lord ! "

Let friend and stranger, one in Thee,
Feel with such power thy Spirit move,
That every man's own speech shall be
The sweet eternal speech of love.

Yea, fill us with the Holy Ghost,
Let burning hearts and tongues be given,
Make this a day of Pentecost,
A foretaste of the bliss of heaven.

OUR BABY.

WHEN the morning, half in shadow,
Ran along the hill and meadow,
And with milk-white fingers parted
Crimson roses, golden-hearted ;
Opening over ruins hoary
Every purple morning-glory,
And out-shaking from the bushes
Singing larks and pleasant thrushes ;
That 's the time our little baby,
Strayed from Paradise, it may be,
Came with eyes like heaven above him :
Oh, we could not choose but love him !

Not enough of earth for sinning,
Always gentle, always winning,
Never needing our reproving,
Ever lively, ever loving,
Starry eyes and sunset tresses,
Lips that knew no word of doubting,
Often kissing, never pouting,
Beauty even in completeness,
Ever full of childish sweetness,
That 's the way our little baby,
Far too pure for earth, it may be,
Seemed to us, who, while about him,
Deemed we could not do without him.

When the morning, half in shadow,
Ran along the hill and meadow,

And with milk-white fingers parted
Crimson roses, golden-hearted,
Opening over ruins hoary
Every purple morning-glory,
And out-shaking from the bushes
Singing larks and pleasant thrushes,
That 's the time our little baby,
Pining here for heaven, it may be,
Turning from our bitter weeping,
Closed his eyes as when in sleeping,
And his white hands on his bosom
Folded like a summer blossom.

Now the litter he doth lie on,
Strewed with roses, bear to Zion.
Go, as past a pleasant meadow,
Through the valley of the shadow ;
Take him softly, holy angels,
Past the ranks of God's evangels,
Past the saints and martyrs holy,
To the earth-born, meek and lowly ;
We would have our precious blossom
Safely laid in Jesus' bosom.

LOUISA.

INSCRIBED TO HER HUSBAND, S. F. CARY.

WHERE leaves by bitter winds are heaped
  In the deep hollows, damp and cold,
And the light snow-shower silently
  Is falling on the yellow mould,

Sleeps one who was our friend below ;
　With meek hands folded on her breast,
When the first flowers of summer died,
　We softly laid her down to rest.

By her were blessings freely strewn,
　As roses by the summer's breath ;
Yet nothing in her *perfect* life
　Was half so *lovely* as her *death.*

In the meek beauty of a faith
　Which few have ever proved like her,
She shrank not, even when she felt
　The chill breath of the sepulchre.

Heavier and heavier still, she leaned
　Upon His arm who died to save,
As step by step He led her down
　To the still chamber of the grave.

'T was at the midnight's solemn watch
　She sank to slumber, calm and deep ; —
The golden fingers of the dawn
　Shall never wake her from that sleep.

From him, who was her friend below,
　She turned to meet her Heavenly Guide ;
And the sweet children of her love !
　She left them sleeping when she died.

Her last of suns went calmly down ;
　And when the morn rose bright and clear,
Hers was a holier Sabbath day
　Than that which dawned upon us here.

A TIN WEDDING CELEBRATION.

DEAR friend, the thought must surely come
  To-night to every thinker,
That he who joined your fates at first
  Was something of a tinker !

For through the ups and downs of life,
  Through fair and stormy weather,
His soldering for *tin* long years
  Has held you fast together.

And since your love has worn so well,
  Another truth we settle :
You are not made of tinsel stuff,
  But true and tempered metal.

And therefore may the gods, on you
  Their choicest gifts bestowing,
Fill up the tin cup of your lives,
  With bliss to overflowing.

May love and friendship smooth the path
  Of life your feet are treading ;
Till happier than this night of *tin*
  Shall be your golden wedding.

And may you hear with hearts as young
  Our last congratulations,
As when your marriage bells first rung
  Their tin-tinnabulations !

FOR THE SILVER WEDDING OF MR. AND MRS. J. C. DERBY.

SOME five and twenty years ago —
Ah! time of youth and rapture ! —
Our host was a bewitching beau
The girls all tried to capture.

Our hostess 't was who won the field,
And honor, then, to her be ;
She justly takes the prize we yield
Because she won the Derby.

A PACK OF TRUTHS.

No matter how strictly according to Hoyle
You may shuffle your cards or your own mortal coil —
How you play out your best cards or what you conceal,
There is one who can beat you and give you the *De'il*.

In the sharp game of life you may win the first trick :
But after you 've cut your last cards and your trick,
Then, deuce take it all, even though you die game,
Whether kings, queens, or knaves, he will take you the
    same.

You will find life at last is a pretty grave joke,
For you can't let it pass, and you cannot revoke ;
Gabriel takes you at last, you may like it or lump,
For he 'll order you up, and he holds the last trump.

SONG.

Oh, always is Eden created anew,
When hearts for each other beat tender and true ;
When bright as a sunbeam the glad moments slip,
And the joy from the heart rises up to the lip.
    Youth, youth, giver of bliss,
Thy greatest is this, aye, thy greatest is this.

But better and sweeter is love that will last
When youth with the bloom of the roses is past ;
Oh ! the warmth of affection that never grows cold,
And the strength of affection that never grows old.
    Blest, blest, thrice blest are those
Who are loved till life's close, who are loved till life's
    close.

But best of all good things it is, to behold
The heart warm and young when the frame groweth
    old ;
For they who walk lovingly here hand in hand,
Together shall rest in the heavenly land,
    Rest, rest, in heaven above,
Forever united with Him who is Love !

THAT CALF.

An old farmer, one morn, hurried out to his barn
    Where the cattle were standing, and said,
While they trembled with fright, — "Now which of
    you, last night,

Shut the barn-door, while I was in bed ? "
Each one of them all shook his head.

Now the little calf, Spot, she was down in the lot,
　And the way the rest did was a shame ;
For not one, night before, saw her close up the door,
　But they said that she did, all the same ;
　For they always made her bear the blame.

Said the horse, Dapple-gray, " I was not up this way
　Last night, as I now recollect ; " —
And the bull, passing by, tossed his horns very high,
　And said, " Where 's the one to object,
　If I say, 't is *that calf* I suspect ? "

" It is too wicked now," said the old brindle cow,
　" To accuse honest folks of such tricks ; " —
Said the cock in the tree, " I am sure 't was n't me ; " —
　All the sheep just said " bah ! " — there were six ; —
　And they thought now *that calf*'s in a fix !

" Of course we all knew 't was the wrong thing to do,"
　Cried the chickens ; " Of course," mewed the cat ;
" I suppose," said the mule, " some folks think me a fool,
　But I 'm not quite so simple as that ; —
　Well ! *that calf* never knows what she 's at ! "

Just then the poor calf, who was always the laugh
　And the jest of the yard, came in sight ; —
" Did you shut my barn-door ? " said the farmer once
　　more ;
And she answered, " I did, sir, last night ;
　For I thought that to close it was right."

Now each beast shook his head — " She will catch it,"
   they said,
" Serve her right, for her meddlesome way ; " —
Cried the farmer : " Come here, little bossy, my dear,
   You have done what I cannot repay,
   And your fortune is made from to-day.

" Very strangely, last night, I forgot the door quite,
   And if you had not closed it so neat,
All the colts had slipped in, and gone straight to the
   bin,
   And got what they ought not to eat ; —
   They 'd have foundered themselves upon wheat."

Then each beast of them all began loudly to bawl,
   The mule tried to smile, the cock crew ;
" Little Spotty, my dear, you 're the favorite here,"
   They all cried : " we 're so glad it was you ! "
   But *that calf* only answered them, " boo ! "

INDEX OF FIRST LINES.

GENERAL INDEX OF TITLES.

Standard and Popular Library Books

SELECTED FROM THE CATALOGUE OF

HOUGHTON, MIFFLIN AND COMPANY.

A Club of One. An Anonymous Volume, $1.25.

Brooks Adams. The Emancipation of Massachusetts, crown 8vo, $1.50.

John Adams and Abigail Adams. Familiar Letters of, during the Revolution, 12mo, $2.00.

Oscar Fay Adams. Handbook of English Authors, 16mo, 75 cents ; Handbook of American Authors, 16mo, 75 cents.

Louis Agassiz. Methods of Study in Natural History, Illustrated, 12mo, $1.50; Geological Sketches, Series I. and II., 12mo, each, $1.50 ; A Journey in Brazil, Illustrated, 12mo, $2.50 ; Life and Letters, edited by his wife, 2 vols. 12mo, $4.00; Life and Works, 6 vols. $10.00.

Anne A. Agge and Mary M. Brooks. Marblehead Sketches. 4to, $3.00.

Elizabeth Akers. The Silver Bridge and other Poems, 16mo, $1.25.

Thomas Bailey Aldrich. Story of a Bad Boy, Illustrated, 12mo, $1.50; Marjorie Daw and Other People, 12mo, $1.50 ; Prudence Palfrey, 12mo, $1.50 ; The Queen of Sheba, 12mo, $1.50 ; The Stillwater Tragedy, 12mo, $1.50 ; Poems, *Household Edition*, Illustrated, 12mo, $1.75 ; full gilt, $2.25 ; The above six vols. 12mo, uniform, $9.00; From Ponkapog to Pesth, 16mo, $1.25 ; Poems, Complete, Illustrated, 8vo, $3.50 ; Mercedes, and Later Lyrics, cr. 8vo, $1.25.

Rev. A. V. G. Allen. Continuity of Christian Thought, 12mo, $2.00.

American Commonwealths. Per volume, 16mo, $1.25.
Virginia. By John Esten Cooke.
Oregon. By William Barrows.
Maryland. By Wm. Hand Browne.
Kentucky. By N. S. Shaler.
Michigan. By Hon. T. M. Cooley.

Kansas.   By Leverett W. Spring.
California.   By Josiah Royce.
New York.   By Ellis H. Roberts.   2 vols.
Connecticut.   By Alexander Johnston.

(In Preparation.)

Tennessee.   By James Phelan.
Pennsylvania.   By Hon. Wayne MacVeagh.
Missouri.   By Lucien Carr.
Ohio.   By Rufus King.
New Jersey.   By Austin Scott.

American Men of Letters.   Per vol., with Portrait, 16mo,
$1.25.

Washington Irving.   By Charles Dudley Warner.
Noah Webster.   By Horace E. Scudder.
Henry D. Thoreau.   By Frank B. Sanborn.
George Ripley.   By O. B. Frothingham.
J. Fenimore Cooper.   By Prof. T. R. Lounsbury.
Margaret Fuller Ossoli.   By T. W. Higginson.
Ralph Waldo Emerson.   By Oliver Wendell Holmes.
Edgar Allan Poe.   By George E. Woodberry.
Nathaniel Parker Willis.   By H. A. Beers.

(In Preparation.)

Benjamin Franklin.   By John Bach McMaster.
Nathaniel Hawthorne.   By James Russell Lowell.
William Cullen Bryant.   By John Bigelow.
Bayard Taylor.   By J. R. G. Hassard.
William Gilmore Simms.   By George W. Cable.

American Statesmen.   Per vol., 16mo, $1.25.

John Quincy Adams.   By John T. Morse, Jr.
Alexander Hamilton.   By Henry Cabot Lodge.
John C. Calhoun.   By Dr. H. von Holst.
Andrew Jackson.   By Prof. W. G. Sumner.
John Randolph.   By Henry Adams.
James Monroe.   By Pres. D. C. Gilman.
Thomas Jefferson.   By John T. Morse, Jr.
Daniel Webster.   By Henry Cabot Lodge.
Albert Gallatin.   By John Austin Stevens.
James Madison.   By Sydney Howard Gay.
John Adams.   By John T. Morse, Jr.

John Marshall. By Allan B. Magruder.

Samuel Adams. By J. K. Hosmer.

Thomas H. Benton. By Theoc ore Roosevelt.

Henry Clay. By Hon. Carl Schurz. 2 vols.

(*In Preparation.*)

Martin Van Buren. By Edward M. Shepard.

George Washington. By Henry Cabot Lodge. 2 vols.

Patrick Henry. By Moses Coit Tyler.

Martha Babcock Amory. Life of Copley, 8vo, $3.00.

Hans Christian Andersen. Complete Works, 10 vols. 12mo, each $1.00. New Edition, 10 vols. 12mo, $10.00.

Francis, Lord Bacon. Works, 15 vols. cr. 8vo, $33.75; *Popular Edition,* with Portraits, 2 vols. cr. 8vo, $5.00; Promus of Formularies and Elegancies, 8vo, $5.00; Life and Times of Bacon, 2 vols. cr. 8vo, $5.00.

L. H. Bailey, Jr. Talks Afield, Illustrated, 16mo, $1.00.

M. M. Ballou. Due West, cr. 8vo, $1.50 ; Due South, $1.50.

Henry A. Beers. The Thankless Muse. Poems. 16mo, $1.25.

E. D. R. Bianciardi. At Home in Italy, 16mo, $1.25.

William Henry Bishop. The House of a Merchant Prince, a Novel, 12mo, $1.50 ; Detmold, a Novel, 18mo, $1.25 ; Choy Susan and other Stories, 16mo, $1.25 ; The Golden Justice, 16mo, $1.25.

Bjornstjerne Bjornson. Complete Works. New Edition, 3 vols. 12mo, the set, $4.50; Synnove Solbakken, Bridal March, Captain Mansana, Magnhild, 16mo, each $1.00.

Anne C. Lynch Botta. Handbook of Universal Literature, New Edition, 12mo, $2.00.

British Poets. *Riverside Edition,* cr. 8vo, each $1.50 ; the set, 68 vols. $100.00.

John Brown, A. B. John Bunyan. Illustrated. 8vo, $4.50.

John Brown, M. D. Spare Hours, 3 vols. 16mo, each $1.50.

Robert Browning. Poems and Dramas, etc., 15 vols. 16mo, $22.00 ; Works, 8 vols. cr. 8vo, $13.00 ; Ferishtah's Fancies, cr. 8vo, $1.00; Jocoseria, 16mo, $1.00 ; cr. 8vo, $1.00 ; Parleyings with Certain People of Importance in their Day, 16mo or cr. 8vo, $1.25. Works, *New Edition,* 6 vols. cr. 8vo. $10.00.

William Cullen Bryant. Translation of Homer, The Iliad

cr. 8vo, $2.50 ; 2 vols. royal 8vo, $9.00 ; cr. 8vo, $4.00. The Odyssey, cr. 8vo, $2.50 ; 2 vols. royal 8vo, $9.00 ; cr. 8vo, $4.00.

Sara C. Bull. Life of Ole Bull. *Popular Edition.* 12mo, $1.50.

John Burroughs. Works, 7 vols. 16mo, each $1.50.

Thomas Carlyle. Essays, with Portrait and Index, 4 vols. 12mo, $7.50 ; *Popular Edition*, 2 vols. 12mo, $3.50.

Alice and Phœbe Cary. Poems, *Household Edition*, Illustrated, 12mo, $1.75 ; cr. 8vo, full gilt, $2.25 ; *Library Edition*, including Memorial by Mary Clemmer, Portraits and 24 Illustrations, 8vo, $3.50.

Wm. Ellery Channing. Selections from His Note-Books, $1.00.

Francis J. Child (Editor). English and Scottish Popular Ballads. Eight Parts. (Parts I.–IV. now ready). 4to, each $5.00. Poems of Religious Sorrow, Comfort, Counsel, and Aspiration. 16mo, $1.25.

Lydia Maria Child. Looking Toward Sunset, 12mo, $2.50 ; Letters, with Biography by Whittier, 16mo, $1.50.

James Freeman Clarke. Ten Great Religions, Parts I. and II., 12mo, each $2.00 ; Common Sense in Religion, 12mo, $2.00 ; Memorial and Biographical Sketches, 12mo, $2.00.

John Esten Cooke. My Lady Pokahontas, 16mo, $1.25.

James Fenimore Cooper. Works, new *Household Edition*, Illustrated, 32 vols. 16mo, each $1.00 ; the set, $32.00 ; *Fireside Edition*, Illustrated, 16 vols. 12mo, $20.00.

Susan Fenimore Cooper. Rural Hours. 16mo, $1.25.

Charles Egbert Craddock. In the Tennessee Mountains, 16mo, $1.25 ; Down the Ravine, Illustrated, $1.00 ; The Prophet of the Great Smoky Mountains, 16mo. $1.25 ; In The Clouds, 16mo, $1.25.

C. P. Cranch. Ariel and Caliban. 16mo, $1.25 ; The Æneid of Virgil. Translated by Cranch. 8vo, $2.50.

T. F. Crane. Italian Popular Tales, 8vo, $2.50.

F. Marion Crawford. To Leeward, 16mo, $1.25 ; A Roman Singer, 16mo, $1.25 ; An American Politician, 16mo, $1.25.

M. Creighton. The Papacy during the Reformation, 4 vols. 8vo, $17.50.

Richard H. Dana. To Cuba and Back, 16mo, $1.25 ; Two Years Before the Mast, 12mo, $1.00.

G. W. and Emma De Long. Voyage of the Jeannette. 2 vols. 8vo, $7.50; New One-Volume Edition, 8vo, $4.50.

Thomas De Quincey. Works, 12 vols. 12mo, each $1.50; the set, $18.00.

Madame De Stael. Germany, 12mo, $2.50.

Charles Dickens. Works, *Illustrated Library Edition,* with Dickens Dictionary, 30 vols. 12mo, each $1.50; the set, $45.00.

J. Lewis Diman. The Theistic Argument, etc., cr. 8vo, $2.00; Orations and Essays, cr. 8vo, $2.50.

Theodore A. Dodge. Patroclus and Penelope, Illustrated, 8vo, $3.00. The Same. Outline Illustrations. Cr. 8vo, $1.25.

E. P. Dole. Talks about Law. Cr. 8vo, $2.00; sheep, $2.50.

Eight Studies of the Lord's Day. 12mo, $1.50.

George Eliot. The Spanish Gypsy, a Poem, 16mo, $1.00.

Ralph Waldo Emerson. Works, *Riverside Edition,* 11 vols. each $1.75; the set, $19.25; *"Little Classic" Edition,* 11 vols. 18mo, each, $1.50; Parnassus, *Household Edition,* 12mo, $1.75; *Library Edition,* 8vo, $4.00; Poems, *Household Edition,* Por trait, 12mo, $1.75; Memoir, by J. Elliot Cabot, 2 vols. $3.50.

English Dramatists. Vols. 1–3, Marlowe's Works; Vols. 4–11, Middleton's Works; Vols. 12–14, Marston's Works; each vol. $3.00; *Large-Paper Edition,* each vol. $4.00.

Edgar Fawcett. A Hopeless Case, 18mo, $1.25; A Gentle man of Leisure, 18mo, $1.00; An Ambitious Woman, 12mo, $1.50.

Fénelon. Adventures of Telemachus, 12mo, $2.25.

James T. Fields. Yesterdays with Authors, 12mo, $2.00; 8vo, Illustrated, $3.00; Underbrush, 18mo, $1.25; Ballads and other Verses, 16mo, $1.00; The Family Library of British Poetry, royal 8vo, $5.00; Memoirs and Correspondence, cr. 8vo, $2.00.

John Fiske. Myths and Mythmakers, 12mo, $2.00; Outlines of Cosmic Philosophy, 2 vols. 8vo, $6.00; The Unseen World, and other Essays, 12mo, $2.00; Excursions of an Evolutionist, 12mo, $2.00; The Destiny of Man, 16mo, $1.00; The Idea of God, 16mo, $1.00; Darwinism, and Other Essays, New Edi tion, enlarged, 12mo, $2.00.

Edward Fitzgerald. Works. 2 vols. 8vo, $10.00.

O. B. Frothingham. Life of W. H. Channing. Cr. 8vo, $2.00.

William H. Furness. Verses, 16mo, vellum, $1.25.

Gentleman's Magazine Library. 14 vols. 8vo, each $2.50; Roxburgh, $3.50; *Large-Paper Edition*, $6.oo. I. Manners and Customs. II. Dialect, Proverbs, and Word-Lore. III. Popular Superstitions and Traditions. IV. English Traditions and Foreign Customs. V., VI. Archæology. VII. Romano-British Remains: Part I. (*Last two styles sold only in sets.*)

John F. Genung. Tennyson's In Memoriam, cr. 8vo, $1.25.

Johann Wolfgang von Goethe. Faust, Part First, Translated by C. T. Brooks, 16mo, $1.25; Faust, Translated by Bayard Taylor, cr. 8vo, $2.50; 2 vols. royal 8vo, $9.oo; 2 vols. 12mo, $4.oo; Correspondence with a Child, 12mo, $1.50; Wilhelm Meister, Translated by Carlyle, 2 vols. 12mo, $3.oo. Life, by Lewes, together with the above five 12mo vols., the set, $9.oo.

Oliver Goldsmith. The Vicar of Wakefield, 32mo, $1.oo.

Charles George Gordon. Diaries and Letters, 8vo, $2.oo.

George H. Gordon. Brook Farm to Cedar Mountain, 1861-2. 8vo, $3.oo. Campaign of Army of Virginia, 1862. 8vo, $4.oo. A War Diary, 1863-5. 8vo, $3.oo.

George Zabriskie Gray. The Children's Crusade, 12mo, $1.50; Husband and Wife, 16mo, $1.oo.

F. W. Gunsaulus. The Transfiguration of Christ. 16mo, $1.25.

Anna Davis Hallowell. James and Lucretia Mott, $2.oo.

R. P. Hallowell. Quaker Invasion of Massachusetts, revised, $1.25. The Pioneer Quakers, 16mo, $1.oo.

Arthur Sherburne Hardy. But Yet a Woman, 16mo, $1.25; The Wind of Destiny, 16mo, $1.25.

Bret Harte. Works, 6 vols. cr. 8vo, each $2.oo; Poems, *Household Edition*, Illustrated, 12mo, $1.75; cr. 8vo, full gilt, $2.25; *Red-Line Edition*, small 4to, $2.50; *Cabinet Edition*, $1.oo; In the Carquinez Woods, 18mo, $1.oo; Flip, and Found at Blazing Star, 18mo, $1.oo; On the Frontier, 18mo, $1.oo; By Shore and Sedge, 18mo, $1.oo; Maruja, 18mo, $1.oo; Snow-Bound at Eagle's, 18mo, $1.oo; The Queen of the Pirate Isle, Illustrated, small 4to, $1.50; A Millionaire, etc., 18mo, $1.oo; The Crusade of the Excelsior, 16mo, $1.25.

Nathaniel Hawthorne. Works, *"Little Classic"* *Edition*, Illustrated, 25 vols. 18mo, each $1.oo; the set $25.oo; *New Riverside Edition*, Introductions by G. P. Lathrop, 11 Etchings and Portrait, 12 vols. cr. 8vo, each $2.oo; *Wayside Edition*, with Introductions, Etchings, etc., 24 vols. 12mo, $36.oo;

Fireside Edition, 6 vols. 12mo, $10.00; The Scarlet Letter, 12mo, $1.00.

John Hay. Pike County Ballads, 12mo, $1.50; Castilian Days, 16mo, $2.00.

Caroline Hazard. Memoir of J. L. Diman. Cr. 8vo, $2.00.

Franklin H. Head. Shakespeare's Insomnia. 16mo, parchment paper, 75 cents.

The Heart of the Weed. Anonymous Poems. 16mo, parchment paper, $1.00.

S. E. Herrick. Some Heretics of Yesterday. Cr. 8vo, $1.50.

George S. Hillard. Six Months in Italy. 12mo, $2.00.

Oliver Wendell Holmes. Poems, *Household Edition,* Illus trated, 12mo, $1.75; cr. 8vo, full gilt, $2.25; *Illustrated Library Edition,* 8vo, $3.50; *Handy-Volume Edition,* 2 vols. 32mo, $2.50; The Autocrat of the Breakfast-Table, cr. 8vo, $2.00; *Handy-Volume Edition,* 32mo, $1.25; The Professor at the Breakfast-Table, cr. 8vo, $2.00; The Poet at the Breakfast-Table, cr. 8vo, $2.00; Elsie Venner, cr. 8vo, $2.00; The Guardian Angel, cr. 8vo, $2.00; Medical Essays, cr. 8vo, $2.00; Pages from an Old Volume of Life, cr. 8vo, $2.00; John Lothrop Motley, A Memoir, 16mo, $1.50; Illustrated Poems, 8vo, $4.00; A Mortal Antipathy, cr. 8vo, $1.50; The Last Leaf, Illustrated, 4to, $10.00.

Nathaniel Holmes. The Authorship of Shakespeare. New Edition. 2 vols. $4.00.

Blanche Willis Howard. One Summer, Illustrated, 12mo, $1.25; One Year Abroad, 18mo, $1.25.

William D. Howells. Venetian Life, 12mo, $1.50; Italian Journeys, 12mo, $1.50; Their Wedding Journey, Illustrated, 12mo, $1.50; 18mo, $1.25; Suburban Sketches, Illustrated, 12mo, $1.50; A Chance Acquaintance, Illustrated, 12mo, $1.50; 18mo, $1.25; A Foregone Conclusion, 12mo, $1.50; The Lady of the Aroostook, 12mo, $1.50; The Undiscovered Country, 12mo, $1.50.

Thomas Hughes. Tom Brown's School-Days at Rugby, 16mo, $1.00; Tom Brown at Oxford, 16mo, $1.25; The Manliness of Christ, 16mo, $1.00; paper, 25 cents.

William Morris Hunt. Talks on Art, 2 Series, each $1.00.

Henry James. A Passionate Pilgrim and other Tales, 12mo, $2.00; Transatlantic Sketches, 12mo, $2.00; Roderick Hudson, 12mo, $2.00; The American, 12mo, $2.00; Watch and Ward, 18mo, $1.25; The Europeans, 12mo, $1.50; Confidence, 12mo, $1.50; The Portrait of a Lady, 12mo, $2.00.

Anna Jameson. Writings upon Art Subjects. New Edition, 10 vols. 16mo, the set, $12.50.

Sarah Orne Jewett. Deephaven, 18mo, $1.25; Old Friends and New, 18mo, $1.25; Country By-Ways, 18mo, $1.25; Play-Days, Stories for Children, square 16mo, $1.50; The Mate of the Daylight, 18mo, $1.25; A Country Doctor, 16mo, $1.25; A Marsh Island, 16mo, $1.25; A White Heron, 18mo, $1.25.

Rossiter Johnson. Little Classics, 18 vols. 18mo, each $1.00; the set, $18.00.

Samuel Johnson. Oriental Religions: India, 8vo, $5.00; China, 8vo, $5.00; Persia, 8vo, $5.00; Lectures, Essays, and Sermons, cr. 8vo, $1.75.

Charles C. Jones, Jr. History of Georgia, 2 vols. 8vo, $10.00.

Malcolm Kerr. The Far Interior. 2 vols. 8vo, $9.00.

Omar Khayyám. Rubáiyát, *Red-Line Edition*, square 16mo., $1.00; the same, with 56 Illustrations by Vedder, folio, $25.00; The Same, *Phototype Edition*, 4to, $12.50.

T. Starr King. Christianity and Humanity, with Portrait, 12mo, $1.50; Substance and Show, 16mo, $2.00.

Charles and Mary Lamb. Tales from Shakespeare. *Handy-Volume Edition.* 32mo, $1.00.

Henry Lansdell. Russian Central Asia. 2 vols. $10.00.

Lucy Larcom. Poems, 16mo, $1.25; An Idyl of Work, 16mo, $1.25; Wild Roses of Cape Ann and other Poems, 16mo, $1.25; Breathings of the Better Life, 18mo, $1.25; Poems, *Household Edition*, Illustrated, 12mo, $1.75; full gilt, $2.25; Beckonings for Every Day, 16mo, $1.00.

George Parsons Lathrop. A Study of Hawthorne 18mo, $1.25.

Henry C. Lea. Sacerdotal Celibacy, 8vo, $4.50.

Sophia and Harriet Lee. Canterbury Tales. New Edition. 3 vols. 12mo, $3.75.

Charles G. Leland. The Gypsies, cr. 8vo, $2.00; Algonquin Legends of New England, cr. 8vo, $2.00.

George Henry Lewes. The Story of Goethe's Life, Portrait, 12mo, $1.50; Problems of Life and Mind, 5 vols. 8vo, $14.00.
A. Parlett Lloyd. The Law of Divorce, cloth, $2.00; sheep, $2.50.
J. G. Lockhart. Life of Sir W. Scott, 3 vols. 12mo, $4.50.
Henry Cabot Lodge. Studies in History, cr. 8vo, $1.50.
Henry Wadsworth Longfellow. Complete Poetical and Prose Works, *Riverside Edition*, 11 vols. cr. 8vo, $16.50; Poetical Works, *Riverside Edition*, 6 vols. cr. 8vo, $9.00; *Cambridge Edition*, 4 vols. 12mo, $7.00; Poems, *Octavo Edition*, Portrait and 300 Illustrations, $7.50; *Household Edition*, Illustrated, 12mo, $1.75; cr. 8vo, full gilt, $2.25; *Red-Line Edition*, Portrait and 12 Illustrations, small 4to, $2.50; *Cabinet Edition*, $1.00; *Library Edition*, Portrait and 32 Illustrations, 8vo, $3.50; Christus, *Household Edition*, $1.75; cr. 8vo, full gilt, $2.25; *Cabinet Edition*, $1.00; Prose Works, *Riverside Edition*, 2 vols. cr. 8vo, $3.00; Hyperion, 16mo, $1.50; Kavanagh, 16mo, $1.50; Outre-Mer, 16mo, $1.50; In the Harbor, 16mo, $1.00; Michael Angelo: a Drama, Illustrated, folio, $5.00; Twenty Poems, Illustrated, small 4to, $2.50; Translation of the Divina Commedia of Dante, *Riverside Edition*, 3 vols. cr. 8vo, $4.50; 1 vol. cr. 8vo, $2.50; 3 vols. royal 8vo, $13.50; cr. 8vo, $4.50; Poets and Poetry of Europe, royal 8vo, $5.00; Poems of Places, 31 vols. each $1.00; the set, $25.00.
James Russell Lowell. Poems, *Red-Line Edition*, Portrait, Illustrated, small 4to, $2.50; *Household Edition*, Illustrated, 12mo, $1.75; cr. 8vo, full gilt, $2.25; *Library Edition*, Portrait and 32 Illustrations, 8vo, $3.50; *Cabinet Edition*, $1.00; Fireside Travels, 12mo, $1.50; Among my Books, Series I. and II. 12mo, each $2.00; My Study Windows, 12mo, $2.00; Democracy and other Addresses, 16mo, $1.25; Uncollected Poems.
Thomas Babington Macaulay. Works, ˙6 vols. 12mo, $20.00.
Mrs. Madison. Memoirs and Letters of Dolly Madison, 16mo, $1.25.
Harriet Martineau. Autobiography, New Edition, 2 vols. 12mo, $4.00; Household Education, 18mo, $1.25.
H. B. McClellan. The Life and Campaigns of Maj.-Gen. J. E. B. Stuart. With Portrait and Maps, 8vo, $3.00.
G. W. Melville. In the Lena Delta, Maps and Illustrations, 8vo, $2.50.

T. C. Mendenhall. A Century of Electricity. 16mo, $1.25.

Owen Meredith. Poems, *Household Edition*, Illustrated, 12mo, $1.75; cr. 8vo, full gilt, $2.25; *Library Edition*, Portrait and 32 Illustrations, 8vo, $3.50; Lucile, *Red-Line Edition*, 8 Illustrations, small 4to, $2.50; *Cabinet Edition*, 8 Illustrations, $1.00.

Olive Thorne Miller. Bird-Ways, 16mo, $1.25.

John Milton. Paradise Lost. *Handy-Volume Edition.* 32mo, $1.00. *Riverside Classic Edition*, 16mo, Illustrated, $1.00.

S. Weir Mitchell. In War Time, 16mo, $1.25; Roland Blake, 16mo, $1.25.

J. W. Mollett. Illustrated Dictionary of Words used in Art and Archæology, small 4to, $5.00.

Montaigne. Complete Works, Portrait, 4 vols. 12mo, $7.50.

William Mountford. Euthanasy, 12mo, $2.00.

T. Mozley. Reminiscences of Oriel College, etc., 2 vols. 16mo, $3.00.

Elisha Mulford. The Nation, 8vo, $2.50; The Republic of God, 8vo, $2.00.

T. T. Munger. On the Threshold, 16mo, $1.00; The Freedom of Faith, 16mo, $1.50; Lamps and Paths, 16mo, $1.00; The Appeal to Life, 16mo, $1.50.

J. A. W. Neander. History of the Christian Religion and Church, with Index volume, 6 vols. 8vo, $20.00; Index, $3.00.

Joseph Neilson. Memories of Rufus Choate, 8vo, $5.00.

Charles Eliot Norton. Notes of Travel in Italy, 16mo, $1.25; Translation of Dante's New Life, royal 8vo, $3.00.

Wm. D. O'Connor. Hamlet's Note-Book, 16mo, $1.00.

G. H. Palmer. Trans. of Homer's Odyssey, 1–12, 8vo, $2.50.

Leighton Parks. His Star in the East. Cr. 8vo, $1.50.

James Parton. Life of Benjamin Franklin, 2 vols. 8vo, $5.00; Life of Thomas Jefferson, 8vo, $2.50; Life of Aaron Burr, 2 vols. 8vo, $5.00; Life of Andrew Jackson, 3 vols. 8vo, $7.50; Life of Horace Greeley, 8vo, $2.50; General Butler in New Orleans, 8vo, $2.50; Humorous Poetry of the English Language, 12mo, $1.75; full gilt, $2.25; Famous Americans of Recent Times, 8vo, $2.50; Life of Voltaire, 2 vols. 8vo, $6.00; The French Parnassus, 12mo, $1.75; crown 8vo, $3.50; Captains of Industry, 16mo, $1.25.

Blaise Pascal. Thoughts, 12mo, $2.25; Letters, 12mo, $2.25.

Elizabeth Stuart Phelps. The Gates Ajar, 16mo, $1.50; Beyond the Gates, 16mo, $1.25; Men, Women, and Ghosts, 16mo, $1.50; Hedged In, 16mo, $1.50; The Silent Partner, 16mo, $1.50; The Story of Avis, 16mo, $1.50; Sealed Orders, and other Stories, 16mo, $1.50; Friends: A Duet, 16mo, $1.25; Doctor Zay, 16mo, $1.25; Songs of the Silent World, 16mo, gilt top, $1.25; An Old Maid's Paradise, 16mo, paper, 50 cents; Burglars in Paradise, 16mo, paper, 50 cents; Madonna of the Tubs, cr. 8vo, Illustrated, $1.50.

Phillips Exeter Lectures: Delivered before the Students of Phillips Exeter Academy, 1885-6. By E. E. HALE, PHILLIPS BROOKS, Presidents McCOSH, PORTER, and others. 12mo, $1.50.

Mrs. S. M. B. Piatt. Selected Poems, 16mo, $1.50.

Carl Ploetz. Epitome of Universal History, 12mo, $3.00.

Antonin Lefevre Pontalis. The Life of John DeWitt, Grand Pensionary of Holland, 2 vols. 8vo, $9.00.

Margaret J. Preston. Colonial Ballads, 16mo, $1.25.

Adelaide A. Procter. Poems, *Cabinet Edition*, $1.00; *Red-Line Edition*, small 4to, $2.50.

Progressive Orthodoxy. 16mo, $1.00.

Sampson Reed. Growth of the Mind, 16mo, $1.00.

C. F. Richardson. Primer of American Literature, 18mo, $.30.

Riverside Aldine Series. Each volume, 16mo, $1.00. First edition, $1.50. 1. Marjorie Daw, etc., by T. B. ALDRICH; 2. My Summer in a Garden, by C. D. WARNER; 3. Fireside Travels, by J. R. LOWELL; 4. The Luck of Roaring Camp, etc., by BRET HARTE; 5, 6. Venetian Life, 2 vols., by W. D. HOWELLS; 7. Wake Robin, by JOHN BURROUGHS; 8, 9. The Biglow Papers, 2 vols., by J. R. LOWELL; 10. Backlog Studies, by C. D. WARNER.

Henry Crabb Robinson. Diary, Reminiscences, etc. cr. 8vo, $2.50.

John C. Ropes. The First Napoleon, with Maps, cr. 8vo, $2.00.

Josiah Royce. Religious Aspect of Philosophy, 12mo, $2.00.

Edgar Evertson Saltus. Balzac, cr. 8vo, $1.25; The Philosophy of Disenchantment, cr. 8vo, $1.25.

John Godfrey Saxe. Poems, *Red-Line Edition*, Illustrated, small 4to, $2.50; *Cabinet Edition*, $1.00; *Household Edition*. Illustrated, 12mo, $1.75; full gilt, cr. 8vo, $2.25.

Sir Walter Scott. Waverley Novels, *Illustrated Library Edition*, 25 vols. 12mo, each $1.00; the set, $25.00; Tales of a Grandfather, 3 vols. 12mo, $4.50; Poems, *Red-Line Edition* Illustrated, small 4to, $2.50; *Cabinet Edition*, $1.00.

W. H. Seward. Works, 5 vols. 8vo, $15.00; Diplomatic History of the War, 8vo, $3.00.

John Campbell Shairp. Culture and Religion, 16mo, $1.25; Poetic Interpretation of Nature, 16mo, $1.25; Studies in Poetry and Philosophy, 16mo, $1.50; Aspects of Poetry, 16mo, $1.50.

William Shakespeare. Works, edited by R. G. White, *Riverside Edition*, 3 vols. cr. 8vo, $7.50; The Same, 6 vols., cr. 8vo, uncut, $10.00; The Blackfriars Shakespeare, per vol. $2.50, *net.* (*In Press.*)

A. P. Sinnett. Esoteric Buddhism, 16mo, $1.25; The Occult World, 16mo, $1.25.

M. C. D. Silsbee. A Half Century in Salem. 16mo, $1.00.

Dr. William Smith. Bible Dictionary, *American Edition*, 4 vols. 8vo, $20.00.

Edmund Clarence Stedman. Poems, *Farringford Edition*, Portrait, 16mo, $2.00; *Household Edition*, Illustrated, 12mo, $1.75; full gilt, cr. 8vo, $2.25; Victorian Poets, 12mo, $2.00; Poets of America, 12mo, $2.25. The set, 3 vols., uniform, 12mo, $6.00; Edgar Allan Poe, an Essay, vellum, 18mo, $1.00.

W. W. Story. Poems, 2 vols. 16mo, $2.50; Fiammetta: A Novel, 16mo, $1.25. Roba di Roma, 2 vols. 16mo, $2.50.

Harriet Beecher Stowe. Novels and Stories, 10 vols. 12mo, uniform, each $1.50; A Dog's Mission, Little Pussy Willow, Queer Little People, Illustrated, small 4to, each $1.25; Uncle Tom's Cabin, 100 Illustrations, 8vo, $3.00; *Library Edition*, Illustrated, 12mo, $2.00; *Popular Edition*, 12mo, $1.00.

Jonathan Swift. Works, *Edition de Luxe*, 19 vols. 8vo, the set, $76.00.

T. P. Taswell-Langmead. English Constitutional History. New Edition, revised, 8vo, $7.50.

Bayard Taylor. Poetical Works, *Household Edition*, 12mo, $1.75; cr. 8vo. full gilt, $2.25; Melodies of Verse, 18mo, vellum, $1.00; Life and Letters, 2 vols. 12mo, $4.00; Dramatic Poems, 12mo, $2.25; *Household Edition*, 12mo, $1.75; Life and Poetical Works, 6 vols. uniform. Including Life, 2 vols.; Faust, 2 vols.; Poems, 1 vol.; Dramatic Poems, 1 vol. The set, cr. 8vo, $12.00.

Alfred Tennyson. Poems, *Household Edition*, Portrait and Illustrations, 12mo, $1.75; full gilt, cr. 8vo, $2.25; *Illustrated Crown Edition*, 2 vols. 8vo, $5.00; *Library Edition*, Portrait and 60 Illustrations, 8vo, $3.50; *Red-Line Edition*, Portrait and Illustrations, small 4to, $2.50; *Cabinet Edition*, $1.00; Complete Works, *Riverside Edition*, 6 vols. cr. 8vo, $6.00.

Celia Thaxter. Among the Isles of Shoals, 18mo, $1.25; Poems, small 4to, $1.50; Drift-Weed, 18mo, $1.50; Poems for Children, Illustrated, small 4to, $1.50; Cruise of the Mystery, Poems, 16mo, $1.00.

Edith M. Thomas. A New Year's Masque and other Poems, 16mo, $1.50; The Round Year, 16mo, $1.25.

Joseph P. Thompson. American Comments on European Questions, 8vo, $3.00.

Henry D. Thoreau. Works, 9 vols. 12mo, each $1.50; the set, $13.50.

George Ticknor. History of Spanish Literature, 3 vols. 8vo, $10.00; Life, Letters, and Journals, Portraits, 2 vols. 12mo, $4.00.

Bradford Torrey. Birds in the Bush, 16mo, $1.25.

Sophus Tromholt. Under the Rays of the Aurora Borealis, Illustrated, 2 vols. $7.50.

Mrs. Schuyler Van Rensselaer. H. H. Richardson and his Works.

Jones Very. Essays and Poems, cr. 8vo, $2.00.

Annie Wall. Story of Sordello, told in Prose, 16mo, $1.00.

Charles Dudley Warner. My Summer in a Garden, *Riverside Aldine Edition*, 16mo, $1.00; *Illustrated Edition*, square 16mo, $1.50; Saunterings, 18mo, $1.25; Backlog Studies, Illustrated, square 16mo, $1.50; *Riverside Aldine Edition*, 16mo, $1.00; Baddeck, and that Sort of Thing, 18mo, $1.00; My Winter on the Nile, cr. 8vo, $2.00; In the Levant, cr. 8vo, $2.00; Being a Boy, Illustrated, square 16mo, $1.50; In the

Wilderness, 18mo, 75 cents; A Roundabout Journey, 12mo, $1.50.

William F. Warren, LL. D. Paradise Found, cr. 8vo, $2.00.

William A. Wheeler. Dictionary of Noted Names of Fiction, 12mo, $2.00.

Edwin P. Whipple. Essays, 6 vols. cr. 8vo, each $1.50.

Richard Grant White. Every-Day English, 12mo, $2.00; Words and their Uses, 12mo, $2.00; England Without and Within, 12mo, $2.00; The Fate of Mansfield Humphreys, 16mo, $1.25; Studies in Shakespeare, 12mo, $1.75.

Mrs. A. D. T. Whitney. Stories, 12 vols. 12mo, each $1.50; Mother Goose for Grown Folks, 12mo, $1.50; Pansies, 16mo, $1.25; Daffodils, 16mo, $1.25; Just How, 16mo, $1.00; Bonnyborough, 12mo, $1.50; Holy Tides, 16mo, 75 cents; Homespun Yarns, 12mo, $1.50.

John Greenleaf Whittier. Poems, *Household Edition*, Illustrated, 12mo, $1.75; full gilt, cr. 8vo, $2.25; *Cambridge Edition*, Portrait, 3 vols. 12mo, $5.25; *Red-Line Edition*, Portrait, Illustrated, small 4to, $2.50; *Cabinet Edition*, $1.00; *Library Edition*, Portrait, 32 Illustrations, 8vo, $3.50; Prose Works, *Cambridge Edition*, 2 vols. 12mo, $3.50; The Bay of Seven Islands, Portrait, 16mo, $1.00; John Woolman's Journal, Introduction by Whittier, $1.50; Child Life in Poetry, selected by Whittier, Illustrated, 12mo, $2.00; Child Life in Prose, 12mo, $2.00; Songs of Three Centuries, selected by Whittier: *Household Edition*, Illustrated, 12mo, $1.75; full gilt, cr. 8vo, $2.25; *Library Edition*, 32 Illustrations, 8vo, $3.50; Text and Verse, 18mo, 75 cents; Poems of Nature, 4to, Illustrated, $6.00; St. Gregory's Guest, etc., 16mo, vellum, $1.00.

Woodrow Wilson. Congressional Government, 16mo, $1.25.

J. A. Wilstach. Translation of Virgil's Works, 2 vols. cr. 8vo, $5.00.

Justin Winsor. Reader's Handbook of American Revolution, 16mo, $1.25.

W. B. Wright. Ancient Cities from the Dawn to the Daylight, 16mo, $1.25.